LETHBRIDGE-STEWART

BLOODLINES
FOREWORD TO THE PAST

Baz Greenland
& Andy Frankham-Allen

CANDY JAR BOOKS · CARDIFF
2020

GEORGE KOSTINEN staggered backwards, and would probably have finished his fall were it not for a pair of strong arms holding him. He glanced back, and smiled at the reassuring form of Archie Lethbridge-Stewart.

Reassuring only because nothing else was. It was a maelstrom of colour. All around him, bouncing and intermixing, colours and shapes, most of which he couldn't even name. Three people were before him. Two women and one… Man? He assumed it was supposed to be a man, but with every blink of an eye the man seemed to change his number of limbs, his very form. One moment there was one of them, and in the next there were three. And he appeared to be in pain, the colours circling around him.

'What's going on?' Archie asked.

'Temporal collapse is imminent,' said one of the women. She moved forward, and for a moment George thought he recognised her. 'The Accord is attempting to hold it together.'

'So, we're too late?'

'Not… yet,' the Accord said.

The woman looked curiously at George. 'I thought you were meant to be bringing Lucy Wilson.'

'So did I, but…' Archie shrugged. 'Change of plans. This is the one I was meant to collect.'

Despite the oddness of the situation, and knowing his entire life had been one long series of odd situations, George stepped forward and offered his hand. 'George Kostinen. You look strangely familiar.'

'That's because she's a relative of Reisha,' Archie said. 'Or at least, one assumes she is in her world. This is Anne Bishop, although her maiden name is Travers.'

Anne smiled at George, shook his hand, then looked at Archie. 'Reisha? I don't recall a Reisha in the family.'

'Granddaughter of your cousin, I think. Erm, Joseph?'

Anne thought about it. 'Oh, I haven't heard from my cousins in years. That's Uncle Vincent's middle child. I know Joe has children, but I don't think they're old enough…'

'George is from 2021. Or at least one version of it.'

'I see. Yes, well, that makes sense. She clearly hasn't been born yet. I'm from 1978,' Anne added, now looking back at George.

'And I'm from 1943,' the other woman said. 'Eileen Le Croissette.'

Now that George was looking at her properly, he could see she was wearing a World War II uniform. She couldn't have been more than early-twenties, with dark hair and a kind smile.

'Okay,' George said. 'So, now we're all here, what are we supposed to do?'

'A good question,' said Archie.

'One might even say, the *right* question,' a new voice from behind them said.

They turned. Standing there, dressed in silver robes, reflecting the light around them, was a man not unlike the Accord. He smiled warmly.

'I am the Silver Guardian of Space and Matter, I hold the atoms of the universe in balance.'

George raised his hairless eyebrows, somehow doubting that was entirely true. But who was he to question such a being? After all, if Harlequin could do all the things he claimed…

'Another of the Accord?' Anne asked. 'He,' she nodded at the other being, 'called you?'

'That is correct. We have found the temporal positions of the disruptions. The epicentre of causal collapse, both happening at the same time. Each outcome weakening the other.' The Silver Guardian held out a hand, on which sat four silver rings. 'Each of you shall wear one. They will guide you on your mission.'

George looked at his companions. Archie was the first to step forward. He took a ring and examined it.

'It looks a little like that ring Bill had. Silver instead of gold, but it contains the same crystal… A time ring?'

'It is a polymer-temporal tracking beacon,' the Guardian explained, 'existing on both a quantum and material plane at…'

Archie raised an eyebrow.

'A time ring,' the Guardian finished. He smiled. 'With additional properties.'

Archie nodded and placed the ring on his finger. Immediately his clothing changed, turning him into something out of an old Sherlock Holmes film.

'The additional properties?' he asked.

'Indeed. It is intuitive, and extrapolates from your mind your intended destination, and then adapts your clothing to help you better blend in.'

'But how?'

Eileen stepped past Archie. 'Just say thank you,' she told him, and took a ring for herself. 'I wonder what I'm going to wear.'

Anne and George quickly followed suit. Soon all four of them were wearing different clothes. Archie and Anne looking like they belonged in the Victorian era, and George and Eileen dressed for the Artic.

The Silver Guardian indicated to Anne and Archie. 'You two will be sent to Paris in 1896. There, something is preventing the union of Alistair Lethbridge-Stewart and Lillian McDougal. You must ensure it happens. Restore time, restore the Lethbridge-Stewart family line.'

'I say,' Archie began, 'you mean my granny and great uncle? Oh. Of course, that's right. Bill told me that it was they who were meant to wed, not Lillian and Archibald. And having Alistair as a grandfather, instead of Archibald, my alter ego, Alistair Gordon Lethbridge-Stewart, would become the great hero of—'

And, in a blink of an eye, Archie and Anne vanished.

'And us?' Eileen asked. 'I assume where we're going it will be quite cold.'

'You will be sent to Tsongkhar, in the land you call Tibet. There you will find Edward Travers. You must ensure his survival.'

'Survival?' George asked.

'Yes. If he dies, all will be lost. There will be no alliance in London, 1969. Edward Travers must meet the Doctor and help defeat the Great Intelligence. Edward Travers must return home.'

Eileen nodded. 'Where he and Margaret will eventually beget Alun and Anne. So, Tibet. 1935? Yes, he's told me about his expedition there.'

'Nobody's told me,' George said.

Eileen explained the little she knew. George listened. When she was finished, he nodded and said, 'Okay, let's make it so.'

And, just like that, the world around him changed once more.

CHAPTER ONE
Paris in Springtime

'—Bill's world.'

A new location shifted into focus around him, shadows and blurred shapes became landmarks and people, distorted sounds sharpened. And the sight before him took his breath away. The bustling, cobbled street on which they now stood was packed with horse-drawn carriages, intermingled with flocks of people. Men and women dressed just like Archie and Anne: men in finest suits with top hats and canes, women with tight corseted dresses and exquisitely decorated bonnets, all moving about their daily business. The sounds of conversation, hoof beats and footsteps on the cobbles filled the air. There was a great deal of commotion. Cities, it seemed, had rarely changed in the past seventy years.

Archie took a deep breath and looked up, feeling the warmth of the sun on his face. The sun broke through the clouds above the city, and while it was warm and welcoming, the stench that filled the air was not. The putrid smell of horse faeces was overpowering and, looking around, it was not hard to see why. Passers-by seemed to navigate the small brown piles with ease.

'Rather unpleasant, isn't it?' he muttered with distaste, thinking the Basil Rathbone films never really did the era justice. He looked to Anne, and was surprised to see that she wasn't quite as taken aback by the stench as he was.

She gave an enthusiastic gasp. 'Oh, how remarkable! That's a real Mekarski!' She pointed to a large juggernaut of a tram that was shuffling along the wide street.

The vehicle that navigated towards them was certainly impressive; a huge double story contraption of metal and steam, packed with passengers. It looked far more unstable than the modern trams he was used to, a tin box only barely resembling a London double decker of his own time.

'Compressed-air propulsion system,' Anne said with awe. 'Air heated with steam, using a bouillotte boiler. A single-stage engine that expands air in one piston and then exhausts it in another.' She grinned as she watched it continue down the busy street, swallowed up by the mass of pedestrians interweaving around the horse-drawn carts.

Anne turned to Archie, still beaming, a glint in her eyes as she continued. 'It's a remarkable piece of engineering for this time. The air is reheated after leaving the tank and before entering the engine. The reheated air bubbles through a hot water tank, picking up hot water vapor to…' She paused, pulling her gaze away with a somewhat sheepish smile. 'As I said, it was quite a remarkable piece of engineering.'

Archie forced a smile. 'I'm sure it was.'

'I would love to ride one, if we can.'

'May I remind you, Anne, that we have a job to do?'

Anne kept her smile, but her eyes hardened. 'I am well aware, Archie.'

'Apologies, I meant no disrespect. This is all rather…'

'Remarkable,' Anne finished for him.

For a moment, he thought he saw something in her expression, sadness perhaps. The sort of look Sabina would give him when she didn't want him to worry about her. But it quickly vanished.

'Yes, I think I will try to appreciate the wonder of travelling back to the nineteenth century and all the delights it brings,' she continued. 'As should you, Archie. It's not like you'll be visiting the past again, is it?'

'Not unless the Guardian allows me to keep this ring, no,' Archie said with a smile, turning the silver ring on his finger. 'Besides, you've already travelled back in time, haven't you? So, you're an old hand at this lark.'

'I've never travelled this far back, though. This is almost like a different world.'

Archie nodded, thinking of George's world, the differences he'd seen there. He could appreciate Anne's enthusiasm. And she was right, he decided, taking in the sights around them. They were in Paris at the end of the nineteenth century. All these people, many long gone by his time, going about their lives without any comprehension that two people from the future had come to this time to put history back on course. A history different to the one he had experienced.

Even after all he had been through, all he had learned, Archie still didn't know how to feel about that. A world in which he, a humble teacher, was a military man? A life where Katherine and Jimmy didn't even exist?

Archie quickly banished that thought. He had a job to do and, if he believed everything he had been told, this was far bigger than him. Or his family. Besides, if he understood things correctly, fixing this timeline would stabilise his own world and then, hopefully, he could go back to his life. Assuming he could make things up to Sabina and his family after he had abandoned them all so abruptly…

'How anyone is expected to breathe in one of these things is preposterous,' Anne grumbled, fussing with her corseted dress.

Archie smiled. 'The wonders of nineteenth century Paris already fading?'

'Let's just say I have mixed feelings.'

He offered out his arm and she linked hers with his. He could already feel the sweat on his brow and his high buttoned collar felt tight against his throat, but he suspected he was suffering far less than his companion. The fact that Anne could still breathe and smile at the same time was a wonder.

'So, we have to make sure your grandparents meet up,' she said, as they walked. 'I assume you know how they met?'

'Well, I know how *Alistair*, my great uncle, and Lillian

were supposed to meet. My grandfather, Archibald, won't meet Lillian for some time, I suppose. Not if time is put back on track. In my world it was quite different.'

Archie went on to explain what Bill had told him during their journey to London… Almost two weeks ago now! Two weeks and over seventy years in the future.

He told her how his *grandparents* were supposed to meet during an interval at the *Palais Garnier*, and then, some years from now while Alistair was off doing his duty, Lillian succumbed to loneliness and spent a night with Alistair's brother, Archibald. This led to the birth of a son, Gordon, who everybody assumed was Alistair's.

'And eventually your alter ego was born,' Anne said.

'Yes, never knowing the truth.'

'And in your world…?'

'Lillian and Archibald met a short time from now, they fell in love, married and Gordon was born.'

'I see.' Anne smiled sadly. 'The *Palais Garnier*. Bill and I visited there only a short time ago. In my world, that is. Okay, let us assume then that we're in the right time and place, it stands to reason that Alistair and Lillian will be attending whatever show is on there this evening. Which, by my reckoning, gives us a few hours to purchase tickets and obtain lodgings for the night.'

'Purchase?'

'Well certainly, if the Guardian wants us to succeed, then he'll have provided all the tools we'll need.'

Archie considered, and patted his coat. With a smile and a flourish, he pulled out a wallet. Which contained some of the largest notes he'd ever seen. 'Good Lord, this is what passed for money?'

Anne grinned. 'A different time, Archie. And like all advances, things seem to shrink in the future. Money among them.'

'Quite.'

'The next logical question is: who or what is stopping them from meeting? We don't know exactly how they met, only that they meet this evening at the interval.'

Archie considered. 'Then our course of action is clear. This evening we keep a very close eye on them. Once we've found them. And we have until the interval to nudge them into each other's orbits, as it were.'

Anne smiled. 'Sounds very simple, doesn't it? But I imagine it won't be, or we wouldn't need to be here.'

'Finding them will be hard enough. I suspect it'll be a full house at the theatre.' Archie cast his eyes around. 'First things first, though. You've been to the *Palais Garnier* before.' He raised his cane to point at the grand sight of the Eiffel Tower rising behind the rooftops before them. 'Is the opera house close?'

Anne shook her head. 'No. We need to head down river towards the *Louvre.*'

'A good idea.' Archie thought a moment. 'We should probably find a hotel close to the *Palais Garnier,* too. Assuming our mission lasts more than just one night.'

'In my experience, Archie, missions rarely end as quickly as you expect them to.'

'A cheery thought.'

Despite the looming presence of the Eiffel Tower over the Parisian rooftops, it took them almost an hour to reach the bank of the River *Seine.* There they charted a passenger boat upriver towards the opera house. The stench of sewage filled the air and their nasal passage, as they waited for the boat to dock and, by the time they were sailing upriver, with the warm spring breeze billowing off the water, Archie felt he could truly breathe once again.

The trip along the *Seine* to the docking at the Pont Royal Bridge was pleasant. Archie noticed the tall, grand buildings overlooking the river seemed a little different to how he imagined them, based on paintings he'd seen in his time. He assumed this to be simply down to artists impression, rather than changes to the timeline. There were some landmarks missing, noticeably the *Musée d'Orsay,* which Anne reminded him was originally a railway station built four years after this time. But, altogether, it was a picturesque little trip through a bustling, vibrant city and for a moment he found that he could almost forget why they were there.

A short time later, they disembarked at the Pont Royal Bridge, where they quickly navigated their way up the stone steps, and made their way around to the *Louvre* Palace that rose off the right bank of the river. After a quick, rather pleasant stroll through the gardens, they found a horse and carriage to take them up towards the *Rue Auber* and the *Place de l'Opéra*, running along the entrance of the *Palais Garnier*. While Anne was somewhat disappointed not to take a trip on a Mekarski, they were both glad of the opportunity to rest their feet some more. It had already been quite an expedition through the streets of Paris and, by the time they reached their destination, they were both tired and hungry; neither of them felt much desire to go and see an opera, but that was where they needed to be tonight.

History depended on them both.

The opera house itself was an imposing sight. Above tall pillars and arches, stood two magnificent golden angels, staring aloof across the city from their spires. In its centre, the green dome with its golden crown gave the *Palais Garnier* a rather majestic feel, as beautiful as anything he had seen since his arrival.

Anne removed her bonnet, and sniffed back a tear. Archie raised an eyebrow at her.

'Sorry,' she said, 'but, like I said, coming here was one of the last things Bill and I did before we got caught up in Copeland's experiments, before Bill...'

Ah yes, Archie considered. In 1978, shortly before the Accord had called on Anne as an agent, her husband had been killed.

'Look, Anne, if this is too hard for you, you can always ...'

Anne shook her head, gathered herself together and took a deep breath. She fixed her bonnet back onto her head. 'The mission. It's important.' She smiled up at Archie. 'I'll be fine. Now, let us hope there are tickets still available for tonight's performance.'

Archie couldn't help but smile.

'What is it?' Anne asked.

'Oh, it's nothing really. Just… If your alter ego is anything like you, then it's clear why you and I became friends in Bill's world.'

'Well, when we return to our version of the future, perhaps we should follow their lead? After all, isn't that the whole point? Lethbridge-Stewarts and Traverses.'

Archie nodded. 'Yes, I'd like that. Although, of course, I'll have to wait nine years for us to re-connect.'

'I'll be waiting.'

With that promise made, the two new friends turned back to the opera house with apprehension. He still wasn't comfortable with the mission, to unite his granny with a man he had always considered his great uncle.

As he kept his gaze on the *Palais Garnier*, Archie sighed heavily. What he did now would change everything he knew.

But then, maybe everything he knew had changed already. Changed the moment Bill first told him about this other future. Archie considered the last couple of weeks. His life had been altered… perhaps irrevocably. When he finally returned home, would he even really be Archie Lethbridge-Stewart anymore? How much of him would be Alistair Gordon Lethbridge-Stewart…?

CHAPTER TWO
The Renowned Explorer

A NEW world opened up around Eileen and George. Solid. Cold. Real.

Eileen felt the ground beneath her feet. She didn't know how long she had been in the other place, but the real world felt like a distant memory. She scrunched her toes inside her snow boots, rubbing the thick soles against the frost and rock beneath her. She was a long way from London now. Standing on a small hill in Tibet, she realised she was a long way from everything.

The young man with the bald head – George, her new companion – stood at her side, rubbing his hands. 'Bloody cold, isn't it?' he grumbled, and put on his gloves.

'Language!' she scoffed, casting him a stern gaze.

He looked at her in surprise. 'Yeah, sorry, I guess,' he said, clearly feeling nothing of the sort.

Eileen looked down at the village a short distance from the foot of the hill. No doubt that was Tsongkhar. At first glance, it looked like a ramshackle collection of huts and stalls, strands of cloth blowing in the wind across structures of stick and stone. Except, on closer inspection, it wasn't quite as rough as it looked. The buildings were sturdy and well-constructed, even if the materials used weren't the most sophisticated. Canopies and wood slats were fitted to keep out bad weather, and even the tents on the edge of the village looked robust. A couple of stone structures had also been built into the hill side, weathered with age, but standing strong.

Quite some distance beyond the village, the slopes of the Himalayas dominated the landscape. They were too far away to make out properly, probably a day's journey, but she could see the huge slopes of grey rock ascending towards the heavens; snow-capped peaks rising majestically against the brilliant blue skies. As the snow caught the sun, it looked to her as if liquid gold was being poured down the mountainside. Eileen's heart swelled as she took in the mountain range. She was certain she had never seen anything quite so beautiful in all her life.

George said with a smile, 'Pretty amazing, isn't it? I thought the Welsh valleys were lush.'

'Lush?'

'Yeah, you know, beautiful?'

'Ah!' Eileen nodded. 'Yes, they certainly are that. Always had a fondness for Wales.'

'Same here.'

Eileen offered him a smile. 'Right then, we can't stand here sightseeing all day, George. We have a purpose for being here, and we're not going to achieve it unless we get a move on.'

As they walked, Eileen considered the mission before them. She recalled Travers' story, of course, but he hadn't furnished her with a great deal of details. She knew he was in Tibet to look for yeti, and she also knew that he'd found some, of a sort. Robotic killing machines controlled by something called the Great Intelligence. The very thought of the Yeti being out there among the snow filled her with a great deal of trepidation. Dealing with those Quarks was one thing – she'd had armed back-up, for a start. But out here in Tibet, all she had was a teenage boy not a great deal younger than her. She couldn't begin to think how they'd survive against Yeti.

They walked through the outskirts of Tsongkhar, and Eileen caught a couple of curious glances from the local population. Nothing too aggressive or insidious, but enough to make her painfully aware that they stuck out like a sore thumb. She exchanged pleasant smiles with a couple of women and a trader leading a yak laden with goods out to the valley. Eileen thought herself a good judge of people, and she sensed no hostility.

'We'll need some climbing gear,' Eileen said, as they wandered down past some tents, thinking more on what to expect in the coming days.

'Are you planning on a spot of mountaineering?' George asked.

'Travers is, and if we're to keep him alive, then wherever he goes…'

'…So go we. All right. You got any cash?'

Eileen stopped, surprised at George's manners. 'If you are asking if I have money, I have some coins on me.' She fumbled for her purse and sifted through the contents. Two shillings, a halfpenny, three farthings and four florins. She wasn't sure if they would have any value here. Eileen imagined Tibet didn't see British currency very often. Some of her coins hadn't yet even been minted.

'Got a two-pound coin!' George exclaimed, pulling out a strange coin, large with a silver ring around a circle of gold. 'I wonder if this will have any street cred?'

Street cred? No, she wasn't going to attempt to understand that one.

They carried on.

After over an hour of looking around Tsongkhar, attempting to talk to the locals, very few of whom understood English, they had discovered a serious lack of Edward Travers.

The sun set, and the village was lit up with delightful lanterns that gave Tsongkhar a fairy tale-like quality. For a moment, Eileen was able to enjoy the beauty and wonder of the village, absorbing a culture and people very different to what she was used to. There was an atmosphere to the place that was enticing. The people were friendly, welcoming to strangers.

At the far side of the village, they came across what looked like a café of sorts. A Caucasian man, wearing the clothing of the locals, was sitting at a table just inside the small building, looking out of the glassless window. There was a cup in his hand and his face was lit up by candlelight. Eileen entered the café, indicating for George to follow. Taking a deep breath, Eileen marched over and held out her hand in greeting.

'Good evening. I'm Miss Le Croissette.'

The man set his cup down and shook her hand firmly. 'Hello, Miss Le Croissette,' he said, with a deep Scottish burr. He eyed her and George with a bit of a frown. 'I didn't ken there were other English people here in Tsongkhar.'

'I'm Welsh,' George replied a little coolly.

The man laughed. 'Ah, it's like the beginning of a joke, eh? A Scot, Welsh and Englishman were sitting in a café…' He laughed again. 'Won't you both join me?'

He indicated the narrow bench opposite him. Eileen waited for George to sit before joining his side.

'We arrived this afternoon,' she said, pulling down her hood. It was distinctly warmer inside the café. 'George and I were wondering if there were many westerners here in Tsongkhar?'

'No as a rule,' the man replied, taking a sip of his beer. 'You're the only other non-locals I've seen in this whole village. You're lucky we met. Tomorrow, Edward and I take the Path of Oddiyana up to Det-Sen.'

Eileen felt the warmth of elation. The Guardian had indeed sent them to the correct place, and at the right time. She searched her memory, wondering if Edward had ever mentioned his expedition partner. If he had, she couldn't recall his name.

'The monastery?'

'Aye. Although the locals tend to call it a gompa.'

Eileen put as much innocence in her voice as possible. 'Oh, I've been thinking of visiting there, too. Haven't we, George?'

George just nodded.

'On your own?' the man asked.

Eileen bristled at the implication. 'One doesn't need to

be chaperoned by a man at all times.'

The man laughed. 'Indeed. But these are dangerous parts for the unwary.'

Eileen leaned in closer. 'Dangerous?'

'Oh, indeed, madam. Have you no heard of the metoh-kangmi?'

George frowned. 'The what?'

'Yeti, Mr George,' the man said. 'Howard-Bury's infamous "wild man of the snow", or as the locals call it, the metoh-kangmi.'

A look passed across George's face. Eileen wasn't quite sure how to describe it. A strange mix of excitement and fear. And something else. Recognition, perhaps?

'Legends, surely,' Eileen said. 'I'm sure we've all heard such stories, Mr...?'

'Ah, how rude of me.' He reached out his hand to shake hers again. 'Mackay. John Mackay, renowned explorer and adventurer, at your service.'

'Renowned?' Eileen laughed politely. 'And Edward... sorry, Professor Travers is in Tsongkhar now?'

Mackay nodded. 'You know him?'

'Only by reputation,' she replied quickly. 'Are you also an anthropologist?'

'Oh, no even remotely. Ever heard of me?'

'Perhaps,' Eileen said, not lying. Edward *might* have mentioned him in passing. 'You are *renowned*, after all.'

'Travers is the star of our little expedition. Full of big ideas. Published academic. His name in lots of well-respected journals...' Mackay sipped his drink, a frown furrowing his brow. 'Here I am, telling my life story and you haven't told me yours. You're no one of Professor Walters' students, are you?'

'Never heard of him.'

'Very well.'

'We're going to Det-Sen Monastery because I want to be a monk,' George exclaimed suddenly, and indicated his bald head. 'I've got the look for it.'

Eileen forced a laugh as Mackay gave them a baffled

expression.

'George here likes to tell jokes. We are going to Det-Sen to study the ancient ways of the monks there. George is a scholar of History and I am his teacher. We like to travel. I find it is much more fun experiencing life in person, rather than in dusty old books.'

George nodded enthusiastically. Eileen wasn't sure if MacKay was convinced. She realised she had better keep the conversation moving forward.

'Have you travelled many places?'

Mackay set his tankard down, his eyes wide. 'Spent a good portion of the last three years in South America. Before that I was in India.'

'Oh, I would love to travel to India someday. I've only spent time in France, Germany… This is your first time in Tibet?'

Mackay shook his head. 'No. I was in these parts about five years ago, which funnily enough, is the reason I'm here now.' He sipped the contents of his cup again and smacked his lips with satisfaction. 'They brew this just for travellers like me. Made with barley, of course. No really beer, no alcoholic content, but the taste… Well, it's delicious stuff. Would you no care for a wee taste?' He offered the tankard in her direction.

She politely declined and held up her arm to stop George, who leaned forward to take up the offer. He couldn't have been much older than fifteen, and far too young in her opinion to be drinking whatever that concoction was.

'Professor Travers hired you?' she asked.

'Aye. But we've met before.' Mackay leaned in a little closer, lowering his voice. 'You see, I saw something up on Mount Jampa the last time I was here. I'm no convinced it was a yeti. It might have just been a bear or something. But it was big, real big.' He pulled back with a grin. 'Anyway, no one believed me when I told them about it. Was laughed out of the room. But Travers, he believed. Knocked on my door a couple of years back, full of excitement over my story. We've been friends ever since. Said he would come here one day. And when Professor Walters decided to publicly humiliate old Edward in front of all his fellow academics, well, there was no other choice. Told Walters he was going to prove him wrong, bring back evidence of the existence of the metoh-kangmi, or the abominable snowmen as that hack Henry Newman once mis-coined it….' He beamed at Eileen and George. 'And here we are, six weeks later. Financial backing from Fleet Street and me along for the ride. Truth be told, I'm rather excited. Wee bit scared too, but that's all part of the adventure. If there's no a slim chance you might die along the journey, it's probably no worth doing.'

Eileen didn't know what to say to that. This man was an incorrigible fellow. She might admire his sense of adventure, even be a little jealous at all the places he had travelled to, but his death wish was worrying. Particularly if he was travelling with Travers up to the Det-Sen Monastery.

Travers must have mentioned him. Eileen thought hard. Was there something about a friend dying on the mountain? She felt sure. It had to be Mackay.

Of course, according to the Silver Guardian, it was Travers they were here to save. Not Mackay. Eileen was very aware of the importance of history, of one's role in it, after all it was one of the many reasons she had decided to enter the Armed Forces; to protect England's history. If history decided it was Mackay's fate to die on this expedition, then she could do nothing to stand in its way.

Travers, however, was a different story.

'You said Professor Travers is nearby?'

Mackay finished his non-beer. 'Out gathering the last of the supplies.'

Eileen looked at George. 'Do you think you can fetch us the supplies we'll need?' As he nodded, she turned back to Mackay. 'If you don't mind the company?'

'Of course not.' He shrugged. 'I think there's about ten in the expedition so far. Two guides, some missionaries, a couple of locals heading to the gompa for enlightenment, plus Travers and myself.'

'Any supplies in particular you think we need?' George asked Mackay, rising from the bench.

'Oh, a good tent and some blankets. It's about a week to Det-Sen and the nights are cold.'

Eileen excused herself, and went outside with George. She handed him the remainder of the coins from her purse, keeping two of the florins back. She was hoping they might be able to use them for food and lodgings that night. She had no desire to sleep in a tent before they left Tsongkhar.

George moved on to the next stall, a big cloth sack draped over his shoulder. He had purchased a tent, some blankets, and a load of salted meats and soda bread. His two-pound coin had paid for most of it, Eileen's the rest. He had a couple of those copper coins remaining. They didn't look like they would fetch much, but he had one thing left to find. A weapon.

He knew this was history, a better world, before the Clown, before the Kruge… But for good or bad, he'd been hardened by his world and he knew you didn't go anywhere you didn't know without a weapon. He was still trying to work out who he was without Happy's influence, and although he was a long way from working it all out, he knew himself enough to know he wasn't going to be taking any chances.

Looking at the various stalls in Tsongkhar's central square, he found very little that could serve as a decent weapon. He wasn't interested in a gun, even if he could find one. He knew the trouble they attracted, and although there were no Volpertinger here in Tibet, he could only imagine how a real yeti would react to the sound of a gun going off.

A real yeti. Now there was a thought. He'd lived with his own robotic Yeti for long enough, got used to Pennyworth's presence, but to meet a real yeti… Well, there had to be a reason the Great Intelligence had modelled its robots on them.

Looking around the village square, lit up all pretty, he realised this was the first time he had been abroad. He had always wanted to go somewhere exotic and strange. An all-inclusive in Malaga had never appealed to him. And now he was finally here. In Tibet. In freaking 1935! He couldn't help but find the whole thing just a little bit exciting.

He discovered a blacksmith, who was closing up his shop. A lot of the items on display were equipment for building or farming, but there were a few knives that caught George's attention. Some pretty wicked arrows too, but he was certain he didn't have the room or money to buy a bow and arrow. Which was a shame, he was a dab-hand with one of those after hours of training with Reisha.

He paused, his mind now on his girlfriend. He hoped she was all right. That she'd still be there when he returned.

One of the knives, a small silver dagger with a brown leather-bound handle, was just the thing he was looking for.

He set the big cloth sack down and took out the two copper coins. He waved his hand to get the blacksmith's attention and pointed at the dagger. Unfortunately, he was met with a rather gruff response. The man crossed his arms and let out something like a harrumph.

George didn't know what to do. The stalls were closing up and it was probably too late to find a knife elsewhere. He did the only thing he could. Look defeated and then flashed him a winning smile. It didn't work. The blacksmith's expression didn't change.

George was just about to give up, when the blacksmith leaned over and inspected the coins in George's hands. He walked off and returned with a dagger about two thirds the size of the one George wanted. The blade wasn't quite as impressive, but it was a weapon.

George completed the exchange and navigated his way back to the café, hoping there might be something to eat waiting for him.

Up ahead, he saw a man that was obviously not local. He was wearing a fur-lined coat, a black knitted hat, with a face bearing the stubble of a few days. The man was laden with supplies and he didn't look happy about it. It had to be Professor Travers.

George hurried up to join him.

It took him a moment to realise he wasn't the only person watching Travers. There was movement in the shadows ahead, a figure lurking by the side of a building Travers was about to pass. The moment he got close, the stranger slunk out of the shadows and unsheathed a sword.

George laid down his sack and ran forward, pulling his dagger free and throwing it towards Travers' attacker. It struck the man in the shoulder. With a scream, the attacker fell back and vanished into the shadows, the dagger still embedded in his shoulder.

George felt a surge of anger; he had lost the weapon before he had even left Tsongkhar.

As he stood there, getting his breath back, a thought struck him. Was that it? He'd been sent to make sure Travers didn't die, that he helped the Doctor defeat the Great Intelligence. If George hadn't been there, would that man have succeeded in his attack? Was *that* the mission? George felt a little let down.

He picked up his cloth sack and approached the professor. 'Are you okay?'

Travers looked at him, his face pale, and nodded slowly. 'Yes, I think so. Thank you.'

George flashed him a smile. 'No worries. I saw that man coming towards you, and…'

'And you saved my life.' Travers offered a small smile.

'Right time, right place, is all. Do you know who that was?'

Travers sighed. 'Alas, no. It may have been one of the Golok people. They have been known to attack people out in the wilderness, but I wouldn't want to make assumptions.' He paused, taking a deep breath. 'I have no idea why he would want to kill me. The people of Tsongkhar are usually so welcoming.'

'Maybe he wasn't from Tsongkhar. I'm heading back to

the café. Me and… my teacher met your mate there. John Mackay?'

'Splendid. Why don't I join you there?'

They picked up their supplies and set off.

'I hear you're heading up to Det-Sen?' George said.

Travers nodded. 'I am indeed. First thing tomorrow.'

'Us too. If you don't mind us tagging along?'

The professor laughed as they continued their walk to the café. 'You are a forward young man. One who has clearly ascertained my identity. Do you have a name?'

'Oh, sorry. Yeah, it's George.'

'George.' Travers smiled. 'Well, George, I assume you are not frightened by the legends of the fearsome yeti?'

George shrugged. 'Oh, they don't bother me. I had one as a pet once.'

'A pet?'

How could he explain that one?

'Never mind,' George said quickly with a grin. 'Just a joke.'

Professor Travers wasn't laughing. 'I think you'll find that up Mount Jampa there'll be very little time for joking. We're talking life and death situations.'

George shrugged. 'What's new?'

Travers gave him a curious look, which only deepened when George grinned at him.

CHAPTER THREE
A Nineteenth Century
Parisian Adventure

LUCK WAS on their side. With tickets for *Hellé* purchased, Archie turned their attention to the next part of their plan. Accommodation.

'What about that place?' he asked, pointing towards a rather opulent hotel across the busy street from the opera house.

Anne's expression was the same as it had been looking at the *Palais Garnier* for the first time. She took a deep breath, dismissing his suggestion with a wave of her hand. '*Le Grand* is rather expensive. I am sure we can find something cheaper nearby.'

Archie could tell there was something else she wasn't saying. Was this the hotel where Anne and Bill had stayed on their anniversary? He had the uneasy feeling that every part of the journey was going to be a deeply uncomfortable trip down memory lane for her.

Perhaps a change of subject was needed.

'What about something to eat before we find tonight's lodgings?'

She hesitated a moment and then gave him a warm smile. 'That would be lovely, Archie.' The sadness on her face changed to curiosity. 'I always wanted to try the food at the famous *Café de la Paix*. It's the one place Bill and I never got to go. Would you care for some nineteenth century cuisine? Make the most of our experience here?'

Archie had no idea what nineteenth century cuisine tasted like. Give him one of Sabina's famous Sunday roasts, or his mother's beef stew and dumplings, any day.

Without waiting for an answer, Anne stepped out onto the *Rue Auber*, navigating her way through the mass of people and horse-drawn carriages. He followed quickly.

An hour later, the bill paid and his stomach full, Archie found himself contently sipping his glass of wine and looking out over the bustle of the *Place de l'Opéra*. He was just about to suggest they start their search for nearby lodgings, when a small group of women in brightly-coloured dresses, bonnets and parasols, caught his eye. All speaking clear English, they appeared to be locked in a debate with the woman in the lead, a young lady in her late teens or early twenties, talking with a soft Scottish accent. Her dress was a bright blue, brighter than that of her companions, and her long dark hair cascaded in curls beneath her bonnet, swaying from side to side as she led her little throng.

'Well, Lyon is most certainly an option, Ruby,' the woman said crisply as the group passed Archie's and Anne's table. 'But the French Riviera is far more agreeable this time of the year.'

The woman immediately behind her, Ruby, clearly, looked somewhat dejected. 'If you think that is best.'

'Oh, I do. Nice and Monte Carlo are a must, but I hear that *Juan-les-Pins* is very up and coming too.'

'Well, you know best, Lilly,' one of the other women acquiesced with a curt smile.

As they moved on, heading towards a vacant table a few seats away from theirs, Anne looked at Archie, her eyebrows raised questionably no doubt at the look of recognition on his face.

'Is that…?'

Archie nodded. 'My grandmother. Bill did say she was travelling with her friend Ruby in Paris.'

Archie had seen photographs of Granny McDougal as a young woman, and there was no denying she looked just as pretty in real life. He remembered stories from visits to the family estate in Appin, stories of her life as a young socialite – always the life of the party.

Anne took a sip of her wine. 'Should we introduce ourselves? It might make our task easier if we can use a friendly meeting now. That way bumping into her at the theatre later will be more natural, and will make our entire mission a good deal easier.'

'A capital idea, Mrs Bishop.' Archie finished the last of his drink and stood. He wondered how one should introduce oneself to one's own granny.

Anne fixed her bonnet and reached out to take his arm in hers. He put on his top hat and grabbed their bags and cane.

'Follow my lead,' she muttered in his ear, and quickly raised her voice as they passed Lillian's table. 'Oh, I can't believe how excited I am for *Hellé* tonight.'

Anne looked at Archie, indicating for him to respond. 'Oh right,' he muttered and raised his own voice. 'Yes, it should be quite the event.'

It was enough to attract the attention of the small group. Not surprisingly, it was Lillian who turned to interrupt them.

'Fellow opera lovers? How lovely!'

Anne smiled. 'Oh, hello. Always nice to meet other Britons abroad.'

'Indeed.' Lillian smiled back. 'Isn't Paris just divine?'

'It's so beautiful. Are you watching *Hellé* tonight?'

'Absolutely. I would not miss it for the world.'

'How exquisite.' Anne matched Lillian's high-pitched tone. 'Well, we must make sure we meet up to discuss it later. I am always keen to discuss opera with like-minded people.'

'Oh indeed!' Lillian beamed. 'I hear Madame Caron's solo is just exquisite'.

'I have heard that, too. Maybe I will see you during the interval?'

'Of course. And perhaps drinks afterwards?' Lillian asked, with a solicitous smile at Archie. 'We are staying at

Le Grand.'

'Just a step away from the *Palais Garnier?*' Anne said, not missing a beat and ignoring Archie's sudden discomfort. 'What a wonderful visit this must be for you.'

'Oh, I am so in love with Paris. I'm Lillian McDougal, by the way.' She turned to her companions, as if noticing them for the first time. 'These are my friends and travelling companions. Ruby Holland, Anastasia Bude, Victoria Nicholls and Wilhelmina Peretti.'

'A pleasure.' Anne beamed. 'I'm Anne Bishop and this is…'

'Matthew,' Archie cut in. Best not to use his real name. 'Matthew Gordon.'

'Anne, Matthew. We look forward to discussing the opera with you fine people.' Lillian turned to her group. 'Don't we, ladies?'

Her companions nodded enthusiastically. Archie wasn't sure they were actually permitted to talk. Although he was more troubled by the look his future granny kept throwing his way.

'Lovely.' Anne grinned. 'Well, we won't take up any more of your time. We'll see you at the opera.'

Lillian laughed. 'Oh yes, absolutely!'

'Goodbye.' Anne tugged on Archie's arm and led him away.

'I think that went rather well,' Archie said when they were out of earshot.

'If we ignore the fact that she rather fancied the look of you.'

'Yes, well, let's just do that.'

'I assume you take after your grandfather?'

'Which one?' Archie asked with a raised eyebrow. 'Either way, yes. The paternal genes are rather strong in my family.'

'Thought so.' Anne laughed. 'Your grandmother makes me want to grind my teeth.'

Archie chuckled at that. 'Well, she does mellow somewhat with age.'

*

They found lodgings, purchased suitable attire for a trip to the opera, and prepared for the night ahead. While he enjoyed a nice warm bath, Archie considered his reflection. Stubble had overtaken his face in the almost-two weeks since leaving Bledoe. He found a razor and some lather in the bathroom, and set about fixing that. He finished his neck and jawline, and was about to start on his upper lip, when he stopped.

'Actually, that looks rather good,' he decided, and washed the lather off, admiring the thin moustache that now adorned his face.

Anne smiled at him when they met in the hotel foyer. 'I must say, Archie, that does rather suit you.'

'Oh, do you think so? I never thought I was much one for facial hair, especially considering my profession, but…'

'Well, if we're ever going to try something different, now is the time.'

And that said, they made their way to the *Palais Garnier*.

They stepped into the grand foyer of the opera house. Before them, the magnificent staircase rose up into the upper levels, glistening in gold and candlelight. Amid the bustle of the opera goers, all dressed in lavish finery, an orchestra played from one of the balconies above, the sweet music echoing out across the chamber. It was an utterly audacious example of wealth and opulence, and most certainly not Archie's sort of thing at all

Once again, Anne was silent. He imagined she was lost in her own memories of her anniversary trip with Bill. Archie could still see the look of love on old Bill's face when they had talked about Anne – and after spending an afternoon in her company, Archie could understand why Bill had fallen so totally for her. Of course, the version of Bill that Archie had met was from the year 2018, many decades after the woman that now accompanied him. And, more importantly, in Anne's time, her Bill had only recently died. But, Archie believed, had he lived, Anne's Bill would have gone on to have as many happy years with her.

Anne took Archie's arm and led him towards the nearest attendant, dressed in a lavish gold cloak.

'Bonsoir. Vos billets, s'il vous plaît?'

Anne held out their tickets. The attendant inspected them closely, then directed Archie and Anne towards the staircase. They joined the throng of people making their way towards the upper level foyer and discovered a bar and cushioned seating area, where more attendants waited with trays of champagne. Another indulgence.

While it wasn't to his taste, he was certain Sabina would have loved it. Perhaps, if he ever got home, he might take her to Paris. As apologies went, that would be fairly magnificent.

Anne sipped her champagne as she eyed the room intently. 'I'm going to mingle, see if I can find Lillian and work on that connection. Why don't you focus on looking for your grandfather?' She hesitated. 'Sorry, your great uncle. Do you know what he looks like?'

'I've seen pictures,' Archie said. 'I just wish I knew why he was here. Opera was always my granny's sort of thing.'

Anne laughed. 'This isn't your sort of thing either?'

Archie smiled. 'No, not really, Anne.' He paused, taking a moment to sip the cool champagne as he collected his thoughts. 'Perhaps I will head to the bar and observe from there?'

'Okay, let's meet up over there.' Anne pointed towards a dark wood door framed with a red velvet curtain. 'The opera starts in twenty minutes. We'll meet in fifteen.'

The room was quickly filling up. Archie knew enough French to manage basic conversation, but the fast-flowing chatter was lost on him. It was a relief when he reached the bar and found a number of vacant chairs. It seemed the people attending *Hellé* were there for the social interaction as much as the opera itself.

A smart young man in his twenties, clean shaven, with slick black hair, was working behind the bar. He approached

Archie with a warm smile.

'*Comment puis-je vous server, monsieur?*'

'Whisky please, straight,' Archie replied before catching himself. '*Sil vous plait.*' He frantically fumbled for the word for whisky in his head, but came up blank.

The bartender laughed warmly. 'Ah, another Englishman!' he said in a thick Mancunian accent. He was already reaching for a whisky glass. 'No worries, sir, I've got your order.'

Archie smiled back, relieved. As the drink was poured, Archie quickly scanned the room, but he couldn't make out anyone that resembled a younger version of his great uncle.

The bartender handed a double to Archie. 'Would you care for anything else?'

Archie shook his head. 'No thanks.' He took a sip of the whisky. It was warm and relaxing; as much as that had been good champagne, this was more his kind of drink. He set the glass down. 'Manchester accent?'

The bartender grinned. 'Born and bred in Salford.'

'Salford is a long way from Paris,' Archie mused, before taking another sip of the whisky.

The bartender laughed. 'You don't get somewhere like the *Palais Garnier* in the North. We've got the Royal in Manchester, but that's not quite on the same level. They did, however, do a terrific production of *A Woman's Revenge* there last year. Are you a fan of Henry Pettitt's work?'

Archie shook his head. 'I am afraid theatre really isn't my kind of thing.'

The bartender sniggered. 'Then what are you doing at the *Palais Garnier?*'

Archie would have been offended by the man's apparent mockery if he had not found the whole affair befuddling and amusing himself. 'Ah… my, ah, female companion wanted to see it.'

'In that case, I'll keep the whisky coming.'

Archie raised his glass, realising he had inadvertently implied he was engaged in some kind of affair. *Sabina, please forgive me.* 'Good man,' he said, reminding himself it was

simply a cover story. An unplanned one, but nonetheless…
'My name is Archie, by the way.'

'Al.' The waiter shook Archie's hand.

Archie froze. He narrowed his eyes. Surely not. 'As in… Alistair?'

The bartender pulled back sharply, and his eyes scanned the room with sudden hesitation. Archie looked at him uneasily. The Mancunian accent had thrown him, but there were other things that he knew about his great uncle that confused him here. He had never heard of Alistair Lethbridge-Stewart being a bartender and he certainly hadn't been born in Salford. If this was the man he was looking for, why was he lying to him, and why was he putting up this frankly bizarre pretence?

'I'm sorry, did I say something to upset you?'

Al stared at him for a moment and then relaxed, his smile returning. 'No, sorry. I just… It reminded me of something that someone once said.'

Archie held up his hand, returning the smile. 'Think nothing of it, Al,' he said, trying to not look at the other man too closely. It was amazing, the more he looked, the more the man resembled a Lethbridge-Stewart. And yet he didn't. It was most perplexing.

'Let me top up your drink,' Al said, reaching for the whisky bottle and adding to Archie's glass without waiting for a reply.

As he sipped his drink, Archie noticed two men in black suits take a seat at the bar, talking in what he thought was a Russian accent. Ever so subtly, Al pulled away, catching the two Russians in his gaze. They didn't seem to be paying him any attention, but Archie was certain that his great uncle was listening to their every word and understanding it.

That at least made sense. During the First World War, Naval Commander Alistair Lethbridge-Stewart had worked with British Military Intelligence in Russia, before switching careers and joining the Army. The war was some years away yet. As far as Archie remembered, at this point his great uncle was still an active officer of Her Majesty's Royal Navy.

But then, the fake accent, the fake background. Al was clearly here undercover. But why? Archie knew so little of his great uncle's career in British Military Intelligence that he couldn't even attempt to guess at the motivation behind such an *assignment*.

For the first time, Archie wished he'd taken more interest in his family's history. That had been more James' interest — a fact Archie's grandad always brought up whenever the opportunity presented itself.

As Al moved to serve the two Russian gentlemen, Archie noticed his body language change, as well as his accent, confirming Archie's deduction that something else was going on here — his great uncle was doing much more at the *Palais Garnier* than simply tending bar.

Archie decided to leave before Al picked up on his suspicions.

By the time he reached the rendezvous point, Anne was already there, chatting away in French with two women, one that looked to be in her twenties, the other her fifties. While certainly dressed for the occasion, their finery wasn't as extravagant as some of the other opera goers. But their expressions were happy, and they seemed genuinely elated to be there. Archie might not have a fine appreciation for the opera, but it was encouraging to see how much joy it brought others.

Anne turned to greet him, another full glass of champagne in her hand. Archie remarked that she seemed in a very good mood, too, even if it might all be a façade.

'How did you get on?' she asked warmly.

Archie hesitated. 'I met my great uncle.' He glanced around. 'Any sign of Lillian?'

Anne indicated the far side of the room, where Lillian and her entourage were standing, in bright full-length gowns, giggling away as they drank champagne. Lillian (he was having trouble with thinking of her as his granny) looked stunning in a full, emerald green gown. Green had always been her colour. As he watched her, the idea of her falling madly in love with Alistair seemed preposterous. He was, so the stories went, so very unlike his brother.

'They just arrived, fashionably late,' Anne noted, turning to her new companions. 'Matthew, allow me to introduce you to Madame Chomette and her daughter, Alexandrine.'

Archie nodded his head in their direction and smiled. '*Bonjour.*'

'*Bonjour,*' the elder woman said, inclining her head.

'Welcome to Paris,' Alexandrine added.

Archie hesitated and Anne laughed. 'Alexandrine here speaks very good English. Entirely self-taught.'

Alexandrine grinned. 'Working in a restaurant, you pick up a lot of languages. And we have a lot of British tourists. Are you a scientist too, like Anne?'

Archie laughed. 'No, not quite. I teach mathematics.'

'I'm afraid I don't understand mathematics all that well.'

'But your English is exceptional,' Archie told her warmly. It was always good to see young people apply themselves and he imagined it was not easy for a young waitress in nineteenth century France to study, no matter what the subject.

Attendants moved to the various doorways. With a bustle of excitement, the mass of opera goers started to make their way to their seats, as staff collected empty champagne glasses quickly. Archie swallowed his whisky with a large, satisfying gulp.

Anne handed her empty glass to a passing attendant and turned to Alexandrine. 'Where are you seated?'

'Fifth tier.'

'Oh, we're just below you on the fourth. Enjoy the show.'

'And you.' Alexandrine beamed, taking her mother's arm and chatting away excitedly as they queued for their seats.

Anne took Archie's arm in her own, and they made their way across the busy room. 'How was your great uncle?'

Archie sighed. 'Not what I expected. He's a bartender.'

Anne raised an eyebrow. 'I thought he was in the military?'

'He was, both before and after his time with British Intelligence. And, as I understand things, up until this point my family's history matches that of my alter ego. Therefore, whatever Alistair is doing here, it's the same thing he was doing in my world, too.'

'That's because right now, this is your world... *Our* world,' Anne said, correcting herself. 'Reality is splintered here, tonight, creating a different timeline to the one your *alter ego* lived in.'

Archie lowered his head. All this time travel lark was damned confusing. He'd thought he was starting to get a handle on it, but interacting with his own history... Well, it wasn't as straightforward as it had all seemed.

'We're going to have to wait until the interval to make contact with Lillian,' Anne said, switching subject.

Archie nodded. 'In theory, all we need to do is observe and make sure they meet each other.'

'And let history take its course.'

They reached the attendant and showed their tickets.

'Shall we enjoy the opera in the meantime?' Anne asked as they passed on through to the seats.

Archie suppressed the urge to sigh. 'Well, it would be a shame not to, now that we are here.'

CHAPTER FOUR
A Place of Death

THE AUDITORIUM was as impressive as anything else Archie had witnessed in the *Palais Garnier*. The inside of the dome was exquisitely painted, framed in gold and, at its centre, a shining chandelier shone like a magnificent jewel. Red velvet seats were lined in rows before the grand stage and across rising levels, separated by golden columns.

Anne informed him that the opera house had a Baroque-style interior decor and *Beaux-Arts* exterior architecture, but it meant very little to him. He was a man of mathematics; he could appreciate the beauty, but he couldn't quite connect with it the way Anne did. Given that she was a scientist, he found her love of art and culture a bit of an enigma itself.

He was learning tonight that people did not always fit the boxes you presumed them to be in.

Soon, the main lights went down, and the opera began. At first, Archie found the urge to fall asleep overwhelming. It had been a long couple of weeks. Certainly, he had slept plenty while in George's world, but it was always fitful, interrupted. The sense of unease he had felt there was absent here – there was an unusual feeling of comfort sitting in an opera house in the past.

After a while, the music won him over, and he began to appreciate it was quite beautiful in its own way.

The applause, the grandeur and the heavenly music echoed throughout the main auditorium and, an hour later, Madame Caron returned to the stage for an encore to the first act. The singer was exceptional, there was no denying it. Her grand, beautiful voice filled the room and Archie was forced to admit the praise his granny had given Madame Caron had been well deserved.

Archie felt a surge of energy within him as Madam Caron began a second verse. As much as he found her voice stunning, he was eager for her encore to be over and for the opera goers to make their way back to the upper foyer. His heart thud in his chest. Everything hinged on what came next.

He wanted to believe it would all be easy. Simply introducing Lillian to Alistair, but recent experiences had taught him that it would be anything but simple. He expected trouble. Lots of it.

He smiled briefly to himself. Was this the kind of life his alter ego lived? If so, Archie could not entirely deny the thrill it brought him.

He looked to a wide-eyed Anne, who had a tear running down her cheek. Archie was about to reach out to her when a thundering crack shook the room.

For a brief moment, everything stopped.

There was no sound.

Before he could catch a second breath, a blinding light followed and he wondered, somehow, how a storm could have erupted from within the opera house. It all lasted a mere second; the thunder, the lightning and the dust crashing down upon them as he stared up at the shadow rushing towards the audience.

The chandelier came crashing down.

The world exploded into chaos.

Anne gasped for air, feeling dust on her face. Her ears were ringing, her eyes still trying to adjust to the flash of light that had blazed out across the audience. Sights and sounds were distorted and, for a moment, she felt a rising panic. This must have been what drowning felt like.

All around, people were screaming and shouting, ripping themselves from their seats. She turned her head and saw Archie frozen, a small cut on the side of his dust-covered face. She quickly checked her arms, moved her neck, looking for any sign of injury. Gingerly, she ran her trembling hand over her face. Dust aside, she was fine.

Anne had no idea what had happened. One moment she had been entranced in the heavenly voice of Madame Caron, managing ever so briefly to put her thoughts of Bill aside, the next, screams of panic filled the auditorium.

Quickly, she scanned her surroundings. People were frantically trying to get away from their seats, many covered in dust, a couple like Archie with light cuts in their hands and faces. Some spectators were even shoving each other aside, trying to climb over the balustrade to jump into the pit below. Attendants and a couple of policemen were already on site.

'Archie!' she shouted over the din. He didn't respond, his eyes wide as he stared out. 'Archie!'

He snapped out of his catatonia, and stared at her in disbelief. 'Anne?'

'Do you know what happened?' she shouted back. The noise of the panicked spectators clambering over seats towards the exits was almost deafening.

Archie raised a trembling hand up, pointing towards the dome above. Anne looked up and her eyes went wide with shock. Part of the chandelier had broken free. She turned her head and saw that a segment of the fifth gallery was gone. The missing section of the chandelier must have torn through the ceiling and floor.

'Oh my!'

Had anyone been killed?

The crowd was starting to disperse as staff moved in to clear the fourth gallery. '*De cette façon, rapidement!*' one of the attendants said gruffly, indicating for them both to make their way to the exit.

As they followed him, Anne glanced towards the stage, where Madame Caron and the other performers were still waiting anxiously, trying to call for calm. A number of spectators closer to the stage were still filing out.

Anne and Archie reached the exit, and a scream of terror filled the auditorium. Panic surged through Anne as she noticed the ceiling around the chandelier begin to catch fire. A barrel of flame rushed along a cable and spilled out onto the intricate artwork above.

Through the large windows at the entrance, she could already hear the ringing of bells outside as the fire department arrived.

'What do we do now?' Archie muttered as they neared the bottom of the staircase. He was still dazed. The small cut on his head wasn't deep, but it was still bleeding. 'Lillian and Alistair…'

Anne nodded thoughtfully, trying to gather her thoughts. Memories of her anniversary with Bill. Grief over his death. Now this. The *Palais Garnier* was the last place she wanted to be. But she was a professional. She'd worked with UNIT for almost a decade; she'd dealt with much worse than a theatre full of panicked people.

'I don't know, Archie,' she said, keeping her voice steady. 'We'll have to reconvene and form a new plan. They're both still in the city, so if we can—'

She was cut off by an anguished scream above as one of the panicked guests burst into tears. It was Alexandrine. Without hesitation, Anne rushed up the staircase despite the protestations of the two attendants behind her. The young woman in her torn grey dress was weeping, her face covered in blood, her hair dishevelled. She was limping on her right foot.

A policeman stepped in to block Anne's path. *'Vous devez retourner au foyer!'* he demanded gruffly.

Anne would not leave Alexandrine, not when she was injured. Anne shot him a cold glare and reached out to take the girl's hand. The policeman relented, seeing the act for what it was.

Alexandrine grabbed her hand in return. There was a deep gash to the side of her face, but for all the blood, that seemed to be the worst of her injuries. Anne looked around. Where was Madame Chomette?

'*Où est ta mère?*' she asked nervously.

Alexandrine wiped blood and tears away from her eyes and looked back to the doorway leading to the fifth gallery. Anne gulped down the nausea in her throat. Alexandrine's mother, with whom Anne had spent a delightful conversation about local French cuisine just an hour before, had to be still in there.

Alexandrine refused to leave until her mother was found, and Anne waited for her as the frantic search began.

Firemen marched into the auditorium to tackle the blaze, while the staff worked to direct the rest of the attendees to safety. She saw Archie join the guests assembled below, and she shot him a reassuring smile as she stayed at Alexandrine's side.

A dust-covered figure was carried out a moment later and Anne felt a swell of hope, until she realised that the woman limping on her leg, a deep gash across her right eye, was not Madame Chomette. After what seemed forever, two more men appeared at the entrance to the fifth gallery, holding a limp body under the cloth.

Anne's heart raced, her gut swirling with nausea. She fought down her own discomfort and ordered Alexandrine to look away as the body was laid down outside the auditorium.

Anne caught a glimpse of the body. It was definitely Madame Chomette; Anne could make out the pink beading on her dress. But the face was unrecognisable, the skull crushed, her right hand and leg torn apart. Anne made sure to direct Alexandrine's face away, until the girl's mother had been completely covered.

An image of Bill, dead on the floor of Copeland's lab, flashed before her and she felt the sting of tears in her eyes. Taking a shallow breath, Anne focused her attention on helping Alexandrine make the descent down towards the lobby where the rest of the spectators were still assembled, subdued in a collective quiet panic.

Archie joined her side. 'Lillian is about to leave,' he muttered in Anne's ear, indicating the entrance where

Lillian and her entourage were making their hasty departure. None of them appeared injured, thankfully.

With Alexandrine still clutching her arm, Anne hesitated over their next course of action. How could she abandon the woman in the wake of her mother's death? At the same time, there was still a mission to complete. Or resuscitate. There was going to be no interval. Lillian could not possibly meet Alistair now.

It had to come down to numbers, didn't it? What was one person's grief compared to the potential lives lost if Anne and Archie failed in their mission?

'Have you seen Alistair?' she asked, scanning the crowd, even though she had no idea what Archie's great uncle looked like.

Archie shook his head, looking back towards the entrance worryingly. 'Lillian…?'

'She'll be fine,' Anne reassured him. 'We know where she's staying. Right now, our priority is finding Alistair.'

Archie agreed with a nod. 'I'll have a look around. See if I can find him.'

Anne wanted to follow, but Alexandrine was still sobbing at her side. She was surprised the young woman was still managing to stand.

Numbers. Anne was a scientist. She couldn't let her heart lead her in this.

As much as she found herself wracked with guilt, she called over to an attendant and asked him to look after Alexandrine. The woman was in such a state that she barely noticed the man take her arm and lead her away.

Anne muttered an apology and hurried after Archie.

They bustled their way through the crowd, quiet enough not to attract the attention of the police, who were growing in number in the lobby. They continued their search. At the far end of the crowd, Anne caught sight of two gentlemen in black suits and top hats moving swiftly through the crowd, away from the entrance. There was something oddly suspicious about them. Anne pushed her way forcibly past a couple of women to reach Archie and tugged on his arm. She pointed towards the two gentlemen.

Archie frowned. 'The Russians,' he muttered quietly.

Anne hesitated. 'Russians?'

'They were at the bar. Alistair was acting rather oddly around them. Evidently something to do with his reason for being here.'

Anne caught a gleam of something silver and froze. One of the men had pulled out a long-barrelled gun. While the second Russian scanned over the crowd, the first took a big step forward and jabbed the weapon into the back of a man wearing a long black coat.

'Alistair,' Archie hissed in Anne's ear.

They watched as Alistair was forcibly marched forward, the revolver digging into his back. The Russians pushed their way through the crowd to the back of the lobby. One of the abductors forced open a service door and shoved Alistair though. The Russians followed him swiftly.

'Let's follow them,' Archie said.

There was a shout from behind them and Anne turned to see a policeman walking in their direction. She hurried her pace and shoved open the door, dragging Archie in behind her before they could be intercepted.

The room beyond was smothered in pitch darkness. Glass broke beneath her feet. A broken lamp? There was a flicker of orange light and she saw Archie's face, reflecting in the small flame rising from the lighter in his hands.

'Do we have a plan?' Anne asked.

'I'm rather afraid I'm making this up as I go,' Archie said with a slight smile. 'All I know is we can't let the Russians do anything… untoward… with Uncle Alistair. Come on.'

Anne nodded, and followed.

Each step took them deeper into the darkness. The air was cold and stale, the unsettling stench of sewage rising the further down beneath the opera house they went. Archie was silent beside her; the only sound she could hear was their heavy breathing. He had put the lighter away, afraid that even the smallest light might attract attention. Anne felt goosepimples on her arms and wished she had a coat. The dress, despite its full-length skirt and covered arms, did little to keep her warm. Her shoes were certainly not what she would have picked to have gone chasing people through dark tunnels beneath the streets of nineteenth century Paris.

The darkness ahead was suddenly broken by a glimmer of yellow light.

Anne stopped and she held out her hand to Archie's chest to halt him. The ground had levelled out. The light ahead revealed tall stone columns before them. Anne gently pushed Archie behind the nearest column, joining him to keep out of sight of whatever it was making the light. Her heart pounding in her chest, she dared to glimpse around the side of the column and saw a figure emerge, carrying a metal cannister in his hand. An oil lamp burned within, protected by a glass door, the whole metal box fixed to a handle.

The light was bright enough to flood his immediate surroundings and Anne was forced to step a little further back to avoid being seen.

Archie remained silent behind her.

Holding her breath, Anne tried to take in the features of the man. He was tall, very tall, with dark eyes beneath thick bushy eyebrows lit up by the glow of the lamp. He was dressed in black finery, obviously one of the spectators at the performance of *Hellé*. Not that he seemed the opera-going sort. He had a cruel and violent look to him.

The man turned on his heels and marched back along the tunnel. The lamp light lit up a series of columned arches leading off into different tunnels. Anne realised just how easily they could have got lost in this maze.

'We have to follow,' Archie said quietly.

Anne swallowed. 'We do.'

Quickly, with as much stealth as they could muster, they took up their pursuit.

At the end of the tunnel, the Russian vanished, the light lowering to the ground. Anne realised he was walking down more steps, leading deeper into the bowels of the city and closer to the smell of rank sewage air.

'You know,' Archie said, 'I do believe I've read something similar to this.'

Anne nodded, thinking the same. She smiled ruefully. 'Probably because the *Palais Garnier* was Gaston Leroux's inspiration.'

'Ah. That explains it.'

'Walking through history, Archie. A singular experience, isn't it?'

Anne glanced up at him, and he lifted an eyebrow at her.

'Not quite how I would have put it,' he said.

They reached the bottom step, and Anne froze as the man stepped away. He joined the other Russian, the one with the colt, who was still holding it against the small of Alistair's back and carrying a second lamp in his other hand. Alistair was facing away, silent and seemingly subdued. For a moment the Russians engaged in conversation, their voices muffled.

Anne took a step back up, ushering Archie behind her so as not to be seen. Only when the Russians moved on, did she approach the lower level. They snuck behind the nearest column out of sight.

At the bottom of the steps, a huge lake rippled like glass beneath the columns and archways, bathed in the glow of the two lamps.

'The Phantom's lair,' Archie said.

The water stretched out into the darkness, lost in the suffocating black that hung beyond the edge of the light. Even without the heavy stench of human waste and musty air trapped within the thick stone caverns, there was something grim and forbidding about the place that made Anne's blood run cold. It was a place of death.

Anne's heart pounded again, and she desperately tried to think of a course of action. The Russians' intent was clear.

They marched their prisoner along the narrow stone

walkway to the edge of the water. Anne had no weapon of her own, and she was sure Archie didn't either, and besides there was too great a distance between them and the Russians.

'Wait here,' Archie whispered in her ear and, without hesitation, slunk away from the column.

Anne watched nervously as the captors argued over Alistair's fate. Archie crouched beneath the next column, his face lit up as he held the lighter aloft. She hoped he wasn't going to do anything stupid.

Archie grabbed a dirty, whitish object from the ground. It was a skull. He threw the skull, aiming for the head of the Russian with the gun. It missed, whizzing past his head, and landed with an almighty splash into the dark water.

Both men turned and, taking the opportunity afforded him, Alistair struck. He wrapped his arms around the neck of the man with the gun. His hands were still tied at the wrists, which created a loop, allowing Alistair to throttle and drag the man down. The revolver fell to the ground with a clang, the sound echoing out through the huge chamber.

Archie ran and Anne joined him, both closing in on the second Russian. His face lit up in shock as he held the lamp aloft before him. In a flash, he placed the lamp on the ground and reached inside his coat, but Archie was at him before he could pull out the weapon.

He landed a fist into the Russian's face. The Russian staggered back to the ground, reaching out to stop himself from falling into the water.

Anne closed in, elbowing him in the stomach. He grunted, sliding back, and lost his grip. With a gasp, he rolled over the edge and disappeared beneath the lake's surface.

Alistair still held the first Russian in his grip, throttling the man. Anne heard a sudden snap and the Russian's head jolted to one side.

Alistair raised his arms and let the body slump to the ground. Without hesitation, Alistair kicked his captor over the edge into the water to join his comrade.

Anne grabbed the second Russian's lamp; the first had fallen and broken in the struggle.

'Who the blazes are you?' Alistair demanded gruffly, looking at first Anne and then Archie.

'I…' Archie stumbled over his words.

Anne wondered what he could possibly say. *Hello, I'm you're great nephew,' perhaps?*

She stepped forward. 'We were at the opera and we saw these men kidnap you. We… well, we came to the rescue.'

Alistair nodded. 'Well, thank you,' he replied, a little more softly. He regarded Archie closely. 'As you can tell, I'm not from Manchester, and neither am I a simple bartender. Commander Alistair Lethbridge-Stewart, British Military Intelligence,' he said.

'And these men?' Archie asked.

Alistair just smiled. 'Don't worry about them. Do you know, I'm not quite sure what I would have done if you two had not arrived at just the right moment.'

'You'd probably be dead,' Anne said coolly.

Alistair gave her a hint of a smile. 'I suspect I would be. Thank you.'

Anne jumped as a splash of water hit the ground at her feet. She spun, almost falling backwards as the Russian she had kicked into the lake pulled himself up from the water, gun in hand. For a moment, she thought that he was going to kill her.

Fortunately, Alistair got there first. Even with his wrists bound, he was able to fire the first shot. The bullet struck the Russian in the forehead and he fell back, plunging back into the water for the very final time.

Anne looked up. Archie took the lamp from her and gave her a reassuring tug on the shoulder. Calming herself, Anne turned to the man that had saved her.

'Thank you,' she said wearily.

Alistair's smile broadened. It was instantly disarming. 'My pleasure, Miss…?'

'*Mrs* Bishop. But Anne is fine,' she replied quickly. He

had a glint in his eye, and he smiled. She had no desire to be swept up in that charm.

'If I may ask,' Archie began, 'just what is going on here?'

Alistair's smile dropped and his posture straightened. 'Well, I suppose there's no point pretending now, is there? You just helped take down two members of the Gilded Serpent Society.' He looked down at the lake, and set off. 'Now… Let's find a way out of here, shall we?'

With little other option, and feeling they'd made some progress in their mission, Anne and Archie followed Alistair Lethbridge-Stewart, Secret Agent of the British Empire.

CHAPTER FIVE
The Path of Oddiyana

WHEN THE sun was high in the brilliant blue sky, the guides led the expedition to a halt on a wide plateau on Mount Jampa overlooking the valley below. The party separated into smaller groups, breaking out their supplies.

Eileen took out a couple of small pieces of soda bread and salted meat and shared them with George. She had no idea what kind of meat it was, but hunger gnawed at her and she was glad to have something in her. They finished off with a few swigs of cold water from a canteen they had purchased.

'You enjoy the view?' one of the guides asked.

'Yes. It's…. Breathtaking.'

The low hills of Tibet rolled out beneath them, rivers curving like silver snakes on the landscape. While Tsongkhar was no longer visible, she could make out a few other communities scattered in the distance. This place of beauty, with its vibrant culture, was unlike anything she had ever experienced in her life.

'I'm Eileen,' she introduced herself.

'I am Wangdak.'

'An interesting name.'

'It was my grandfather's name,' the guide explained, his English clear, if highly accented. 'And it will one day be my grandson's name.'

Eileen smiled. 'Your son is due to be a father?'

Wangdak laughed. 'No, Chözang is only four years old. But is tradition in my family, every other generation first son is called Wangdak.'

'That's a nice tradition. We have something similar in the UK. Names are passed down.'

Wangdak bowed his head. 'The Buddha is kind.'

'Yes, and his people have an incredible land.'

'A land that is contested. I brought my family to Tsongkhar to keep them safe, so that we may fully embrace the blessings of Mount Jampa. As Buddha says, those who are awake, live in a state of constant amazement.' With a smile, Wangdak departed so he could attend others in the camp.

Eileen watched him. She took in a deep breath, feeling her chest swell, a tear running down her cheek. Being among Tibetans was not something she would soon forget.

'Are you okay?' George asked, walking over to her.

She looked at her companion and smiled. 'I am well,' she replied, wiping the tear from her face. 'I am just taking a moment to appreciate this.'

George nodded. 'Terrific, isn't it?' He swallowed the last piece of salted meat, chewing thoughtfully. 'I thought we would be higher by now.'

'Ah, Mackay explained this to me. We snake along the base of Mount Jampa for a couple of days first. We only gain altitude after that.'

Movement behind alerted them to the packing-up of the rest of the expedition. It was time to move on.

'Do you think that man will come back?' George asked, as they began packing away their own supplies.

'I expected him to have struck again by now.' Eileen lowered her voice so that the rest of the group, particularly Travers, couldn't hear her. 'If he was so determined to kill Travers, I suppose he could have come back that first night while we slept, or laid a trap for us outside Tsongkhar.'

'That's a comforting thought,' George muttered grimly.

'All we need to do is keep Travers alive, make sure he meets the Doctor, so that in thirty-five years they can ally themselves again in London alongside Archie's alter ego.'

'Which will put the universe back?'

Such a big concept, Eileen wondered how she was able to even fit it inside her head. She tried not to think too hard on it.

'That's what we were told.'

The rest of the day continued without incident. The trail became a little trickier to navigate, though they didn't appear to be gaining any more height. Wangdak and his fellow guide were highly skilled, navigating a slight landfall and taking the party around a woodland outcrop back onto their path. When the sun started to set, they made camp in a small outcrop of caves. The guides performed a quick check that they weren't disturbing any local wildlife and set up a couple of fires in adjoining caverns.

As Eileen settled down on the cold rock floor, Mackay stepped over to join her. He had a big grin and a hip flask in hand. 'Fancy a tipple?' he asked, holding the flask out to her.

Eileen hesitated. 'No, thank you.' She wanted to keep her wits about her.

Mackay nodded and put the hip flask away. 'Do you mind if I join you?'

She offered him a smile. Just because Travers didn't recognise her in his future, that didn't mean she needed to isolate herself completely.

'Of course not. Please, I would appreciate the company.'

He sat down and removed his gloves, warming his hands against the fire. She was glad of the warmth too. There was a nasty chill in the air already, despite the shelter of the cave.

'Will we see any yeti tonight?' she asked, half expecting to see one of the mythical creatures appear at the entrance to the cave.

Mackay laughed. 'Certainly no this close to civilisation. They tend to live much higher up the mountain. They will likely be more cautious of us than we are of them. At least, that's always been my understanding of wild animals. Unless you're a leopard, of course. Did I no tell you about the time I was nearly eaten by one in the Amazon?'

Eileen smirked. He liked his stories. 'Yes, in the café. And again, at camp last night.'

Mackay laughed again. 'Ah, well it's a good story, Eileen.' He rubbed his hands against the chill and held them out to the fire again. 'This cave should provide a decent shelter tonight. We'll no even need the tents, as long as we cover the entrances.'

Eileen was glad of that. She might consider herself worldly, but sleeping in cramped conditions next to a sixteen-year-old boy was hardly appropriate.

'How high up the mountain were you when you saw the yeti?'

'Oh, a long way from where we are now, for sure. It's another four days to the Det-Sen Gompa. We will be hard pressed to find any sign of them before then. I—'

He was interrupted by a scream that echoed around them. Eileen jumped to her feet, and joined the rest of the party. The sound seemed to come from outside. Without hesitation, Eileen rushed to the entrance, George at her heels.

'Where's Travers?' she asked him. 'The other cave?'

'I… I don't know,' George replied, concern now crossing his hairless features.

'He went for a walk to clear his head,' Mackay said, coming up behind them.

'He would. You two wait here.'

'Now see here,' Mackay began, but Eileen was already heading out of the cave.

She heard footfalls behind her. She didn't expect either of them to obey.

It was bitingly cold outside, the wind billowing against the slope was so icy that she had to catch a breath. Eileen could hardly believe how quickly the temperature had plummeted. Unfortunately, there was no time to go back for her gloves. To her right, one of the villagers stood trembling, his face white with shock, his eyes wide as he looked down the path.

Travers stood a little further down, his arm bleeding from a gash in one of his coat sleeves. Behind him stood a man, eyes wide and fierce, a dagger to Travers' throat. She suspected this was the same man that George had fought off the other night. And the patched-up wound on his shoulder proved it.

'Okay, let's calm down,' Eileen said. 'There's no need for this. Just tell us what you want, and maybe we can see about giving it to you.'

The man sneered at her. Out of the corner of her eye she noticed George creep behind a group of rocks, hidden from the man holding Travers. Eileen tried to shake her head no, but with the man watching, she could barely twitch. Besides, something told her George would not listen.

'We are on a pilgrimage,' she continued, no longer to just calm the situation, but to distract the man.

He showed no sign of caring, so Eileen continued talking anyway. Behind her she heard the frightened mumblings of the expedition party, and a quick glance told her that Mackay was rummaging in his pack, no doubt for some sort of weapon. Which was the last thing the situation needed.

She gently waved him down. The man holding Travers noticed and tensed, bringing the dagger that bit closer to Travers' skin.

Eileen held her hands up. 'We don't need weapons. Words are all we need to solve things, don't you think?'

It was obvious the man did not. But that hardly mattered anymore. George had reached him. He moved fast, quicker than Eileen would have expected. He launched himself on the man's back, at the same time grabbing the dagger and pulling it away from Travers' neck. Travers leaned forward and rolled onto the ground. George and the man struggled, each vying for control of the dagger.

Eileen was surprised at George. Not only at his bravery, but at his skill in close quarters. In the few days they'd been in Tibet they had talked very little of George's life, but what he had said indicated a dark world, perhaps even darker than the war Eileen herself had left behind. It was tragic to see someone so young, so full of life and possibility, hardened in such a way. She was not one for mollycoddling, of course, but children should be allowed to be children.

George had grown up far too quickly.

Soon, George had the upper hand and the man tumbled backwards, down the sloping path. Such was his momentum, that he couldn't stop himself from slamming his head against the jutting rock. With an awful crack, he fell still.

Eileen and Mackay rushed down the path, Mackay to check on Travers, Eileen to check on George.

'Are you okay?'

'I…' George looked at the dead man. 'I've never… Reisha and Bowden were the ones who… They carried all the weapons. I mean, I've defended myself, but I never…'

'George.' Eileen tried to take his attention off the body. But his eyes wouldn't move.

'I didn't even want to use Pennyworth. Not unless I absolutely had to. I've seen death, of course, but it's not the same. Is it?'

Now he finally looked at her, Eileen saw the scared boy hidden beneath George's hardened exterior. She wished she knew what George had been talking about, but she got the gist.

'That was very brave of you,' she told him.

'It was,' Travers said, his voice almost a croak. He walked over to George. 'That's twice you've saved my life.'

George grinned, his façade returning in an instant. 'Told you, it's why I'm here.'

'Yes, you did say that.' Travers frowned a moment, then looked down at his attacker. He booted the dead body. 'If I'd wanted a shave, I would have asked,' he quipped, and Eileen smiled slightly.

A short time later, Eileen joined George in the cave. He was sitting by the fire, sipping some warm Tibetan butter milk tea, no doubt to calm the nerves now the excitement of the fight had settled.

Eileen held out the dagger that had been used on Travers. 'To replace the one that you lost.'

George grinned. 'This *is* the one I lost. The bastard must have taken it with him.'

'Language!' Eileen warned sharply.

George nodded sheepishly, his smile dropping. She gave him a curt smile and a friendly pat on the shoulder.

Travers entered the cave. 'Thank you again. I must say, you're quite handy for a student of history.'

As quick as a flash, George said, 'I'm a student of many things.'

Travers let out an unconvinced *hmm.* Mackay joined them, his expression troubled.

'They say he had the mark of an assassin. Someone hired him to kill you, Edward.'

'That's preposterous!' Travers growled. 'Who would want to kill me?'

'Could Professor Walters no be behind this?'

Travers shook his head, letting out a sort of rough laugh. 'No, that's ridiculous. He might think me a fool, but he wouldn't go as far as to kill me to stop me proving my theories.'

'Then who?'

'Have you met anyone recently that seemed strange to you?' Eileen asked. 'Someone who seemed out of place? Acted oddly?'

Mackay thought for a moment and then nodded. 'There was this one man, do you remember, Edward? He was at that village, just outside Lhasa? Very talkative.' Travers nodded, and Mackay turned back to Eileen.

'What was he like?' she asked.

Mackay shrugged. 'Nothing too remarkable, apart from his clothes. All dressed in black, some kind of leather. No any kind of fashion I've come across before. Tall. Curly blond hair. Had a wee bit of an unusual accent too. Seemed awfully interested in who we were and where we were going.' He creased his brow, thinking for a moment longer and then sighed. 'Of course, he might have just been interested to see another traveller in these parts.'

'Like we were, you mean?'

Mackay smiled slightly. 'Well, aye, I suppose so. Of course, you and George have rather proved yourselves.'

Eileen smiled in return.

'You could say that,' Travers agreed. 'Come, George, walk with me. I want to introduce you to Sonam. A lovely young woman, you'd like her.'

George tried to object, but Travers insisted, and, with some amusement, Eileen watched George stalk away with him.

It took George a while to fall asleep, replaying the fight over and over in his mind. He knew he couldn't have done anything differently, and he hadn't meant to kill the man, but still… Knowing you were, at least indirectly, responsible for taking someone's life. He didn't know how Bowden had lived with it. He supposed, like him, George had to remember the stakes. Travers *had* to live. What was the life of one assassin against the loss of millions… billions, even? Whole worlds, actually, if George really considered the fallout.

It was too much for his mind to grasp.

He was free of Happy's influence now, no longer guided and prodded by the Clown, he was finally free to be the man he wanted to be.

He just wished he knew who that would be.

Such thoughts remained with him as sleep finally won out.

The next morning, they set off early. And, after a couple of hours, the party came to a stop before a gap in the path where part of the mountainside had crumbled away. George made his way to the front, eager to find out what was happening. Shale and small boulders littered the trail ahead, the remnants of a small rope bridge hanging off the side of the cliff edge below. Mackay began chatting with Wangdak, while the other guide inspected the gap in the path. Travers joined George and looked over at the bridge.

'How's the arm?' George asked.

'It will heal. I'm glad you got your knife back.'

'Yeah, sorry he almost killed you with it.'

'And I'm sorry Sonam was not to your liking.'

'Yeah, she's nice enough, I suppose. But I… well, I've got a girl back home.'

'Splendid. What's her name?'

'Reisha Tr—' George stopped himself just in time. 'Trevithick,' he finished lamely. 'What about you? Got a wife?'

'Yes, my darling Margaret awaits me in England. A wonderful woman, very patient with my…' Travers chuckled. 'Obsessions, shall we say?'

For a moment they were silent.

'If you hadn't been there in the village at the right time, I would never have got this far,' Travers said honestly.

George smiled. 'Are you excited to see the yeti?'

Travers nodded. 'They are my life's work. Ever since I was sixteen I've wanted to see one, to prove they exist.'

Mackay joined them.

'What is happening?' Travers asked.

Mackay frowned. 'I'm no sure. Some kind of rockfall. Wangdak says there's another path about a mile back. A wee bit steeper, but he thinks we can make it.'

Having little choice, the party continued on. George remained close to Travers, just in case.

The new trail took a steep incline up the side of the slope, half-hidden by a wall of rock that shielded the way. The path led them to another rope bridge that ran across a huge chasm. The bridge looked much longer than the broken one, and much narrower. George didn't think it looked strong enough to hold everyone's weight. Cautiously, he peered over the edge. It was so dark below that he couldn't even see the bottom.

'I usually don't have a problem with heights,' Eileen muttered next to him. 'But that is quite a drop.'

Mackay had his hip flask again and took a quick swig. 'Calm your nerves?' he said, offering it to Eileen.

She hesitated and took the flask, having a short sip. She let out a gasp of disgust. 'Oh dear! What is that?'

'Something special I picked up in Lhasa. Makes you feel all nice and warm inside, doesn't it?'

Eileen nodded. 'Well, it certainly does that.' She looked across to the two guides who were already walking across the bridge, indicating for the rest to follow. 'Shall we get this over and done with?'

George went to ask for a drink too, but Mackay had already returned the hip flask to his coat. With a sigh, George followed Eileen, Mackay and Travers onto the bridge.

Everyone looked a little nauseous as they took each rickety wooden slat, one step after another, shuffling their hands against the rough rope handrail. A gust of cold wind blew across the chasm and for a moment there was a panic among the party as the bridge rocked side to side. Fortunately, it held steady. The bridge had obviously had its fair share of travellers in its time.

George grabbed the next bit of the rope behind Travers, feeling another gust of wind cut against his face. His nose had gone numb and his eyes watered from the cold, tears streaming down his face. Another blast of icy wind hit them, and he held onto the rope for dear life.

As Wangdak reached the other side, George looked back. There were four others behind him, all just as scared as he was. Behind them, a shape moved on the path close to where the bridge started. He dared to pull a hand free from the rope to wipe his eyes and focused.

His heart pounded in his chest. No one else had noticed.

Awkwardly, he indicated for the others to move around him as he held his position, trying to make out what was happening.

'George!' Eileen called out behind him. 'Keep moving!'

'Hold on, something's happening!' he cried back as the last of the expedition party shuffled past him.

A man, dressed all in black, moved to the edge of the bridge. A man with blond hair, just like the one Mackay had described. George felt a wave of panic as he saw the man pull a silver gun from his belt and aim it at one of the ropes fastened to a thick wooden post. There was a flash of red light. Instantly a wisp of smoke rose from the ropes.

George turned on his heels, no longer taking slow, steady steps.

'Run!' he screamed. 'He's cutting the bridge! We have to get off!'

CHAPTER SIX
The Warrior Monks

THE FINAL two villagers were still ahead of him, desperately running for the end of the bridge, all trepidation gone. Eileen, Mackay, and Travers made it to the far end and were screaming for George and the two villagers to move.

There was a second snap behind him. The bridge fell from beneath him. One of the two villagers had just about reached the end, and was thus able to grab hold of the cliff edge. But neither George nor the female villager were as fortunate. The woman screamed, and they both clung in terror to the ropes. With a heavy thud, they slammed against the cliff face.

His body ached from the impact, the muscles in his arms stretching as he clung on for dear life.

The woman above lost her grip, slipped. George stumbled, his gloved hand sliding down the ropes as he frantically reached to grab one of the loose wooden slats where his feet had been. The woman scrambled, grabbing another slat, her boot slamming against his shoulder as she fought to gain a footing. George winced, slipping down further, grabbing the next slat down.

Another rope fell into his eye-line.

'Take the rope!' he heard Mackay call out.

The woman above him continued to slip.

George twisted himself around, trying to grasp hold of the new rope. The wooden slat creaked under the pressure of his grip. He'd almost managed to grab the rope when, with a final creak, the wood snapped and for a brief second there was nothing but air beneath him.

His hands flailed out, and in a blind stroke of luck, they latched on to the rope. His weight pulling it taught, allowed the woman to reach out for it too. The wind continued to beat at them, knocking them against the face of the cliff.

'Hold tight!' Mackay shouted down.

Yeah, wouldn't have thought of that, George wanted to shout back, but he didn't have the breath.

It took what felt like hours, but was probably only minutes, for George and the woman to be pulled up. For a while he lay on the safe ground, gasping for breath. He tilted his head sideways, to see the woman being helped to her feet by other villagers. Eileen knelt down beside him.

'How are you?'

George struggled to his feet, flexed his hands gingerly and touched his ribs. 'I'll be okay, thanks. Probably have a few bruises for a while, but no broken bones as far as I can tell.'

'And you would be able to tell, mark my words,' Travers said, joining them.

Mackay remained by the cliff edge, looking across. Remnants of the bridge clung to the posts on the other side, but there was no sign of the mysterious man.

'What happened?' Eileen asked.

'Bridge finally gave up,' Travers supplied, before George could answer. 'It's been used for decades, bound to collapse eventually.'

'No, it wasn't that.'

Travers frowned at George. 'What was it then?'

'It was that man. The one you saw outside Lhasa.'

Mackay heard the revelation and came over. 'Blond hair, dressed in black?'

George nodded. 'He was… He cut the bridge while we were still on it. He tried to kill us.'

Travers rubbed the bristles on his chin. 'Could it really be Walters? So jealous that he hired an assassin…?'

'I don't think so,' Eileen said. 'In fact, I am certain this has nothing to do with Professor Walters.'

'Then what, dear lady?'

'The yeti,' George said. 'Whoever is behind this doesn't want you to find the yeti. Doesn't want you to reach Det-Sen.'

'But who?' Mackay asked.

'Who cares?' Travers growled in derision. 'If they think a couple of attempts on my life will stop me…'

'Three,' MacKay corrected him. 'And this time we could have all died.'

Eileen nodded, her expression firm. 'They're taking a risk, being careless. Next time they might tip their hand, reveal themselves.'

Mackay let out a *hmm.*

'I say we keep going,' Travers said gruffly. 'But stay alert. There is still a long way to go before we get to Det-Sen.'

And probably plenty more opportunities to try and stop you, George thought glumly.

The next day and a half of their journey passed without incident. As they gained altitude, so the bitter weather increased. The winds grew strong, and snow began to settle. There was a sense of anticipation spreading through the Tibetans, but for both George and Eileen, the trepidation continued to grow. The closer they got to Det-Sen, the more likely the mysterious time meddler would up his game. And they had to be ready. Too much was at stake.

The fourth day continued more or less as the previous one had. More walking, more stopping for rest, more dips in the weather. It was after their lunch rest-bit that something else finally happened. Not that George and Eileen minded the peace, better than being attacked, but they knew something more was coming, sooner or later.

They both rather it was over and done with.

George was packing the water canister into his sack and hoisting it over his shoulder, when he saw five men enter the camp and make their way to the two guides. Mackay and Travers quickly moved in to investigate and, with a quick nod to Eileen, George joined them, one hand on the hilt of his dagger.

The men wore long black robes and carried staffs about four feet in length. On their shoulders were curved pads adorned in a thick, white wool trim and they all wore tall black pointed hats with flaps running down the side of their face. Two were clean shaven, two others with wispy beards that trailed down to their chests. But it was the leader of the group that caught George's eye. A black half moustache ran down the side of each cheek, while his upper lip remained clean shaven. His eyes were black and fierce, and he looked like he meant business. George knew immediately that this new man shouldn't be underestimated.

Wangdak debated furiously in Tibetan with the man. Wangdak tried to take a step forward, but the two strangers either side moved forward, blocking his way threateningly with their staffs.

'What is the meaning of this?' Travers asked, charging up to the front of the party.

The leader of the strangers turned his attention to Travers, his stare hard and fierce. 'You must turn back, stranger,' he replied with perfect English. The tone was sharp. 'The path ahead is filled with danger.'

The fact that the leader could speak English took Travers by surprise. It was enough to put a hole in all his bluster.

'Good man, we are travelling to the Det-Sen Monastery.'

'Det-Sen is closed to outsiders.' The man slammed the butt of his staff to the ground. 'You *will* turn back.'

'I cannot.'

The action had not quite ruffled Travers' feathers as George first thought.

'I come to seek the metoh-kangmi.'

The leader seemed a little startled by Travers' admission. He hesitated, considering the professor's response. George took a step closer to the edge of the party.

Eileen joined him.

'The metoh-kangmi have grown wild, stranger. The mountain has grown dangerous. Your lives are in danger if you continue. You will turn back.'

'But…' Travers was about to continue his tirade, when Mackay put an arm reassuringly on his friend's arm.

'Be careful, Edward. Unless I am mistaken, these are the warrior monks of Det-Sen. They are more dangerous than they look.'

'Warrior monks?' Travers was clearly confused by this. 'Why would monks need to be warriors?'

'Tibet is always under threat, stranger,' the warrior monk said. 'From outsiders. Many gompas have been destroyed, but Det-Sen remains standing.' He turned to look at Mackay. 'You have been to Det-Sen before, stranger?'

'Not quite,' Mackay replied quickly. 'But I was on Mount Jampa a few years ago. And I saw a yeti once. It didn't attack me though.'

'Only recently do the metoh-kangmi attack so openly.' The monk straightened his back, his eyes wide. 'Perhaps I will listen more. My name is Khrisong.'

Travers nodded. 'A pleasure, Khrisong. I am Professor Edward Travers, and my travelling companion here is John Mackay.'

Khrisong considered the four westerners. 'Why do you wish to find the metoh-kangmi?'

'We wish to study them, to learn from them,' Travers said eagerly. 'I must confess, everything I have read about them suggests they are not dangerous. No more dangerous, certainly, than a mountain lion.'

Khrisong regarded Travers and nodded. 'You are right, Professor Edward Travers. In the past, they have been at peace with the mountain. But now they move openly, killing all that come near. Det-Sen has closed its doors, less it become overrun by the metoh-kangmi.'

Travers looked to Mackay, scratching his beard thoughtfully. He turned back to Khrisong. 'Can we help? Perhaps my studies will allow you to find out why they have turned so dangerous.'

Khrisong's eyes went wide with suspicion. 'You would help the monks of Det-Sen?'

'Absolutely!'

Khrisong turned to his warrior monks, muttering quietly in his native language, before addressing the expedition party who stood behind Travers and company. He uttered a command in Tibetan, and murmurs erupted among the group. The meaning was clear. Travers looked ready to explode, but Khrisong turned to his two men at the front.

'Professor Edward Travers and John Mackay will be allowed to come with us back to Det-Sen. We will accept the offer of help against the metoh-kangmi.'

With Travers calmed, Khrisong spoke once more to the expedition party. George didn't know what was being said, but it seemed to be polite. Khrisong indicated two of his monks; they were clearly being assigned to escort the party back down the mountain.

Eileen nudged George, indicating for him to take a step back. He nodded and headed slowly to the end of the party with Eileen, trying not to arouse suspicion.

'We need to get away quickly,' Eileen whispered, 'and follow Travers and the others.'

'Can't we just ask to join them?' George whispered back.

Eileen shook her head. 'Not without changing our cover story. Det-Sen will not be open to a teacher and her student, no more than it is open to the pilgrims. I think the best course of action is to sneak away now and track Travers and Mackay at a distance.'

George nodded. He wasn't convinced sneaking and tracking warrior monks was the safest of options, but she was right about raising suspicion. They needed to stay near Travers, particularly now that they were so close to the monastery.

CHAPTER SEVEN
Family Connections

A BELL rang out in the night, echoing across the empty streets of Paris eleven times. As they walked along the empty path, Archie counted each toll, surprised that it wasn't later. It certainly felt as if they had been walking through the dark, smelly tunnels beneath the city for hours. Time travel – perfect for messing up one's own sense of time.

At his side, Anne was silent, appearing lost in contemplation over the events that had befallen them that night, while Alistair was a few feet ahead, looking for signs of the enemy. They had been following him for a while, both of them at a loss after the abject failure of their mission. Between the falling chandelier and fighting Russian spies in the bowels of the city, it seemed impossible now that Alistair and Lillian would ever meet.

'That was very brave, what you did.'

It was the first time Anne had spoken since they had escaped the tunnels.

'I did nothing,' Archie said. 'I didn't even hit that man. I was aiming for his head.'

'If you had hit his head, he may have stumbled and knocked me into the water too,' Alistair said, stopping ahead of them. 'I am rather pleased I didn't go for a swim down there.'

Anne and Archie came to a halt before Alistair. The man looked at them suspiciously.

'Okay, I think the danger has passed. Who are you both?

Really?' He took in Archie fully, his gun still held firm in his hand. 'You seemed to recognise me at the bar.'

What was Archie supposed to say to that? The truth? That he was his great nephew from a possible future? Fortunately, Anne stepped forward before he could answer, her arms raised in an open gesture.

'You can trust us. We are not the enemy.'

Alistair regarded her coolly. 'Then why did you follow me?'

Anne smiled. 'I believe we were following the two Russian gentlemen attempting to murder you.'

Alistair responded with a hollow laugh, but he didn't lower his gun. 'That is very true. But I still don't know who you are, or what you are doing in Paris. Don't tell me it was to see the opera.'

Anne crossed her arms. 'The opera wasn't our only reason for coming to Paris.' She took a step forward, looking rather unfazed by the weapon in Alistair's hand. 'And I will give you the answers you seek. But first, are we expecting to encounter any more Russians tonight?'

'I don't believe so. But we should make our way off the streets as soon as possible. We have a safe house not far from here. I'll take you there, but then I *want* those answers.'

'We'll be happy to provide them,' Anne said. She beckoned him along. 'Lead the way.'

Satisfied, at least for now, Alistair nodded, and they all set off. Archie looked at Anne, and she merely smiled. He wondered what answers she had in mind.

The safe house was a small apartment on the top floor of a large Parisian townhouse. Alistair led them into one of four rooms, where three cots had been laid out with a few blankets and a small table. Two other armed men were present, but failed to share their names. They only spoke to demand who the 'strangers' were. Both Anne and Archie soon found themselves locked inside the room.

Anne laid down on one of the cots, rubbing her arms and legs and grabbing a blanket to wrap around her body.

As he sat down on one of the cots and grabbed a blanket of his own, Archie fought off the rising sensation of nausea that came with fighting off cold and exhaustion.

They adjusted to the warmth, neither of them having the energy to speak. Archie rested his tired head and leaned back against the wall behind the cot. The longer they waited, the temptation to lie down and sleep became overwhelming.

With the sound of footsteps and creaking floorboards outside, Anne sat up sharply.

'Follow my lead,' she whispered.

Archie nodded. What else could he do? It had been hard enough to adapt to George's world, but to lie to his great uncle, interact with his own past…? Archie was finding that a lot more difficult than he'd expected.

Alistair walked in. Thankfully, he no longer carried his gun. Instead, he held two steaming tin cups, and handed them to Archie and Anne.

'Sweet tea to calm your nerves.'

Archie took the mug gratefully and sipped. The tea was a little milky for his tastes, but that didn't matter. It was good to feel the warmth as it trickled down his throat. Alistair sat down on the third cot, allowing them both a moment to drink as he watched them.

'Okay,' Alistair said. 'Let us talk some truths. Who are you?'

Anne set her mug of tea down. 'We're part of the British Intelligence Branch too.'

Archie barely managed to hide his surprise. Alistair looked at her keenly, measuring his response. Archie would have felt deeply uncomfortable under that gaze, but Anne held it without hesitation, even picking up her mug to take another sip of her tea, without looking away.

'The Intelligence Branch?' Alistair asked, his expression somewhat bemused.

'Yes,' Anne replied firmly. 'Department MI10.'

Alistair raised his eyebrows. 'Can't say I recognise the name.'

'You shouldn't. It's still quite new. We primarily deal with foreign military attachments.'

Alistair wasn't entirely convinced, and Archie couldn't blame him. The Directorate of Military Intelligence wouldn't be separated into individual departments until the First World War.

Alistair held Anne's gaze and nodded. He turned to Archie. 'And him. Is *he* Intelligence too?'

Archie felt very small. He wasn't so practised in this sort of thing, like Anne. He was just a simple teacher of mathematics from Cornwall. In his line of work, he encouraged honesty at all times.

'Let's just say he works for me,' Anne replied, thankfully stopping him from having to lie.

'I see,' Alistair said slowly. His eyes narrowed, and he turned to Archie. 'You seem awfully familiar. Have we met?'

'The first time I saw you was at the opera house,' Archie said cautiously.

'Odd. You remind me of someone. But damned if I can tell who…' Alistair trailed off, his gaze lingering just a little uncomfortably long, before turning back to Anne. 'And what proof do you have?'

Anne laughed. 'I'm in Intelligence. I don't carry a badge with the words "Hi, I'm a spy, how can I help?".'

'Quite.'

'I can tell you what your file says though,' Anne added. 'Your full name is Alistair Conall Hamish Lethbridge-Stewart.' She turned to Archie. 'Would you care to tell Alistair here what else we know about him?'

Archie resisted the urge to smile. Of course, there were things only a family member would know. 'You were born in Carmunnock, Lanarkshire, Scotland. Your grandfather was…' He paused to recall the name. 'Conall Lethbridge-Stewart, and your father is Hamish Lethbridge-Stewart. You have a brother, Archibald Hamish Lethbridge-Stewart, who serves with the British Army.'

Alistair smiled. 'That's a very good recollection of my family history. Can you tell me what my childhood cat was called?'

Archie paused. A cat? How was he supposed to know a thing like that? But a flash of memory hit him. His grandad sneezing uncontrollably during a family visit to a cousin in Scotland. They had two cats and his grandad had complained the whole time.

'You never had a cat,' Archie said confidently. 'Your brother was allergic.'

Alistair held his gaze a moment longer and then smiled. 'Okay, you passed that test.' He turned back to Anne. 'If you really are in Intelligence, what were you doing at the *Palais Garnier*? That was *my* mission.'

'Keeping an eye on you.' Anne sipped her tea. 'I had heard that someone from the Society was on to you. And obviously, I was right.'

Alistair sighed. 'Perhaps. Perhaps. They have a base of operations working out of *Le Grand*. Maybe they recognised me.'

Archie felt his heart skip a beat. '*Le Grand?*' That was the same hotel in which Lillian and her friends were staying.

'At least three more members are based out of there. Whatever trade they are planning, it will take place at the hotel.'

Archie stood. 'I should get back there,' he said wearily, desperately trying to fight off exhaustion. 'I have a rendezvous I can't miss.'

'You're in no fit shape,' Alistair said, taking Archie's arm and guiding him back down onto the cot.

'He's right,' Anne added. 'I'm sure *everyone* will be safe in their beds right now. There is nothing to worry about.'

Alistair sat down on the edge of the third cot. 'We're clearing out the safe house at dawn. Stay here and rest and we'll re-plan in the morning.'

'I think that's a very good idea,' Anne said, stifling a yawn. 'Don't you, Matthew?'

Archie yawned, nodding as he fought back a second. 'I'll head to *Le Grand* in the morning.'

'I'll be in the next room if you need me,' Alistair said,

rising from the cot. He closed the door behind him as he left, but didn't lock it.

Anne turned to Archie. 'Lillian will be fine. I doubt she's caught up in all this. Her meeting with Alistair was a happy accident, and now that she hasn't even met him… Well, she'll be safe in her bed asleep.'

Archie nodded. 'Okay. You're probably right. But we still need to get them to meet.'

'Without dragging her into Alistair's world.'

'Something tells me that won't be so easy to do.'

Archie awoke to see the pink skies of dawn breaking over the rooftops of Paris. As he lay on the cot, staring out of the narrow, dusty window, he could feel the aches in every muscle in his body. Slowly, he sat up, stretching his limbs, feeling a couple of uncomfortable cracks in his neck and back.

Anne stirred in her cot. She gave him a wry smile. 'Good morning.'

Archie smiled back. 'A pleasant sleep?'

Anne sniggered and stretched out her arms. 'Oh, the very best.' She sat up, rubbing her eyes. 'What time is it?''

'I have no idea.' Archie muffled a yawn with his fist. 'It's getting light outside.'

Despite how tired he still felt, he forced himself to stand. There was no time to rest. Not with Lillian in a hotel populated by a dangerous criminal organisation.

'We need to go,' he said, grabbing his shoes from the side of the cot and hurriedly putting them on.

He had no idea what he was going to do once he got to *Le Grand*; he didn't even know what rooms Lillian and her friends were staying in. But he couldn't just sit there, hoping that a situation would present itself. The falling chandelier had put an end to that.

'Hold on,' Anne said, rising. 'We have to think. The entire situation is fraught with danger. For all we know, this Gilded Serpent Society was behind what happened at the *Palais Garnier*.'

'They were not.'

Archie hadn't even noticed Alistair standing there in the opening doorway. His great uncle was wearing a grey overcoat and bowler hat. He looked very different to the young bartender he had met last night.

Anne frowned. 'They weren't?'

Alistair shook his head. 'Apparently, one of the suspension wires holding the chandelier wore down and sparked a fire, causing one of the counterweights to break free. There was no sabotage as far as we can tell, though a workman due to complete maintenance on the chandelier was ill yesterday. A young man by the name of Frederick Goff. If anybody's to blame, it's him. Intentionally or not.' He sat down on the cot, removing his hat.

'Goff?' Anne asked, the colour draining from her face. 'Are you sure?'

Alistair nodded. 'You know him?'

Anne considered a moment. 'Goff is my mother's family name. I don't recognise the Christian name.' She hesitated. 'I'm sure it is a coincidence, that's all.'

She didn't seem so sure to Archie. And he could see why.

This whole thing was happening because of the importance of his family line, and Anne's. They were destined to be entwined, to work together, to secure the future of millions. Although it was the meeting of Archie's alter ego with Anne in 1969 that was the first time such an alliance saved the world, it now seemed that their families were connected even further back.

It wasn't beyond the realm of possibility that if Frederick Goff hadn't been ill, then he would have seen the issue with the chandelier and it wouldn't have fallen. And Alistair and Lillian would have met as history said.

Frederick Goff's illness was no accident.

'Are we certain the Society had nothing to do with his absence?' Anne asked, clearly on the same line of thought as Archie.

Alistair sighed. 'I cannot say for certain. We are still trying to determine the Society's next move.'

Archie didn't have time for deliberations. He needed to make sure Lillian was safe. 'It's time I checked in with my… friend at *Le Grand*.'

Alistair regarded him a moment, perhaps trying to deduce who this person at *Le Grand* was. Finally, he nodded. 'Let me find you some breakfast first. You must be famished.'

Archie could not disagree with that. His great uncle left the room, closing the door behind him.

'I should stay here,' Anne said nervously.

Archie frowned. 'You think we should split up?'

Anne nodded. 'You absolutely have to make your way to *Le Grand* and keep an eye on your grandmother. If we lose her now, this mission is over. But we also need to keep watch over Alistair, too. He thinks we're spies; I can play into that. You locate Lillian and I'll find a way to position Alistair into making his way to *Le Grand*. With any luck, we can engineer some kind of encounter and hopefully get the future back on course.' She paused. 'Besides, I want to be certain there's nothing more to Frederick Goff's illness.'

'He's your… what, great, great…?'

Anne shrugged. 'I wasn't lying. I don't recognise the name, but he's clearly a distant ancestor. The first time, I assume, your family and mine crossed paths. Indirectly, at least.'

'Yes, I surmised the same thing.'

'Keep Lillian close,' Anne said. 'Find a way to engage with her if you can, but don't act suspiciously. Can you do that?'

'I will try my best.'

CHAPTER EIGHT
Reflections on Destiny

ARCHIE TOOK a carriage to *Le Grand*. He found a small café en route, where he enjoyed a little something more substantial. Despite the second breakfast, he still felt exhausted. He walked down the *Rue Auber*, and the familiar grand domes of the *Palais Garnier* rose into view. He was relieved to see that the fire had not spread to the rest of the opera house. Before the steps leading into the *Palais Garnier*, a large crowd had gathered. On the steps stood two well-dressed gentlemen, accompanied by four stern looking policemen, trying to appease the rather tense throng of people.

Archie cautiously made his way to the back of the crowd, trying to pick up what was being said. Unfortunately, his French wasn't strong enough to keep up. He was, however, able to sense the mood of the crowd. And it was deteriorating fast.

He was surprised to catch sight of Lillian in the crowd a few feet away. Dressed in a pale, lavender dress and matching bonnet, she appeared to be alone; none of her travelling companions were with her. With tensions rising in the crowd, Archie moved closer, trying to work out what he would say to her.

'Lillian McDougal?' he said softly, stepping to her side.

Lillian looked at him and frowned. Her eyes seemed cold and distant; his childhood memories were of a woman with a warm smile and a glint in her eye.

'Yes?'

'How are you?' he asked rather awkwardly. 'I trust you escaped last night's incident unscathed?'

She hesitated. 'Yes, I am fine, thank you for asking.' She looked back to the men on the steps again, returning her attention to what was being discussed.

Archie didn't seem to be making much progress. 'I think…'

She cut him off, frowning again. 'My apologies, sir, have we met?'

Archie smiled. 'Oh, I'm sorry. Yes. Yesterday afternoon at the *Café de la Paix*.'

Lillian sighed, as the memory dawned. 'Oh, you were with your delightful friend. Do forgive me. Last night was… trying… to say the least. Were you at *Hellé* too?'

'I was. Such a tragedy.'

'Yes, it was. That poor woman…' Lillian broke off, her face solemn. She took a deep breath. 'Oh, it is fine. I wasn't hurt. None of my friends were injured.' She hesitated, her hand rising unsteadily as she pointed to the cut on his forehead. 'But you were?'

Archie waved his hand dismissively. 'It was nothing. A minor graze, nothing more.'

'Well, I am most glad of that… Matthew, wasn't it?'

'Yes,' Archie said, and offered a smile. He supposed he would have to get used to that name.

A rumble of angry mutterings rippled across the crowd.

'Do you know what he is saying?' Archie asked. 'My French is a little rusty.'

'Rusty, what a peculiar phrase,' Lillian mused, turning back to the speaker. '*Monsieur* Lépine, the local police superintendent, and *Monsieur* Guénin, the district superintendent, are trying to assure the crowd that this was an accident, but they refuse to admit culpability.'

Archie sighed. Bureaucrats in any time period were much the same. 'Even with the death of Madame Chomette?'

Before Lillian could respond, several people erupted in uproar and a number of men towards the front of the crowd began pushing their way forward. The policemen immediately marched towards the crowd, batons ready. Two men behind Archie and Lillian began muttering away angrily, and shoved their way forward. Lillian gasped as she was shoved to the side. Archie rushed to grab her arm, stopping her from falling. He quickly wrapped his arm around her shoulder and marched her away from the angry mob.

Lillian gasped, catching her breath as they stopped, several feet away from the angry crowd.

'What ruffians! You saved my life, Matthew,' she added, fluttering her eyelashes at him.

Archie smiled awkwardly. 'Not quite, but I'm glad you are safe.'

She brushed down the folds of her dress and readjusted her bonnet. 'Oh nonsense. You are my hero. How can I ever repay you?'

'Your safety is all the reward I need.'

'Heroics like that deserve a proper reward. What can I do to show my gratitude?' Lillian paused a moment in thought, and then grinned excitedly. 'I shall buy you dinner tonight at the *Café la Paix*. If that is not too forward of me?'

Archie hesitated again. For this time period, it probably was. But if there was one thing he remembered about his granny, it was that she was a boundary pusher. She wasn't someone who let herself be constrained by the rules of society.

He considered her proposal. Dinner at least would allow him to keep an eye on her.

'It would not be too forward at all, Lillian,' he said with a smile. 'But I want to make sure you are okay. Do you have plans for the rest of the day?'

'Alas, my companions and I are off to the *Louvre*. And then a trip down the Seine to the Eiffel Tower.'

At least she would be away from *Le Grand*. He couldn't do much more, unless he started stalking her from a distance, and now that he had made proper contact, he didn't want to jeopardise that.

'Well, I hope you and your companions have a lovely

time. I will see you tonight for dinner.'

'Wonderful!' she gasped with delight. 'Then I shall await your company this evening. Would you care to meet me in the lobby of *Le Grand* at six o'clock, Matthew?'

Lillian certainly knew what she wanted.

'Six o'clock,' Archie agreed, warmly.

'Oh, how delightful! Well, good morning to you, Matthew. I shall see you for dinner tonight.'

Archie bowed his head. 'I look forward to it, Lillian.'

She swept up the skirts of her dress and marched back to her hotel. Archie watched her go nervously, reminded of Anne's remark last night. He would have to play it carefully. He couldn't have his own granny falling for him before she even had a chance to meet the man with whom she was destined to start a family line upon which Archie's life depended.

What a thought, he considered. Not only did he now have to ensure that Lillian and Alistair met so that the timeline was restored, but now he had to make sure that *he* wasn't the reason for erasing himself from existence.

And that didn't even take into account the potential threat posed by the Gilded Serpent Society.

Anne wrapped the blanket around her, glad of the warmth as she sat on the bench overlooking the River Seine. She was still dressed in her dark blue ball gown from the opera, with only a blanket to cover her, but she didn't really care. Even the rank smell rising from the waterway couldn't distract her from the moment of solace, watching the busy city of nineteenth century Paris pass her by.

Archie had been gone for a couple of hours now, and Alistair and his men were clearing out the safe house at the end of the street. Rather than get in their way, she had chosen to find a place where she could gather her thoughts and consider her next plan of action.

Like Archie, she found herself at a loss as to how to proceed. The disaster at the *Palais Garnier* had sent their mission perilously off course.

She had faced disasters before, come up against nefarious villains, hot-headed thugs and her fair share of monsters. Her life working in UNIT had shown her that you had to think on your feet, keep your wits about you even when the next step felt impossible, when the odds felt overwhelmingly against you. But this time felt different. While Archie had certainly proven his worth last night, the truth was she felt alone, more so than she had done in a very long time. No Spencer Pemberton, no John Benton.

And no Bill.

Since being scooped up from that Parisian hospital by the Accord, she hadn't really allowed herself time to grieve. But being back in Paris, it was difficult to *not* think about her husband.

She could at least take some comfort in knowing their daughter, Samantha, was safe at home with Anne's mother. Anne wasn't sure what would happen when she returned home. She expected the Guardians to return her to the same spot from which they'd taken her, so in a manner of speaking her life was literally on hold. All the pain, the hurt, the loss, all of it was on hold while she completed her mission. Saved the universe, saved her own future.

She wiped the stray tear aside as a ray of sunlight gleamed off the side of the Eiffel Tower in the distance, a radiant burst of gold against the edge of the cityscape. Anne squinted, took in the light, and her mouth parted, surprising herself as a smile formed on her lips. For a moment, her memories of Paris with Bill were not filled with grief, but a surge of happiness. Memories that she treasured dearly.

'I love you, Bill.'

She pulled the blanket tightly about her, sitting up as two figures approached. Alistair and one of his fellow intelligence officers. Cedric, she thought his name was. She had been bombarded with several names that morning.

Alistair came to a stop before her, indicating his hand to the space on the bench beside her. She smiled and he sat down in silence. Cedric took a step towards the railing running alongside the river, looking up and down the quiet street.

'The safe house is cleared,' Alistair told her. 'We are ready to move to our new location. Are you with us?'

Anne nodded. 'I am.'

'Good. Then we should make a move soon. We found Frederick Goff.'

Anne held her breath. She had no idea how Frederick fit into her family line, or whether he was simply a distant cousin, but whichever way she looked at it, he was proof that her family was an important part of events in 1896. Of ensuring the union between Lillian and Alistair happened.

'Is he okay?'

Alistair nodded. 'He seems to be recovering from whatever illness had inflicted him. Cedric here was the one to visit his home,' he added, beckoning for his colleague to join them. 'Tell Anne what you told me.'

Cedric nodded, his back straight and hands clasped behind him as he delivered his report. 'Frederick Goff was struck ill after his shift at the *Palais Garnier* two nights ago. He made a quick stop at an inn close to his apartment. One drink later and he was barely conscious. He seemed surprised that he made it home in one piece.'

Anne frowned. 'Was he poisoned at the inn?'

Cedric shrugged. 'We cannot be certain. The only thing he could recollect was chatting briefly to a tall man with plain black clothing and curly blond hair.'

Anne considered. Clearly Frederick's drink had been spiked.

'It was the only thing he could remember between leaving the *Palais Garnier* and waking up violently ill the following morning,' Cedric said. He paused, removed his hat and wiped his brow. 'If it was poison, it does not appear to be fatal.'

No, it wouldn't be, Anne thought. Just strong enough to prevent his work on the chandelier. To make sure Lillian and Alistair did not get to meet.

'Do we know who this man with the blond hair is?' Anne asked.

Alistair sighed. 'That is the question. Judging by Goff's description, he doesn't appear to bear any resemblance to the members of the Gilded Serpent Society we have observed. That is not to say he isn't one of them though.' He returned the bowler hat to his head and stood. He looked nervously up and down the street. 'Are you ready, Anne?'

'More than you will ever know, Alistair,' Anne said, and stood. 'Let's move out.'

CHAPTER NINE
The Wild Men of the Snows

EILEEN AND George followed Travers, Mackay and the warrior monks at a safe distance. Khrisong clearly knew some shortcuts up the mountain, off the main pilgrim path, and it wasn't until the sun began to sink beneath the horizon that the monks finally stopped for a breather. They came to a halt at what looked like remnants of a camp side.

Eileen and George snuck in behind a narrow rock formation, crouching low so not to be seen, but close enough that they might listen. There was some debate going on, and Eileen wanted to be prepared.

'We came across this camp this morning,' Khrisong was telling Travers and Mackay. 'We tracked him coming down from the mountain.'

'He looks dead,' Travers said. 'What happened to him?'

Dead? Eileen didn't like the sound of that.

'He came to hunt the yeti,' Khrisong said, no doubt using the Westerners term for their benefit. 'They hunted him.'

'He looks like he was injured badly,' Mackay said. 'I guess he tried to escape and died of his injuries in the night.'

'That is what we believe,' Khrisong agreed. 'He should not have come for them. The Wild Men of the Snows are not to be trifled with.'

'Aye, for sane men like you and me, that might be true,' Mackay said. 'But I've met enough big game hunters to know they are all driven by ego and pride, and an absolute certainty that they are right in what they do. This man would have no stopped hunting his prey for anything.'

'The hunter became the hunted.' Travers laughed gruffly. 'I find that rather satisfying.'

Eileen saw Khrisong stamp his staff on the ground. 'He deserved his fate.'

At the sound of rustling, Eileen dared to peak her head higher over the ledge. She saw Mackay retrieve two weapons from the tent. They looked like hunter's rifles. Khrisong immediately raised his staff. She caught a glimpse of the monk's face. He was not happy.

'You would hunt the yeti?'

Mackay backed off. 'No. Of course not. We are here to help. But Edward and I have no weapons. It would make sense that we have something to defend ourselves, if we needed to.'

The warrior monk considered his words and then nodded. 'Defence only, John Mackay. Never for attack.'

Mackay nodded. 'Of course, Khrisong.' He handed one of the rifles to Travers.

Khrisong stamped his staff on the ground again. 'We should leave. We will camp at nightfall. There is more mountain to cover before then.'

As the group continued on their path, George turned to Eileen. 'I think we should see if there are any supplies left,' he whispered. 'We're running a bit low.'

Eileen looked at him aghast. 'You would pick at a dead man's corpse?'

George didn't back down. 'He deserved what he got. Eileen, in my world you learn to do what's needed to survive. The more food, water, blankets we can get, not to mention something better to carry our stuff in than these cloth sacks, the better chance we have of managing to survive the next couple of days.'

Eileen sighed. He had a point. 'Okay, let us give them some more distance and then we will see what we can find.'

A deafening roar, echoing across the mountain, jolted Eileen awake. She instinctively reached for the first thing that looked like a weapon; a small pick used for mountain climbing. George sat up beside her, rubbing his eyes.

'What was that?' he asked, half yawning.

Eileen clambered out of the tent. They had set up camp near Travers and the monks. The roar came again, something guttural that chilled her to the bone. She stood, holding the pick before her.

She waited.

George climbed out of the tent beside her, his dagger brandished. Together they scanned their surroundings, but found nothing. The sun was masked by heavy clouds that cast the mountainside in gloom. The Transhimalayas, stretching out around them, looked forbidding, a harsh grey landscape that offered no sign of life.

No more sounds came and eventually they gave up. If there had been a yeti attack, they would have heard something from the monks' camp.

They ate a quick breakfast of dried meats and water inside the tent, before packing up for what should have been their final day's journey to Det-Sen.

Slowly, quietly, they moved down the path in the direction of the other camp. They found only the ashes of an extinguished campfire. Travers, Mackay and the warrior monks must have set off at first light. Eileen cursed herself for sleeping past dawn. They had no idea whether Khrisong had taken any more secret trails off the Path of Oddiyana.

'We'll need to pick up our pace,' she told George.

'Don't worry about me.'

Eileen smiled at the young lad. It was like he was born for the life of an adventurer.

The path seemed to get steeper all the time. Eileen's leg muscles burned as they walked. She was cold too, so very cold, and George looked no better. Before long they resorted to wrapping their sleeping blankets over them, which made each step more difficult to manage. The sun barely appeared through the clouds. A gust of snow came upon them so fast they were forced to stop and seek shelter in a small cave formed by two large slabs of fallen rock.

The lack of sun offered little direction and they marched on up Mount Jampa.

Finally, Eileen stumbled across footprints in a clump of snow that had settled on the trail. She looked to George and they exchanged a hint of a smile. It had to be Travers.

With a glimmer of hope, they picked up their pace, battling against the wind as the path became even more treacherous.

Eventually the path came to a natural end, leading out onto a large rocky plateau, sprinkled with snow. There were visible footprints ahead; four, maybe five tracks, two from the boots worn by Travers and Mackay. With the landscape levelling out, they hurried ahead, hoping to catch sign of the group.

That same, terrible roar rolled like thunder over the snowy plateau. Eileen and George froze in their tracks. It was much closer than it had been that morning.

'That's definitely a Yeti,' George exclaimed. 'I would know that sound anywhere.'

Eileen looked at him. 'Oh yes, your robotic pet.'

'It's not the real ones we have to worry about, remember? It's the robotic ones.'

Eileen nodded. She had talked so much about the yeti with Travers and Mackay that she'd almost forgotten that it wasn't the real, gentle versions that Travers was destined to find. But rather, remorseless killing machines controlled by the Great Intelligence.

With that happy thought in mind, they continued cautiously across the plateau and, before long, the familiar sight of the five men came into view. They were standing at the top of a ridge.

Eileen and George scrambled behind a large boulder. Over the wind, she could barely make out the words.

'…to Det-Sen,' Khrisong was saying. 'I will return when I can.' He continued speaking, but the wind muffled his words.

Travers shook his head. '…will camp over there, on that smaller plateau. It will create a natural camp site for us.'

'Are you sure, Edward?' Mackay was understandably cautious. 'I know you want to study them up close, but you heard that roar and you've listened to Khrisong's warnings. It no safe.'

'Pah!' Travers dismissed his friend with a wave of his hand. 'We have the rifles. And the monastery is not far from here. At the first sign of danger, we will run.'

'The gates of Det-Sen will be open to you,' Khrisong said, bowing his head. 'Good luck to you, Professor Edward Travers and John Mackay.'

'Thank you, my friend.' Travers clapped the warrior monk on his shoulder.

With a formal bow, the three monks turned and marched away, leaving Travers and Mackay to walk down to the campsite.

Eileen's eyes followed Khrisong, and in the near distance she spotted the slope of a valley. And there, tall stone walls rose up.

'Det-Sen Monastery.'

'At least it's not far,' George whispered back. 'What do we do now?'

They set up their own small camp in a cave not far from the plateau. They discussed the blond man, the one who was intent on killing Travers. Coupled with the danger posed by the robotic Yeti, and knowing that any day now the Doctor would no doubt arrive, it was essential they be ready for anything.

Once the sun had set, Eileen and George set out, and quickly they found Travers' and Mackay's camp. The two men were cooking over a small fire, debating their next move. Mackay offered caution, while Travers wanted to head out at first light in search of the yeti. Eileen wished the professor would listen to the counsel of his friend, but he seemed determined to walk into the lion's lair. She hoped those hunting rifles would offer them some protection if things got out of control.

With the surrounding area seemingly clear of any

immediate danger, Eileen and George returned to their cave and rekindled the small fire. As they sat warming their hands, Eileen considered their next move.

'I think we should sleep in shifts,' she told George, fighting down the urge to yawn.

'Agreed. The blond guy is getting brazen, but the cover of darkness will be his best opportunity.'

'And with the robotic Yeti roaming about…'

'The perfect weapon. All he needs do is herd them near Travers' camp.'

Eileen yawned. She really wasn't made for such journeying. Too used to cars and planes.

George smiled at her. 'Okay, Eileen. Get some sleep. I can see you're fighting it and I'm feeling okay at the moment.'

She didn't argue. She gave him a smile of gratitude, finished the last of the lukewarm tea in her tin mug, and wrapped herself up in her blankets.

She was asleep instantly.

CHAPTER TEN
A Part of History

WHEN GEORGE woke her several hours later, the cave outside the tent was almost bright with the glow of the full moon. Eileen rubbed her eyes, stretching her tired limbs and sat up. It was deathly cold.

'Anything to report?' she asked.

George's face was grim. 'There's something outside the cave.'

She reached for the pick, pulled on her hat, and threw aside the extra blankets.

They both climbed out of the tent. George had his dagger, though she doubted what use their weapons would have against a Yeti. The fire had already been doused, a grey, wispy smoke still lingering inside the cave.

George put a finger to his lips and crept silently out of the cave. Eileen followed, her heart pounding in her chest. She could barely breathe, her mind settling into a subdued panic. Outside the cave, a path of white moonlight hung eerily across the mountainside, everything else plunged into pitch darkness. It reminded her of the air raids in London, except everything was deathly silent. Even the wind had died, the air settling into a bitterly cold calm. It was like the whole mountain was holding its breath with her.

Then she saw two lights glowing nearby, two pale orange eyes cutting through the black night. The sight of them chilled her very soul. Slowly, a shadow shifted around it, a massive black hulk creeping slowly towards them. It was bigger than she expected, much bigger, so much so that she was staggered by the lack of noise. Something else glinted, reflecting in the moonlight. Long claws at the end of strong arms.

'How do we stop it?'

George narrowed his eyes. 'I've got an idea. When I say run, follow me.'

Eileen didn't argue. Of the two of them, George was the expert here.

'Run!'

George broke into a sprint, running close enough to the creature to get its attention, but not so close that it could reach him. The Yeti turned, letting out a low, rumbling growl, while Eileen followed from a distance, navigating the ice and snow on the ground. She didn't want to imagine what would happen if she slipped. George was almost leaping from one step to the next as he made his way closer to the edge of the plateau.

George skidded to a halt at the edge of the plateau, peering out over the drop below. Eileen raced as quick as she could towards him, the Yeti closing in. She slowed a couple of feet before the edge, not trusting herself not to fall if she lost her balance. The creature stumbled into the path of moonlight and she gasped in horror, taking in its full form.

Glowing orange eyes, sharp fangs, huge claws. The hulking bear-like creature was the stuff of nightmares. Eileen could barely believe it was a robot. It was the complete opposite of those deceptively cute-looking Quarks she'd encountered in Sheffield.

'How good is your aim?' George asked.

'Good,' Eileen said, hefting up the pick, testing its weight.

'When I say, throw that at the Yeti. Aim for its eyes. And take a few steps away from me.'

Eileen nodded, gasping for breath as she found a firmer footing clear of the ledge. She wasn't quite certain what was happening, but she suspected the young man was trying to use himself as bait.

The creature lunged, one huge claw swiping towards George's face as it closed in upon him. George ducked, barely avoiding the claw, and threw himself clear of the ledge, kicking the Yeti as he did so. For a moment, it seemed to stumble.

'Now!' George yelled.

Eileen thought of the fairgrounds she visited as a little girl, of the darts she'd thrown at cards to win toys. This was no different. No different at all.

Focusing, ignoring the threat of the Yeti, Eileen flung the pick through the air. It spun and spun, and for a moment Eileen wondered if perhaps she'd been wrong about her aim. But the pick struck home, lodging itself between the eyes of the beast.

It howled, a terrifying, anguished howl, and seemed to slip backwards.

It felt pain.

That realisation created a pit of guilt in Eileen's gut.

It may have been a robot, but it was somehow living too. She didn't understand how the Great Intelligence could create such things, how robots could feel, but now she had to question what she was doing. To kill a living thing that was but a slave itself…

Eileen didn't like it. Not one bit.

George clambered to his feet and charged the creature, slamming the full force of his body against it. The Yeti roared with anger and fell, stumbling over the edge of the plateau and down into the chasm below.

George barely managed to stop himself from falling with it, pushing himself backwards and landing in the snow with a heavy thud. Eileen rushed to his side.

'Are you okay?' she asked nervously, worried that the claws might have struck George.

He took a couple of deep, heavy breaths and shook his head. 'No, all fingers and toes present. I'm okay.'

Eileen helped him to his feet. He stumbled a couple of times to regain his balance. She held firm, supporting him.

'You were very brave,' she said softly. 'A little foolish

too, but very brave.'

George smiled weakly. 'Just a little something Bowden once taught me.' He looked back at the edge. 'To be honest, I didn't think it would work.'

Eileen shook her head, amazed but not entirely surprised. It wasn't only the blond assailant who was more than a bit brazen.

'George,' she began unsteadily. 'The Yeti. Are they alive?'

George looked at her, puzzled a moment. 'What do you mean?'

'It felt pain. I saw it. Heard it.'

'I…' George was quiet for a minute, thinking. 'Well, I suppose. You're from 1943, right?'

'Yes.'

'And you haven't heard of artificial intelligence?'

Eileen considered. 'Possibly.'

'Well, there are some who think an artificial intelligence can gain sentience. Even if it's a robot, it can still be alive.' George forced a smile. 'Alive, but with an off switch.'

'Like the Yeti?'

'Yup. Pennyworth was alive, I suppose, up to a point.'

It was as Eileen had surmised. 'Then the Yeti, they're aware. Are they willing soldiers of the Great Intelligence?'

'I… I don't know. Never really thought about it.'

No, and neither had Eileen, until now.

'Have you slept yet?' she asked abruptly, changing the subject. George shook his head. 'Okay, can you make it back to the camp?'

'I think so,' he muttered weakly. 'Why?'

'I want to check on Travers and Mackay.'

'Come on then.'

'No, George. You need rest too. Go. I'll be back shortly.'

George nodded reluctantly. 'Fine, but you know I won't sleep until you return.'

'I didn't think so. But at least you'll be resting. Go on,' she added, ushering him away.

When George was almost at the small cave, Eileen

dared to peer over the edge of the plateau into the chasm below.

There was no sign of the Yeti, not that she could see much of anything below really. Taking a deep breath, she marched towards Travers' camp.

A figure lurked by the tent as Eileen approached. It wasn't large enough to be a Yeti, but she knew how shadows could play tricks. She hurried as quickly as she could. Just because there were giant creatures out on the mountain ready to tear them to shreds, didn't mean there weren't more assassins lurking nearby. Or the mysterious man in black.

The shape revealed itself to be a man holding a long rifle. Mackay. Eileen considered heading back before he saw her, but after what had happened, it was better to warn him. She wouldn't forgive herself if she returned to her cave, only to discover later that more Yeti had killed the men while they slept.

Mackay noticed her a moment before she reached the tent, and quickly held the rifle in her direction.

'Who's there?' he hissed.

Eileen held out her arms, to show him she meant no harm, and approached slowly. 'Mackay, it's me.'

He frowned. 'Eileen, what are you doing here? I thought you and George left with the others?'

She didn't have time for explanations. 'Don't worry about that now. Is Travers here too? Is he safe?'

'Aye, he's asleep inside. Dreaming, I think. Having an argument with Professor Walters in his sleep.' Mackay paused, lowering his gun. 'I woke up and heard something outside. Sounded like a yeti, and there was shouting too. Was that you?'

Eileen nodded. 'I'm afraid so.'

'I was worried this would happen. We should have gone to the gompa. Is the yeti going to come back?'

'It fell off a cliff.'

Mackay considered, clearly unsure of the right response. He settled for a smile. 'Are there more?'

'Not that I have seen, but I wanted to look around and be sure. It's not safe on the mountain.'

'Clearly.' He looked back at the tent. 'I'm going to wake up Edward in a minute and get our things packed up. I'm no going to feel safe until there are stone walls between us and them.'

'That sounds like a very good idea. I will do a quick sweep of the perimeter and check there are no surprises waiting for us.'

'Then you should take this.' He stepped forward and offered her his rifle. 'You are trained to use a gun?'

'Unfortunately, yes.' Eileen accepted the weapon. She'd been trained to use a sten gun, like all women in the WAAF, but she'd never fired a rifle before. Still, she decided, it couldn't be that difficult to work out. 'I will be back shortly.'

Gun in hand, she stepped away from the tent and headed down the side of the plateau, scanning the area as best as she could. The moon offered some light, but otherwise the cold, dark night made visibility almost impossible.

She approached the edge of the plateau, and caught sight of something in the snow beneath her. A large print, bigger than a boot, wide and flat, like something with webbed feet. Panic rose within her.

More Yeti!

She turned to run back to Travers' camp, to warn them, and heard a blood curdling scream.

'Travers!' she yelled into the night air, and set off at a run.

The camp came into view. Travers emerged from the tent, rifle in hand. He didn't notice Eileen in the darkness. He raced off in the direction of Mackay's screams.

'Damn,' Eileen hissed.

She followed quietly. She didn't want Travers to be spooked and turn his rifle on her.

Mackay struggled in the Yeti's big arms. Eileen watched, horrified, as Travers tried to yell out. The Yeti, shrouded in shadows, little more than a terrifying mass of fur, flung

Mackay aside. The body landed like a broken doll.

Eileen set off, but before she could reach Travers, the Yeti yanked his rifle from him and flung it to the ground. Eileen was too far away. She stopped and raised the rifle. But she was too late. The Yeti swiped Travers with its heavy arm, smashing him into the snow. He was out cold.

It advanced on Travers.

'Yeti!' Eileen yelled.

The creature stopped, turned to her.

Eileen braced the rifle against her shoulder, and felt momentarily hesitant to fire. If she was right, then the Yeti was being controlled. He no more wanted to attack them, than his natural-born cousins. But if Eileen didn't take action, whether the Yeti was in control or not, he would surely kill them all.

'I'm sorry,' she whispered, and fired.

The Yeti staggered backwards, before lunging a second time. Eileen fired again. She slipped against the force of the rifle, but the bullet struck true, hitting the Yeti in one eye, which shattered.

With a groan, he stumbled in her direction, this time a little more aimlessly. She held the rifle up in defence. The Yeti reached forward, grabbed the weapon and stumbled back. He lumbered towards Travers' camp.

Eileen struggled to her feet and followed at a safe distance, hoping against hope that he would not climb further up the mountain towards the cave in which George was resting.

The Yeti paused near the low burning campfire, and flung the rifle onto the ground. Broken and bent out of shape. With a growl, he retreated into the night.

For a moment, Eileen stood there. Amazed she had survived a second Yeti attack. She glanced up at the cave, glad George was still safe.

'Travers,' she said, suddenly remembering.

She darted off, but what she found was only one body. Mackay's. Travers was gone.

She felt a surge of panic, and looked around wildly.

She let out a breath of air.

In the distance she could see Travers stumbling, clearly still in a daze, in the direction of Det–Sen and, she suspected, history.

The Doctor would soon arrive.

She had saved Travers, kept him alive long enough.

Eileen knelt down beside Mackay's body and closed his eyes. He'd been a good man, and if circumstances had been a little different… Eileen shook her head. Thinking like that wouldn't help her. She simply had to remember the wonderful man she'd known for a short time.

'I'm sorry,' she said, tears stinging her eyes.

CHAPTER ELEVEN
Surprise at Dinner

ARCHIE STRODE into the foyer of *Le Grand*, feeling something of a caricature in his top hat, long, high-collared black coat and cravat. The bronze base of his cane tapped the marble floor, echoing out across the entrance to the hotel, but didn't seem to attract any sort of attention. If anything, it made him blend in with his surroundings even more. He arrived at the reception desk and checked the time on the ornate gold clock hanging above the desk. He had a few minutes before six o'clock came upon him; enough time to see if Anne had left him a message with their contact at the hotel.

There were two men working behind the desk. He approached the first, a man with an impressive handlebar moustache.

'*Bonjour,*' Archie said.

The man smiled. '*Bonjour. Bienvenue au Grand. Combien de fois je t'ai aidé?*'

Archie felt a swell of panic. '*Bonjour. Êtes-vous Thomas?*' he asked with some hesitation.

The man frowned and responded, his accent strong and his speech very fast. Archie struggled to craft a response that wasn't *can you repeat that again slowly and in English.* The second man, wearing thin round glasses, stepped over.

'*Êtes-vous monsieur Anglais?*'

'*Oui.* Yes,' Archie said quickly.

The man muttered something to his colleague, who stepped away to attend another gentleman at the desk.

'I am Thomas,' the man said quietly.

'Ah, good.' Archie sighed with relief, lowering his voice to match Thomas'. 'I was wondering if you had any messages for me?'

Thomas nodded. 'Certainly, sir. The name?'

'Matthew Gordon.'

'And the room?'

'Eleven four eight?'

Thomas paused a moment, his eyes creasing, perhaps trying to suss out Archie's intentions. Archie resisted the urge to adjust his collar. Once again, he was reminded that he was not a man who involved himself in covert missions and consorted with spies. He was a simple teacher of mathematics, nothing more.

'There are no messages at this time, sir,' Thomas finally said. 'But if you wish to leave a message of your own, I can see that it is passed on.'

Archie wasn't certain whether the lack of message from Anne and his great uncle was a good or bad thing. It had been nearly twelve hours since he had left the safe house.

'Oh right, yes of course, a message. If anyone asks, please tell them I will be having dinner with Miss McDougal at the *Café de la Paix* this evening.'

Thomas smiled. 'Certainly, sir. Enjoy your evening.'

Enjoyment was the last thing on Archie's mind.

He waited for Lillian to arrive, glancing around the lobby nervously. Was the enemy here, right now, watching everyone? Watching *him*? Even without the threat of this new enemy, he still wasn't sure how he was going to handle this frankly bizarre situation. How did he keep Lillian close without concocting an elaborate cover story? He was not a man who liked deceit. Honesty had always been his game, something he had instilled in Katherine and Jimmy from a young age. If you led by decency, always being open and honest, it would encourage the same in others.

He continued to wait. Five past six. Ten. For a brief moment he felt a swell of panic, wondering if, somehow,

Lillian had fallen foul of the Gilded Serpent Society. He didn't profess to fully understand the logic of time travel, but surely if she was killed, then neither his future, nor that of his alter ego, would come to pass. If she died, then his father wouldn't be born, and neither would any version of him. And if that was so, would he simply blink out of existence?

Archie felt a headache coming on.

His heart was heavy, wishing for the millionth time that he could be back home with Sabina and the children. Or teaching. He would have been very happy with a stack of marking right now. The ordinary was far more preferable to the extraordinary. His life in Bledoe had never felt so far away.

Finally, at a quarter past six, Lillian arrived, gliding into the lobby in a pale green dress, her hair glistening in the golden sunlight pouring through the sky light. She was quite a sight.

'Oh, please forgive me, Matthew. I lost track of time. Our expedition to the *Louvre* took longer than we expected and my friend Ruby met this charming gentleman, and… Oh, here I am talking and talking. Have you been waiting long?'

Archie smiled. He was more relieved than cross. 'Oh, not long.'

She took his arm and wrapped hers around it. 'Marvellous. Shall we go to dinner?'

The walk to the *Café de la Paix* was a little awkward, but Lillian didn't seem to notice. There was no need to create a cover story. The moment they set off, she began recounting every moment of her travels. The boat from Dover to Calais, their journey to Lille where they encountered some delightful local cuisine, the train to Paris. Ruby's scandalous flirtations with a number of young men. Their trips to the Eiffel Tower, Notre Dame, the *Champs-Elysées* and the *Louvre*. How she was completely enthralled by the culture and was looking forward to her journey on to the south of France and then Italy. She was living quite the continental adventure, unchaperoned and with just her closest friends for company.

He had heard his granny recount these adventures many times before, but to hear this young woman who was so unlike the granny he knew talking of fresh experiences was quite disconcerting.

Every few steps, she would rub his arm fondly, or pass him a warm smile with a mischievous glint in her eye. Archie felt his heart pounding as he struggled to find a way to gently pull free from her affection. He had no idea whether this was just appreciation for saving her or something else more… no. He didn't want to think about *that*.

It was a relief, then, when they were taken to their table and they had something to keep her physically apart from him. Even then, the candlelight was somewhat off-putting, the violinist playing a piece of music that was a little too… romantic. When the waiter brought them a bottle of red wine and Lillian insisted on clinking their glasses in celebration, he had the dreaded realisation that she had more on her mind than just thanking him for his aid outside the *Palais Garnier*.

'Here I am, talking on and on again. My father always tells me I dominate a conversation. Tell me about you, Matthew.'

Archie looked up, his glass of red wine halfway to his mouth. 'Sorry?'

'Tell me about you,' she repeated, a broad smile on her lips. 'Who is this man that so dashingly saved my life this morning?'

He took a long gulp of his wine, trying to ignore the solicitous smile and her wide eyes shining in the candlelight.

'Oh, there is not much to tell. I am not on a big European adventure like you.'

'What job do you have, if I may be so bold?' she asked, leaning a little closer towards him.

If I may be so bold? He was fairly certain Lillian McDougal was being bold enough already. He had always known his granny to be a force of nature. She often spoke of his grandad, Archibald, sweeping her off her feet. He suspected it might have been the other way around. Although, of course, that was not meant to be.

He wondered if Alistair had instead. Or was their meeting at the interval simply love at first sight?

'I am a teacher of mathematics, in a grammar school in Liskeard. In Cornwall. I…' He hesitated to speak of family, less he veer too close to the truth. He didn't want her to remember too much in the future, and then recognise these details in her grandson… Although, of course, his alter ego's future would be quite different.

Time travel…

He decided a portion of the truth was better than an outright lie. If only so *he* could keep track of things.

'A mathematics teacher?' Lillian sounded almost disappointed. 'I took you for some bohemian writer. A poet, perhaps?'

Archie laughed, a little too awkwardly and a little too loudly. 'I am not quite so creatively inclined.'

Lillian took a sip of her wine, a somewhat dangerous look in her eye. 'And yet here you are in Paris, a city of culture and creativity and *passion*. Are you just a teacher of mathematics enjoying the opera, Matthew? Or is there something more to you?'

He took another gulp of his wine, his heart racing. What could he say?

'Ah, yes. The opera. I was informed it was an experience I couldn't afford to miss. I thought I would try it while I was passing through Paris.'

'Then you are not staying in the city long?'

He stopped himself from gulping down the rest of the wine. His head was spinning already. 'Just a couple of days.'

Lillian paused to reflect and then smiled. 'Well, I shall be heading for the south of France tomorrow. I intend to experience as much of the continent as I can, before I return home.'

The waiter arrived to take their order, offering a small respite in their conversation. Being as forthright as she was, Lillian chose to order for both of them, much to the surprise of the waiter. It was the second time Archie had his meal picked out for him at the *Café de la Paix*. He suspected he was going to get a reputation for it.

There was plenty of small talk during their first course, but Archie managed to navigate himself through most of it without the need to lie or divert her advances. In fact, Lillian seemed to have cooled her approach, more content to chat idly rather than focus her attention solely on him. Despite his assertion that he wasn't creative, she recounted her thoughts on the fine art she had seen on her travels, asking his opinion, forcing him to fake a few responses. Fortunately, he had seen enough pictures of the Mona Lisa to keep that conversation going all the way to the main course.

He was tucking hungrily into his meal, finally starting to enjoy the experience, when Lillian reached out and laid her gloved hand firmly on his.

'I really am enjoying your company, Matthew,' she said with a breathless tone. 'Matthew, such a delightful name. Do you happen to know what it means?'

'I'm afraid not, no.'

Her eyes were wide and glistening again and he started to feel just a little bit trapped. A fly in a spider's web was the best analogy he could think of right now.

He tried to pull his arm free, but she held it firmly. 'Thank you, Lillian. I, too, am enjoying this time together.'

She smiled. 'Oh, I am glad.' She paused for a sip of her wine. 'I began these travels to escape the boredom of home. My father isn't rich, but he had enough put aside to fund these travels, and my friends… Well, they come from enough money to allow us this expedition.'

He wasn't sure where this conversation was going, but the fact that she still held his hand was really worrying him now.

'What I am trying to say is, in my own simple way…' Lillian took a small breath, as if to compose herself. 'I am a bit of a romantic soul. My mother always said so. And I wondered, just maybe, if I might find myself meeting someone on my travels. A Parisian gentleman at the opera. Or a young poet or an artist on the French Riviera…'

She leaned a little closer. He leaned a little bit back.

'But I never dreamed my Parisian travels would result in me meeting you, an older, distinguished maths teacher from Cornwall.' She laughed. 'Isn't life odd sometimes?'

Archie laughed. A loud and forceful laugh that attracted at least a couple of fellow diners. It caused enough of a startled reaction from Lillian to give him the opportunity to yank his hand free.

'Listen, Lillian,' he began desperately. 'You are a very nice woman and I find you quite inspiring. You don't let society tell you what to do. You know what you want. But…'

'But what?'

He had the awful feeling that he was about to hurt her feelings.

'But…' He took a deep breath. 'I'm sorry. I…'

He froze as Anne walked up to the table. Lillian didn't notice at first, her attention still focused on him and his lack of response. Archie hesitated, unsure whether to get up from his seat. At least Anne had saved him from continuing this rather *dangerous* conversation.

'Sorry to interrupt,' Anne said quickly, reaching the table. 'I must speak with Archie.'

Lillian's smile dropped as she looked to Anne and back to him. 'Archie?'

'Matthew!' Archie shouted, before he could stop himself.

'Yes, Matthew…' Anne hesitated. 'Sorry, Archie is his middle name and we often use it…'

Lillian frowned. 'We met yesterday?' And then everything clicked into place. She turned back to Archie, her expression becoming a scowl. 'This is where we met…' Her eyes caught the wedding rings on Archie's and Anne's fingers, and suddenly one and one made three. 'You're married!'

'Well, yes, that's what I was trying to—'

Lillian rose abruptly from her chair, grabbed her wine glass and flung the contents into his face. He choked as the wine splashed down onto his shirt, stinging his eyes, startled at how quickly things had escalated.

'Is this some kind of game?' Lillian demanded. Her face was now filled with fury. 'You pretend to save me, coerce me into having dinner with you and then try to *seduce* me? What kind of woman do you think I am?'

Anne desperately tried to step in. 'Lillian, this isn't what you think. I…'

'I feel very, very sorry for you.' Lillian scowled at Anne. 'You deserve better than this, this…this *old* maths teacher from Cornwall!'

Before either Anne or he could craft a response, Lillian stormed away from the table, leaving him dripping with wine and Anne standing somewhat awkwardly in a café full of startled onlookers.

'I'm sorry.' Anne sighed, taking Lillian's seat. 'Are you okay?'

Archie grabbed a napkin and began to dab his face dry. 'Well, I was not expecting that.'

Anne sighed. 'I'm glad I found you. And I'm sorry, but this isn't over yet.'

Archie set the napkin down, noticing the interest from the room and leaned in to avoid the stares. 'Why?'

'Because your grandmother's life may be in danger.'

Of course Lillian McDougal's life was in danger.

Archie stared at Anne, letting out a heavy sigh as a drip of wine ran down his brow. Sitting there in his soaked shirt, he was uncomfortably aware that people were still watching him from their own tables. But he was past caring. Nothing about this nineteenth century Parisian adventure was going to plan.

'Archie, are you listening to me?'

He looked up, snapping out of the mental malaise he had fallen into. 'What have I missed?'

'We need to get somewhere more discreet. We don't know who could be listening.' Anne stood. 'Come on. Let's go.'

Archie noticed the waiter hurrying towards them as he rose from his seat. 'I'll have to pay the bill first.'

Archie followed Anne out of the *Café de la Paix*, where three men stood waiting for them. Their expressions looked very serious. Especially Alistair's.

'What happened to you?' he asked without any hint of bemusement.

Archie wiped a drip of wine that had run down his cheek. 'A misunderstanding, nothing more. Anne tells me Miss McDougal's life may be in danger?'

'Let us get off the street. We don't know who is watching.'

The Gilded Serpent Society, of course.

Alistair indicated for them to follow, and they made their way across the *Place de l'Opéra*. The two men, the British Intelligence officers he had seen at the old safe house, fanned out, their expressions alert as they scanned the area. Alistair led Anne and Archie to the side of an empty shop, not far from the *Palais Garnier*. He cautiously checked their surroundings one more time and retrieved a small brass key from the inner pocket of his coat. Unlocking a small wooden door, Alistair indicated for them to enter.

More secret places. More danger. Archie sighed, and stepped into the narrow dark space, followed by Anne and his great uncle.

He was growing sick and tired of all this hiding. This was not his life.

A narrow wooden staircase rose into pitch darkness before them. With a creek, the door shut behind them, cutting off the light. Archie heard the key turn in the lock. He had nothing to fear from either of his companions, but he still felt a knot of anxiety in his stomach as he stood in the small space; the cold, stale air only adding to his unease. It was a sensation he was becoming grudgingly more used to.

He heard a shuffle in the dark and a sudden glow of yellow light as Alistair lit a small oil lamp behind them.

'Go up,' he muttered softly.

With the light bright enough to guide them, Archie took the first step. The encroaching darkness did nothing to sate his discomfort, but he thought himself a fool for being afraid. He was not a school child facing a bogeyman at the end of his bed. The other two followed, their feet tapping each wooden step the only sound as they made their ascent.

At the top of the stairs was another wooden door, which Archie opened gingerly. A wash of natural light awaited them as he stepped into a small room with a large window overlooking the *Place de l'Opéra* below.

Alistair closed the door and blew out the lamp. The room itself was sparse, containing a single cot and blanket in a corner. A couple of tin mugs had been placed on the floor and, oddly, a telescope positioned in the direction of a large building in the distance.

Le Grand Hotel.

Archie's patience was quickly wearing thin. 'What are we doing here? And why is Lillian McDougal's life in danger?'

Alistair frowned. 'McDougal? Ah yes, a member of the British travelling party at *Le Grand.*'

Anne stepped between them, her expression at least attempting to be something resembling reassuring. 'I have been helping Alistair track the movements of the Gilded Serpent Society this afternoon. We believe Lillian's travelling companion, Ruby Holland, has been targeted by one of the members.'

'They're going to kill her?'

Alistair shook his head. 'Not quite. The society has obtained some sensitive papers that they need to smuggle out of the city before the French authorities close in. They know they won't make it out of Paris with them in their possession. Unfortunately for young Miss Holland and the rest of her party, the society is going to use them to smuggle out the papers for them.'

Archie could hardly believe what he was hearing. 'Miss Holland and Miss McDougal. They are going along with this?'

'No, of course not,' Anne scoffed, a little too boldly for his liking. 'This member of the organisation we have been tracking, a local man called Antoine, targeted Ruby after the events at the opera house. It would seem his plan is to seduce her and sneak the papers in her luggage when your… when Lillian's party head to the south of France tomorrow.'

'Well we must stop him!' Archie demanded fiercely. The moment he saw Anne's face, he felt a little foolish. As if what he had said was anything different to what they were already thinking.

'We will,' Anne said. She gave him a firm smile and a reassuring hand on his shoulder. 'Which is why I am going to try and take her place.'

Archie raised an eyebrow. 'You are?'

Anne nodded, pulling her arm away. 'I'm going to pose as a young socialite on her way back to England. I'll engineer a meeting with this Antoine and pretend to fall for him. With any luck, he will see me as easier prey and pass the papers to me.'

'After which, Anne will transfer the papers on to me and my associates,' Alistair added.

Archie wasn't sure he liked this idea, but at least it might direct the Society's attention away from Lillian's travelling party. 'What are in these papers, may I ask?'

'From what we have been able to deduce so far,' Alistair explained, 'a number of sensitive disclosures about prominent government ministers, including our own.'

'And this information is dangerous, I presume?'

'In the wrong hands, yes. We already suspect the Gilded Serpent Society to be behind a number of significant events in Europe in the last decade. The *Banca Romana* scandal in Italy three years ago. The attacks on the *Fasci Siciliani* movement. Now with the Italian defeat at the Battle of Adwa in Ethiopia a couple of months ago, the situation in that country is growing more and more unstable.'

Alistair began to pace the room, letting out a heavy sigh. 'My associates in Rome believe they are moving to aid Prime Minister Crispi in some more nefarious schemes that will have wide reaching consequences across the continent.'

'I still don't understand what this has to do with British Military Intelligence.'

Alistair stopped in his track, looking at him intently. 'Evidently your department MI10 isn't as well-informed as it should be. There are rumours that the Society is starting to infiltrate high ranking positions here in France and England. This division, in particular, has a number of ties to local criminal enterprises back in England.'

Alistair stepped away again, seemingly lost in thought as he stared out over the *Place de l'Opéra.*

'Fortunately, a number of intelligence agencies have begun to identify their members in Europe, and it is our hope that with a number of surgical strikes, we may be able to stop them.'

'Can't you just arrest them now?' Archie asked.

Alistair turned back to him and shook his head. 'Not without those papers. If we move too soon, we risk the Society going into hiding. It has taken British Military Intelligence far too long to locate this particular division and determine what they are up to.'

'I will deal with this Antoine,' Anne said firmly. 'With Alistair's support, of course. But we need your assistance too.'

Archie didn't know what he could possibly do to help. He was no spy. Even his military training was years old and his experiences in Korea were nothing like this.

'Time is moving quickly,' Alistair continued. 'Miss Holland's travelling party leave Paris by train at five o'clock tomorrow afternoon. Which means Mrs Bishop only has this evening to entice Antoine away from his original target.'

Archie sighed. 'Yes, but what do you want me to do?'

Anne looked at him a little awkwardly. 'You need to convince Lillian that Ruby's life is in danger and keep them safe. You have to tell her exactly what is happening.'

Archie knocked nervously on the door to Lillian's hotel room. His mouth was dry, his heart racing. Despite having run through all the details with Anne and Alistair twice, he feared the moment he opened his mouth it would all fall apart. Getting Lillian's room number from Thomas downstairs had been the easy part. Now he needed to convince her of what was happening with the Gilded Serpent Society and still lie about who he was. He hated the thought of deceiving her.

'You're a fool, Archie Lethbridge-Stewart,' he muttered to himself as he knocked again.

He was a teacher, a father, a grown man. So why did he feel like an awkward child, terrified that his grandmother would stay angry at him?

The door opened. Lillian McDougal's face turned sour as she looked at him.

'I have no desire to converse with you,' she said coldly, her hand already moving to close the door.

'Wait. I must talk with you.'

She raised an eyebrow. 'So that I may listen to more of your lies?'

Lies. Yes, it was all lies.

'I apologise for not being truthful with you. But you must understand that I never meant to hurt you, and my intentions...' He hesitated, fighting down the feeling of nausea at the very thought of what he was about to say next. 'My intention was never to seduce you. Far from it.'

At least that was the truth. A disturbing moment of self-reflection in this whole maddening affair.

Lillian looked as if she was going to slam the door shut, but she hesitated. 'Okay, what were your intentions? And I warn you, I am not a weak, vulnerable woman far from home that you can have your way with. My companions are inside my room. One scream from me and I will have you arrested.'

Archie did not doubt the conviction in her words. He checked the hotel corridor to make sure they weren't being watched, and leaned in a little closer.

'I am with British Military Intelligence,' he said, he *lied*, his voice barely a whisper.

Lillian McDougal looked as if she was about to laugh. Archie forced the urge not to clear his dry throat or bite his lip nervously. If he failed to sway her now, then everything was lost.

'British Military Intelligence?' she muttered back.

He nodded. Slowly. He couldn't break his composure, not now. He *had* to convince her.

'Yes. I am here to warn you that Ruby Holland's life is in danger. Possibly all of your lives.'

A moment of silence as disbelief and then incredulity ran across Lillian's face. Fury began to settle her features.

'What do you mean by that?' she demanded loudly.

'Can I come in, speak with you in private?' he asked earnestly, checking the corridor again.

Lillian eyes narrowed. He held her gaze, desperately afraid that she might see the lie for what it was. He remembered something his grandad had once told him, something that Archie often used with the unruliest of students.

'Look directly at your target, but imagine a snowstorm swirling around you. Imagine the cold, imagine the sensation of wind and snow on your face. Be in the blizzard.'

It worked. He held Lillian's gaze, and eventually she opened the door wider, stepping back to allow him entrance to the room. He moved inside and felt more eyes upon him. Two stern-faced young women sat in chairs near the tall window. Both wore sour expressions, but none more so than Lillian, who now stood with her back to the door, her arms crossed over her chest and her eyes fixed on him.

'You remember Anastacia and Victoria?' she asked, her tone cold and uninviting.

He nodded at the two women but forced himself not to

smile. They would probably see it as a sign of weakness. 'Good evening, ladies.'

They did not return the greeting. He averted their gaze, scanning the rest of Lillian's room. It was small but exquisitely furnished, with dark green leather chairs, gold embraided curtains and a mahogany table, chest and mantlepiece. A small fire burned in a furnace and a second door led to what he presumed was the bedroom. The window had an amazing view out over Paris.

But this wasn't the full travelling party.

'Where is Ruby?'

If she was with Antoine, Anne's plan would fall apart.

'Miss Holland is at the theatre with Miss Peretti,' Lillian replied curtly. 'After the disaster at the opera house last night, they wanted to experience some Parisian culture before we left the city. The rest of us were rather tired.'

She took a step towards him, threateningly. 'Of course, I had plans to dine with a dashing gentleman who saved my life. But we all know how *that* ended.'

One of the two companions let out a harrumph of agreement. The other shot him an icy glare. Archie stepped back nervously, adjusting the collar of his shirt.

'I am sorry I deceived you,' he said cautiously. 'I was trying to make sure you were safe.'

'Safe?' scoffed one of the women, possibly Anastacia. 'She would be safer without you.'

'Well that's not quite true.' He looked at Lillian, ignoring the heat of Anastacia's glare on his face.

'Then please tell us,' Lillian said, 'Mr British Military Intelligence. What is so dangerous as to cause our lives to be in danger?'

Archie took a deep breath, relieved that he could put aside the lies for now. 'Ruby Holland has been targeted by a man called Antoine, a member of a rather dangerous criminal organisation.'

Victoria gasped. 'Antoine? But he seemed so charming.'

Archie nodded, his heart pounding in his chest. 'That was the point. He is attempting to smuggle stolen information out of Paris, and he is planning to use Miss Holland to do it.'

Lillian glared fiercely. 'Ruby is no criminal. She would never—'

'She won't realise what he is doing,' Archie cut her off, feeling somewhat emboldened. A dash of truth in the lie helped. 'Antoine is very skilled, very dangerous. He'll manipulate her to do what he wants. She won't realise what he is doing.'

Lillian's glare dropped, but her body posture was still hostile. 'How do we know you are telling the truth?'

He sighed. He had no proof. 'What do I have to gain?'

Lillian frowned. 'Our encounter this morning. That wasn't a coincidence?'

Archie shook his head. 'No, it wasn't. I needed to talk to you. We knew your travelling party had been targeted by this criminal organisation, to be used to smuggle stolen information out of Paris. As the women in charge, I came to you.'

Lillian's face softened. 'Why the charade over dinner? Why lie about your identity?'

'I needed to know which member of your party had been targeted. I needed to gain your confidence and I was trying to do it without revealing my true purpose and scaring you.' The half lie rolled off his lips surprisingly well. He wasn't sure if that made him a bad person. He would never have lied so brazenly to anyone before.

'We since found out that Ruby was that target, that Antoine targeted her this morning. Everything that happened was engineered to serve his own agenda.'

'Dear God, poor Ruby,' Victoria sighed, deflating in her chair.

Anastacia's reaction was less meek. 'How are you any different from this Antoine?'

'I'm not,' Archie said quickly. 'Both of us forced encounters with members of your travelling party for our own ends. But I assure you, I am solely concerned with trying to stop him and ensure that you all remain safe and out of harm's way.'

He paused, taking a moment. 'When is Ruby meeting Antoine next?'

'She has arrangements to meet Antoine for lunch tomorrow, in the restaurant downstairs,' Lillian said.

That was the information he needed. Now all he had to do was let Anne know before she engineered an encounter of her own.

'When Ruby returns, you must find a way to convince her not to go to this lunch. Tell her the truth if needs be, but make sure she does not meet with Antoine again,'

Lillian nodded. 'I can do that.' He was surprised that she was so willing to accept his proposal.

'Will he come after us?' Anastacia asked loudly, seemingly less convinced. Victoria let out a gasp of anguish.

Archie shook his head. 'No, one of my colleagues is planning to divert Antoine's attention, use herself as bait to lure him away from your party.'

'Shall we leave Paris early?' Lillian asked nervously, the first real sign that she was unsettled by all this.

'No, you should keep your five o'clock train out of Paris.' Archie had no idea if that was correct, but the subject had not come up. The last thing he wanted was to have Lillian's party flee early and attract the attention of the Gilded Serpent Society. Not to mention the fact that he still needed to find a way for her to meet Alistair.

Lillian nodded. 'Okay. We will do as you wish.'

Archie smiled, relieved that something at least was going according to plan.

'I will be close by if you need me,' he told her, feeling genuine for a moment.

CHAPTER TWELVE
The Seduction

ANNE TRIED to hide her anxiety as she walked into the grand foyer of the hotel. It was the first time she had been in *Le Grand* since she and Bill had checked out after their wedding anniversary. Of course, that wasn't to happen for a long while yet.

Walking into the foyer now, she realised not much had changed in the seventy years between now and their trip. It was as grand and beautiful as ever and, like the *Palais Garnier*, a stark reminder of what felt like her last moments of happiness before her world had been torn apart.

Even without all the memories weighing her down, Anne had much to be nervous about. She was wittingly putting herself in the grasp of a dangerous criminal, one who would seek to use her for his own nefarious ends. She was no stranger to action. But once again, she felt alone, without the backup of those she trusted. Without Bill. It felt like she was missing a limb.

Past her would have scoffed that she could ever feel incomplete without a man. She had been strong, all her life. Whether it was battling controversy as she forged a career in science alongside such friends as Maddie Bonnaire, Eliza Shaw and Patti Richards, or proving herself a leading member of UNIT. She had fought the establishment, followed in her father's footsteps. In many ways, she was still that strong, wilful young woman, ready to face danger head on. But in recent years, she had learned she could do that as Bill's partner, in love and in war. Without him, she had lost something.

She didn't even have Samantha. Nothing else mattered more than seeing her daughter, and if putting herself on the front line was what it took to get the mission back on track and get back to Samantha, then that was what Anne would do.

She took a deep breath to gather her thoughts, scanning her surroundings intently. The foyer was relatively quiet, but she felt rather exposed, dressed ridiculously as she was in her tight bodice-bound dress, and stupid wide-brimmed hat. She blended in with the local fashion, certainly. But no woman, in any time period, should be made to hoist themselves into a dress so tight they could barely breathe and then finish it off with something the size of Luton on their head. Bill would have found the whole thing hilarious. But then, so would she, if she didn't have to wear it.

At the far end of the foyer, the lift doors rattled open and an apprehensive looking Archie stepped out. He was a strange fellow, a simple teacher that looked out of his depth most of the time and yet was willing to step up when needed. He balanced a self-depreciating charm with moments of arrogance and wisdom, traits she associated with many of her teachers in her past. He had exhibited moments of bravery too; she wondered just what the timeline zero version of Archie was like, and just how well they worked together. Timeline zero Bill, who she had met a couple of times, certainly suggested an extremely loyal and rewarding relationship shared between the three of them.

Was it any wonder she and Archie got on so well? She was no believer in predestination, but recent events were testing that resolve.

Archie caught sight of her, and hurried over. She picked up her many, many skirts and shuffled towards him.

'Any luck?' she asked quietly.

'Ruby is going to meet Antoine for lunch at the hotel restaurant tomorrow,' he said, without stopping.

Anne stepped past him without missing a step. The last

thing either of them wanted to do was attract the attention of the Gilded Serpent Society lurking in the hotel.

'Which one is Thomas?' she asked.

'Brown hair and glasses.'

'Thank you.'

Without hesitation, Anne advanced towards the concierge desk.

'Thomas?'

He flashed her a small smile. 'Good evening, how may I help you?'

'Any messages for Matthew Gordon in room eleven four eight?'

Thomas shook his head. 'I am afraid not, Mrs Bishop. However, I believe the man you are looking for is in the hotel bar. He is wearing a burgundy cravat.'

'Thank you.'

Turning on her heel, her skirts swishing irritatingly around her ankles, Anne stepped away from the concierge desk and crossed the lobby to the bar, where a number of guests were already seated. Fortunately, she was not the only woman in the room; the last thing she wanted to do was be mistaken for a woman of another profession.

Her target was seated at a table with two other gentlemen, dressed in their finest attire. Anne stealthily navigated her way to the closest table, making sure she was within Antoine's sights. She was just a little too far away and she couldn't make out their muted conversation, but their expressions told her there was some tension between them.

Carefully, Anne removed her hat and placed it on the vacant seat next to hers. She shifted slightly, so as not to be in direct eyesight with Antoine, but clear enough that she could attract his attention when she needed to. He hadn't noticed her yet, too caught up in his tense conversation with the other gentlemen. That was good. She didn't want to rouse suspicion the moment she sat down.

For a few brief moments she waited, calming her beating heart, building up the courage to ensnare this man.

He was a dangerous criminal and she had no back up. She had to do this right.

'Wish me luck, Bill,' she muttered, realising she hadn't even attempted to court the attention of another man in almost a decade. She hoped she wasn't too rusty.

She began to cry. Crocodile tears, of course, but believable enough that to anyone nearby she would come across as terribly upset. In any other situation, she would have felt foolish, angry at the thought of appearing weak and emotionally unstable.

It worked. It took a few heavy sobs and the three men at the next table stopped their conversation. There were a few curious glances from other hotel guests too. Anne laid her face into her hands, trying to keep up the pretence as long as possible. She needed to come across as genuinely vulnerable, the perfect target for Antoine.

She lifted her head, rubbing her eyes and casually looked directly at her target. Antoine flashed her a smile; a very warm, disarming smile. She held his gaze a moment longer, allowing him the briefest glimmer of a smile in return before turning away rather dramatically and *bursting* into tears again.

As she tilted her head back, she saw Antoine speaking briefly with his colleagues and rise from his seat. He quickly walked around to her table and sat down opposite her.

'*Oh, mademoiselle, qu'importe?*' he asked, his voice soft and smooth.

She looked up, sobbed and wiped away the fake tears. 'I am sorry. I do not *parle* much *Français,*' she said meekly, sobbing once more for dramatic effect.

He smiled, flashing rows of white teeth. His dark eyes glinted in the light of the chandelier above. Anne felt somewhat uncomfortable, looking at the man opposite her with his chiselled cheekbones and dark, wavy hair. It nearly took her breath away just how damned attractive he was.

'Then I will happily speak English,' he said, his voice rolling like velvet off his tongue. 'Now, whatever is the matter, *mademoiselle?*

'Oh, it's silly really.' She paused for a weepy sniff. 'I… I just…' She froze, let her lower lip tremble.

Antoine reached out and touched her hand, rubbing his thumb over hers soothingly. 'Come now, you are in Paris. A woman as beautiful as you in a city as beautiful as this, should never be so sad.'

His words were dripping with cliché. In any other situation, she might have laughed. Instead, she choked back her 'tears' and smiled.

'Oh, you are too kind.'

'Kindness costs me nothing, *mademoiselle*,' he said, keeping his hand on hers. 'Now what could possibly make you so melancholy?'

Anne glanced towards the next table, where the two men were waiting somewhat impatiently. 'Please don't worry about poor old me. I will be fine. I will be back in England in two days and all this will be a rather foolish memory.'

'Hush.' Antoine looked to the next table and nodded sharply.

The two men got up to leave, somewhat exasperated, but Antoine hardly paid them any attention. He was obviously the senior operative among them, which meant he was the right target. Now all Anne needed to do was *persuade* him to leave Ruby alone and focus on her instead.

'You are returning to England?'

'I…yes…I…'

Antoine lapped up every moment of hesitation.

'I plan to. Except… oh!' Anne pulled her hand away abruptly, pretending to fight back the tears.

Antoine leaned closer. 'Please do not cry, *mademoiselle*. Tell me what is wrong, and I will do my very best to help you.'

Anne sniffed and let out a weary sigh. She almost felt sorry for him, the way he was being so easily manipulated. *Almost.*

'I was travelling with my brother. We were holidaying in the Champagne region and decided to take a quick trip to Paris before returning home. Unfortunately, my brother was called away on business urgently and I, rather foolishly, decided to stay behind.'

'A wise choice, *mademoiselle*. There is nothing quite like Paris in the springtime.'

'I wholeheartedly agree.' Anne sighed wistfully.

'Good.' He grinned. 'My name is Antoine,' he said, picking up her gloved hand and kissing it.

'Anne,' she said coyly.

'Now that we know each other, why don't you tell me what troubles you. Do you regret staying behind in Paris when your brother left?'

Anne shook her head. 'No, not at all. The last couple of days have been wonderful. But… but my uncle was due to arrive in Paris today and I was to travel back with him. Oh, alas!' She sighed heavily. 'He has fallen ill, and I find myself here, all alone, seeking passage back to England on my own.'

She looked at Antoine, forcing the meekest expression she could muster.

'You must think me pathetic, sitting here weeping so openly in public at the very thought of travelling without company. But you must understand, this is my first trip abroad. I am just a single woman, travelling alone. I fear the courage I found, staying here in Paris, has been my undoing.'

Antoine smiled as he laid his hand on hers again. 'You are not weak, *mademoiselle*. I am inspired by your courage, your determination to experience the beauty of Paris, even without your brother for company.'

'Your words give me comfort.' She could just as easily play into these clichés, and she was almost starting to have fun playing the simpering young woman. 'But I still fear that the journey ahead will be terrifying. I'm not sure I can travel alone.'

His brow furrowed. Antoine looked to be pondering her words. Anne tried to avoid staring too directly at his face; it was far too handsome for her own liking. She felt a twang of guilt. Even pretending to be seduced by a man as good looking as Antoine really did feel like a betrayal of Bill.

'Perhaps I can help,' Antoine said softly. 'I am leaving Paris myself tomorrow too. I could offer myself as company…?'

That was a surprise. Anne had imagined it would take more work to convince him to change targets so easily. She had to take advantage of the moment.

'I cannot ask that.'

'Nonsense, beautiful Anne. Now tell me, how are you planning to leave Paris? By train?'

She nodded, sniffing as she bit her trembling lip. 'Two trains. The first will take me north to Lille, the second to Calais.' She spoke with some hesitation. She needed to make him believe he was helping her. Or in any case, manipulate him into pretending to help her at his own manipulative hands.

'Hmm. I have business in Picardy,' he said after a moment's thought. 'Perhaps if I offered myself as company on part of your journey? That might perhaps relieve the stress of your travels home?'

She had to plan her next words carefully. 'I'm sure that would be too much trouble. You must be *terribly* busy.'

'If I cannot make time to help a lady in need, then what kind of man would I be?'

'You are such a gentleman.' Anne gave him a broad, fake smile. 'My train does not leave until the afternoon. Perhaps then, if you don't mind me asking…'

'Ask away.' He beamed.

'Could we… perhaps, meet for lunch here in the hotel and travel to the station together?'

For the first time, there was real hesitation from Antoine. 'I have already arranged to meet a friend for lunch tomorrow before I leave for Picardy.'

'Oh, Antoine,' she sighed. 'I understand. I can dine alone. My last meal in Paris before returning home. I don't mind eating alone, if I must.'

Antoine hesitated again and then smiled. 'Oh, we cannot have that. This is Paris. No one should ever dine alone. I can change my plans. If you are sure you don't mind the company?'

Anne pretended to hesitate. She had him, but she didn't want to sound too confident. 'But what about your friend?'

'My friend…' Antoine paused. There was that glint in his big blue eyes again as he grinned. 'I think I might be able to cancel my lunch plans. As long as you are absolutely certain you don't mind me taking the train with you?'

'I would love the company.'

'Wonderful!' Antoine grinned. His eyes were wide, and she felt uncomfortably like a prey caught in a hunter's trap. 'Alas, beautiful Anne,' he continued soothingly. 'I have plans tonight, otherwise I would suggest dinner too. Dining with you in candlelight, I'm sure you would look even more beautiful than you do now.'

What a creep.

'Dinner with your friend?' she asked cautiously.

Antoine shook his head. 'No, unfortunately I have business with my associates. They will be waiting for me outside.'

Anne let out a despondent sigh. 'Oh, please, Antoine, do not fear. I have already eaten this evening and I am tired. I… I feel that I should take my leave and rest. I will need it for the journey tomorrow.'

He kissed her hand again. 'My heart will weep until we meet again.'

She forced the urge not to vomit in her mouth. 'I look forward to it.'

'I am glad, beautiful Anne.' He paused, gazing deep into her eyes. Damn, his eyes were beautiful. 'The restaurant here does a wonderful fish course. The best in Paris. I will arrange a table.' Antoine kissed her gloved hand again. 'Shall we meet in the lobby at midday?'

'That would be wonderful.' Anne pulled her hand gently away and grabbed her hat. 'I will see you tomorrow, Antoine.'

He bowed his head. 'Tomorrow, my dearest Anne.'

As she left the bar, Anne looked back to see Antoine

still watching her and gave him one last inane smile before turning back to make her way out of the hotel. Only then did she notice the woman in a pink dress and bonnet standing in her way. Before she realised what was happening, the woman slapped her hand across Anne's face. She stumbled, recoiling from the shock and her stinging cheek. The woman who had attacked her had a face filled with fury.

'What are you doing with my Antoine?' she screamed, seemingly unafraid of who was listening. 'Are you trying to steal him from me?'

Anne froze. So caught up in the act was she, that she hadn't even realised it was Ruby.

She was barely twenty years old, skinny, beautiful with long curls of reddish-brown hair and a face like thunder. Anne had three options. Retaliate, though she wasn't sure what good that would do. Run, but then her plan to coerce Antoine away from Ruby was over. Or involve Antoine and try and salvage the situation.

She absolutely detested the final option. Turning Antoine against a woman whose only crime was jealousy? Allow the man, a criminal, to protect her from her vengeful attacker? Anne felt nauseous as she considered her next step. This was not her. She was ashamed for even thinking it. But as the man of their 'affections' hurried nervously in their direction, she realised she had little other choice.

'Oh, Antoine!' she gasped, falling melodramatically into his arms. 'Please, help me!'

'How dare you!' Ruby screamed. She obviously didn't care what kind of scene she was creating in the middle of the hotel lobby. Anne was embarrassed for her.

Antoine gently pulled Anne away and turned to face the red-faced, red-haired woman. 'Ruby, hush. This is not like you.'

His soft, smooth tone seemed to soothe her. The moment Ruby took in his big wide eyes and smiles, the anger melted away and she seemed more like a simpering schoolgirl than a grown woman. Anne did not like her.

'I don't understand,' Ruby said meekly. 'You said I was the most beautiful woman in Paris. You only had eyes for me. And then I see you holding hands with this old crone!'

Old Crone! Anne wasn't *that* much older than Ruby. But now was not the time to argue. Taking a cue from Ruby's melodramatics, Anne attempted to put on the waterworks and flung herself back into Antoine's arms.

'Oh, she attacked me, Antoine! I was feeling so lost and you were so kind. I didn't feel quite so alone anymore. I… I…' She pretended to sob, burying her face in Antoine's chest.

Anne didn't need to see Ruby's face to feel the heat of her anger flare up.

'But… Antoine?'

'Hush, ladies,' Antoine said, just as calmly as before. Anne could feel his racing heartbeat in his chest. He was just as nervous, trying to fix the situation.

He pulled Anne away again and held her arms softly as he looked to Ruby. 'You are beautiful, young Ruby. Just as you are, Anne,' he added hastily, looking to Anne too. 'I have been deeply honoured to have the pleasure of both your company.' He paused. 'I wish to cause neither of you any harm, or heartache. I wish only the best for both of you.'

'Then leave this crone and come with me,' Ruby said pleadingly.

It was sickening. Anne was almost ready to walk out and leave her to her fate. She was fairly certain Ruby deserved it.

But even a woman as foolish as this one deserved to be saved from the likes of Antoine. Anne calculated her next words. Play up the simpering, needy victim, or perhaps a little bit of reverse psychology? Not that Ruby would understand that if it bit her on the bottom.

'I see I have caused you both so much inconvenience.' Anne sighed, pulling away from Antoine. 'Fear not, kind Antoine. I thank you for everything you have offered, but I will find a way… somehow… some way…to make it back home. Alone.'

She bit her lip, pretending not to cry and, with that, she had him.

'Dear Anne, I cannot allow you to be so abandoned to your fate…'

Ruby wasn't having any of it. 'But, Antoine, you said…'

Antoine reached out to take her hand and kissed it. 'Dear Ruby. The sad truth is that tomorrow's lunch would have been our last meal together. You would have left Paris and we would never have seen each other again. As much as it breaks my heart, I think we should leave our brief acquaintance as what it is. A fond memory.'

The foolish young woman looked as if she were about to cry. 'But…Antoine…'

He kissed Ruby's hand again. 'I know in my heart you will be fine. You have your travelling companions and much of Europe still to explore. Young Anne here has no one. It would be dishonourable of me, un-gentlemanly of me, if I didn't help her in her hour of need.'

And I make a much easier target, Anne thought. *One without friends to potentially disrupt your plans.*

'I hope you can understand, I do this with a heavy heart and a need to help a young woman, like Anne, who requires my aid,' Antoine said.

Ruby wavered a moment and then nodded. Antoine was a manipulative monster, hiding behind charm and good looks and Ruby had fallen foul of him at every step. Anne did feel a little bit sorry for her.

'Will we meet again?' Ruby asked, her whole body deflated.

Antoine smiled. 'Perhaps. Will your travelling party come to Paris on your trip home?'

Ruby's face lit up. 'Yes! We have rooms here on the ninth and tenth of June.'

Antoine's smile widened as he took Ruby's hand again. 'Then I will endeavour to be in the city when you return.'

Ruby squealed and wrapped her arms around Antoine's neck. 'Oh, that would be lovely!'

Her suitor held her embrace a moment longer, before

gently pulling her away. 'Until then, sweet Ruby.'

Ruby took in Anne, a flash of a scowl on her face before returning her beaming gaze upon Antoine one last time. 'My heart will wait for you.'

With that, Ruby spun around, her skirts swishing as she made her way towards the lifts where her rooms awaited. Antoine looked at Anne, who wore a sheepish smile on her face.

'Please don't think ill of me. I know it is just an infatuation on her part, and I just wanted to be her guide in the city.'

Trying to pass his seduction of Ruby off as a mere crush while still trying to charm her… Anne resisted the urge not to give him a few choice words.

'Oh, this has been rather tiring,' she said, feigning a weak sigh. 'I must rest. But I look forward to seeing you again tomorrow. If you are still certain that you want to?'

Antoine took her hand and kissed it. 'With all my heart. Until tomorrow, sweet Anne.'

She slowly took her hand away and made her way to the lifts. She didn't have rooms here at *Le Grand*, but Antoine didn't know that, and she had to keep up the pretence. All the way to the end of what had become another long, long day…

Half an hour of hiding out on the fourth floor of the hotel later, Anne finally made her way back to the secret room above the shop overlooking the *Place de L'Opéra*. Archie was sitting on the cot, drinking tea out of a tin mug. Alistair was pacing near the window. He turned to her with a look of surprise.

'Mrs Bishop? Did Philip let you in?'

Anne nodded. 'He told me to tell you he was going to take a pass around the square.'

Alistair smiled. 'Good. And how did your mission fare?'

Anne looked to Alistair and then to Archie who was rising eagerly from the cot.

'Well, on behalf of all women everywhere, I find myself

profusely apologising for my behaviour. That aside, I have him. I will be meeting Antoine for lunch at midday tomorrow in the hotel.'

'And Ruby?' Archie asked.

Anne felt her blood boil at the very thought of that confounded woman. 'Miss Holland is an *interesting* person, but yes, she is safe. Antoine has turned his sights solely on me.'

Alistair nodded. 'That is good. Well done, Anne.'

'Thanks.' She was oddly gratified by his appreciation. 'Any more word on the mysterious blond man in black who poisoned Frederick Goff?'

'None,' Alistair said grimly. 'If he is a secret member of the Gilded Serpent Society, he has yet to surface.' He looked out to the window. The sun was low now. Sunset would come within the hour. 'I think you should both get some food and rest. Tomorrow will be a momentous day.'

'Ah yes, because the last couple of days have been an absolute breeze.'

Anne sighed. She knew she was being sardonic, but she was too tired to care. They were so far beyond trying to match up Alistair with Lillian, that she had no idea how they were going to get their mission back on track.

CHAPTER THIRTEEN
The Pyramid

BY THE time George awoke, the sun was pouring through the cave mouth, and Eileen was gone. Her blankets were still as she had left them. It took him a moment to gather his thoughts, feeling every cut, bruise and ache on his body.

Climbing out of the tent, he splashed some cold water from the pan, which had cooled over the dead fire, and pulled on his gloves and hat. There was no sign of Eileen in the immediate area. Concern set in. She obviously hadn't returned to the cave, which could only mean…

Something must have happened when she went off to check on Travers and Mackay.

'George?'

His panic washed away at the sound of her voice. Eileen emerged from behind a boulder. Her face was drawn, deep circles under her eyes. She obviously hadn't slept in hours. Probably all night.

'What happened?' he asked, and sat on a rocky ledge beside her.

'John is dead,' she said with a heavy sigh.

Her words were like a punch to the gut. George had liked the intrepid explorer with his sharp quips and fondness for strong alcohol.

'What about Professor Travers?'

George didn't want to sound callous, but if they'd failed at their mission…

Eileen took a deep breath. 'Alive. He escaped to the monastery. I managed to stop the Yeti from killing him.

History is on track.'

There were tears in her eyes.

George nudged closer and put his arm over her shoulder, pulling her to him. Eileen sighed as she closed her eyes. He felt her breathing as he held her, staring out across the snow-capped mountains around them.

'Get some rest,' he said finally. 'I'll go check around.'

She pulled away and nodded. 'Okay. I could do with a nap.'

George stood, stretching his aching limbs. 'You should have woken me before.'

'You needed sleep, too. Be careful, George.'

He nodded and watched her return to the cave.

Mackay dead. Travers at the monastery. History back on track, as Eileen had said. However, clearly their mission wasn't yet over. He didn't know how the time rings worked, exactly, but he suspected they'd return him and Eileen to Calabi-Yau Space when they'd succeeded.

The assassin was still out there. He would try again.

Dagger in hand, George made his slow trek to Travers' camp. Snow crunched beneath his feet. He had no desire to see Mackay's remains, or to come across any more of the Yeti, but he needed to make sure there was no immediate danger.

Halfway to the camp, a strange noise caused George to stop. He listened. It sounded mechanical; a wheezing and groaning, like the air itself was being torn apart. He spun around. On the side of the mountain nearby, a blue box had appeared. He'd seen something like it before, on the news. A Police Box, standing outside Earl's Court Underground Station in London. Only this one looked a little different.

It hadn't been there before.

Could it be…? George smiled. It had to be.

Keen to avoid history, he hurried on to the campsite.

The tent had collapsed under the snow and the fire had been extinguished. Amid the ash and twigs, one of the rifles had been bent out of shape. George scanned the area nervously and saw the shape of a man nearby, partially covered by snow.

John Mackay.

George wanted to walk over, to pay his respects, but he wasn't sure he could handle the sight of his friend, dead in the snow. He had lost many friends over the years. One more was just too much.

Taking a deep breath, he looked instead to the walls of the monastery, barely visible over the tip of the valley.

He had to make sure Travers had arrived safely, reconnoitre the place for any sign of the blond man.

George approached the monastery and stopped. Now he was there, he wasn't sure what to do next. He couldn't just knock and ask for Travers. Khrisong had made his feelings pretty clear, and somehow George doubted the warrior monk would be very impressed to learn that he and Eileen had followed them.

So, George masked his tracks and headed over to a small group of boulders on the hillside close to the monastery's large wooden gates. He waited, hoping that there would be a sign of Travers. But as the sun rose higher over the mountain, none came.

He looked around, and spotted a figure some distance away, just about poking out over the edge of the valley lip. The shape was unmistakable.

A Yeti!

Maybe it had tracked him?

Steeling himself, he made to move. He had to make sure it didn't come too close to the monastery. He moved up the slope of the valley, keeping the Yeti in sight all the time. But as he drew nearer he realised it wasn't a Yeti at all. It was a man in a large fur coat – too large for him, in fact – with a crop of dark hair.

The way the man hopped about, he was clearly new here. Moving with keen interest, peering through a brass telescope down the valley towards—

George ducked quickly.

The man was looking at the monastery. He did a little jig – there was no other word for it – and then turned and rushed off. Presumably the way he had come.

George hadn't passed anymore pilgrims, and certainly hadn't seen any other strangers on the slopes of Mount Jampa. The only thing that had changed since last night was the arrival of the Police Box.

George smiled. He knew who the man was.

With no sign of the Yeti close by, George scurried away quietly, careful to not attract the attention of Tibet's latest visitor.

George and Eileen spent most of the day in the cave recuperating, allowing history to run its course in the monastery. Eileen didn't know a great deal about the events of Travers' first expedition, but she knew the general details. Soon the Doctor would attract the attention and ire of both Travers and the warrior monks.

George was just packing up their supplies when Eileen rushed into the cave, her eyes wide. She hadn't been gone long.

'They're back,' she said grimly, catching her breath. 'Several Yeti on the mountain.'

George grabbed his dagger and attached it to his belt. 'Any sign of Travers?'

Eileen nodded. 'He was with two others I didn't recognise. Two teenagers. Hard to believe, I know, but the boy was wearing a kilt, of all things. They were heading towards Det-Sen.'

'And the Yeti?'

'Converging on the monastery. There is plenty of commotion coming from there. I saw a number of the warrior monks guarding the gate, but didn't dare get any closer. They are obviously preparing for some kind of battle down there.'

'Did Travers tell you about a battle?'

Eileen thought a moment. 'Not as such, but he did mention that the Yeti attacked the monastery. I seem to recall something about someone being used as bait.'

'Nice,' George said sarcastically. 'What do we do?'

'Not get directly involved. We can't. But we have to get close to Travers. The blond man will make a move soon. He has to.'

The mountainside was already dark and treacherous by the time they stepped outside. No new snow had fallen, but there was plenty on the ground to make walking tricky. The moon was even fuller than the previous night, giving them at least some light on the path ahead.

Not far from the remains of Travers' camp, George spotted an ominous black shape lurking beside the Police Box. He cautioned Eileen to stay silent as they stuck to the darkness, moving as quickly as they could against the rocky, icy terrain. Two more Yeti were on the path ahead, their eyes glowing eerily in the darkness, while three other creatures lurked silently on the Path of Oddiyana.

George and Eileen moved away from the main trail. Hidden behind boulders, they spotted seven Yeti in total, all lurking in the vicinity of the monastery, which was lit up by torchlight. George could see several warrior monks on the wall above the gate, bows and arrows ready to attack anything that came too close. It seemed that even if they could make their way undetected past the Yeti, the chances of not getting hit by friendly fire before they reached the gates would be close to impossible.

They waited, neither of them saying a word. They huddled under their blankets, watching for any sign of movement. It was a stalemate between the monks of Det-Sen and the Yeti outside. But, eventually, there was movement at the gate of the monastery.

George strained his eyes, trying to make out the figure that was slinking outside. He couldn't believe anyone would be foolish enough to leave the protection of Det-Sen. For a brief moment, the face of the man in the heavy coat and hat was lit up by the flicker of torchlight.

It was Travers.

George looked to Eileen quickly and she nodded, a scowl on her face.

'I saw him too. What on God's green Earth does he think he is doing?'

Without another word, they left their hiding spot, and as quick footedly as they could manage, they navigated their way across ice, snow and loose rock.

Travers moved quickly back in the direction of his old camp, seemingly unperturbed by the dangers lurking around him. George and Eileen followed, keeping once more to the darkness. Aside from the Yeti up near the Police Box, there didn't seem to be any more of the robots nearby.

Eileen and George crossed the main path and scrambled up the far hillside, tracking Travers to a nearby cave, concealed from the main path by a huge boulder.

George hadn't noticed the cave before. It was far larger than the one he and Eileen had slept in. Just what Travers wanted with it, he had no idea. The professor settled down, huddled in his thick coat and waited. George and Eileen looked to each other.

Nestled in a small rocky crevice a couple of feet higher than Travers, they had a good sight of the cave, the professor and the road to Det-Sen. All they could do now was wait, huddled in their blankets and hope that more snow would not come.

Morning broke, a brilliant golden light spilling over the side of Mount Jampa. Travers barely seemed to notice; his attention was still focused on the cave as he munched on some of his supplies. George looked up and felt the sunrise on his face, warm for the first time in ages. It wasn't enough to take the chill away or remove the aches in his muscles, but it was welcome nonetheless.

Down on the path, there was movement. George grabbed Eileen's arm and pointed. Three Yeti moved into view, their silent, furry hulks striding through the snow in the direction of the cave, and they weren't alone. In their midst walked a man with a long white shawl over his dark robes and a strange hat that looked a bit like a fin. Travers evidently recognised the man, watching him intently with wide eyes.

'A monk of some standing,' Eileen said, 'judging by his robes.'

'How do you know?'

'Well, compare them to what Khrisong and his warriors wore, it's the only obvious conclusion.'

The monk took something from one of the Yeti, a strange silver sphere, while a second creature lifted the enormous boulder like it was made of polystyrene. Once the monk had entered the cave, the Yeti became motionless. Like they had been deactivated.

'Do we try and get Travers out of here?' George muttered.

Eileen looked to him and shook her head. 'He's not in direct harm right now, and since there's no sign of the blond man, I think it's safe to assume this is all a normal part of historical events. Let us see what happens next.'

George didn't like waiting, not with three of the Yeti just a couple of feet away from Travers – and them. Deactivated or not, they still posed a considerable threat. But Eileen was right. They were here to make sure history played out the way it was intended, not to interfere and disrupt things.

The monk soon appeared from inside the cave and headed in the direction of Det-Sen. The three Yeti lumbered after him, silent as ever. The entrance remained open.

Travers began to move in the direction of the cave. Eileen held George back a moment. He wondered for a moment why, and then noticed a light coming from within the cave.

'Okay,' Eileen said. 'But let's be cautious.'

Slowly, they followed Travers into the cave.

There was a long tunnel at first, supported by strong, wooden girders and, at the far end, the pulsating light. Each burst was accompanied by a high-pitched noise. George pulled his hat down to protect his ears, and Eileen did the same. It drowned out a little of the sound.

In the centre of the cave stood a pyramid, the pulsating light coming from it. George and Eileen nestled behind a large stalagmite formation. Travers kept going, moving ever closer to the glowing object.

'What do we do?' George whispered.

Eileen didn't take her eyes off Travers. 'I don't know. Be ready. Do you know what that thing is?'

'Something to do with the Great Intelligence obviously.'

'Yes, thank you, George. I guessed that myself.'

The light grew brighter. The pyramid started to expand. George almost jumped up to stop Travers then, but Eileen nudged him back.

'Wait,' she muttered quickly. 'History, remember.'

George nodded. He didn't like it, but he watched as the professor took a step closer to the pyramid. The light intensified, and the pyramid grew and grew, the flow of light around it fluctuating. The more he looked at it, the more George was afraid of it.

Travers ignored the high-pitched sound, and stepped closer.

He collapsed suddenly, his hands to his ears, screaming.

The pyramid split open, and a strange web-like substance spewed out of it, spilling onto the ground. Travers continued to scream and, in that moment, George saw utter madness in his eyes. Whatever that pyramid had done, it had messed with Travers' brain.

He jumped to his feet, completely oblivious to them and ran to the entrance of the cave.

George barely had time to react before a man blinked into existence before Travers, blocking his path. A tall man in black with blond, curly hair. There was a cruel smile on his lips, and he raised a silver gun; the same one he had used to destroy the bridge.

Travers barely noticed. He was still screaming.

George raced forward, pushing Travers to the ground. The professor rolled to his side, eyes lit up like he was on drugs, jabbering incoherently. George winced as Travers' head struck a rock. In that same moment, a flash of red light soared past George's shoulder, hitting a stalagmite, which shattered into a hundred pieces.

'You won't stop me, you brat,' the man in black hissed, pointing his gun at Travers.

George jumped, using his feet to propel him off a small ledge, and landed straight onto the attacker, knocking him to the ground. They both grunted as they hit solid rock, the air knocked out of their lungs.

On his periphery, George saw the still screaming Travers run from the cave.

'Get Travers to safety!' George shouted at Eileen. She nodded and ran out of the cave.

Exhausted, George rolled to his side. The attacker tried to get to his feet, but George grabbed his ankle, sending him crashing to the ground again. As the man struggled to regain his balance once more, George pounced, throwing himself onto his opponent's back.

The man swung violently, trying to shake George off, but he hung on for dear life. He wrapped his arm tightly around the man's neck and squeezed as hard as he could.

The assailant couldn't be allowed to kill Travers.

That was the last thought George had before everything changed…

CHAPTER FOURTEEN
Oysters and Snails

ONCE AGAIN, Anne was back in the lobby of *Le Grand*, ready to continue with the charade. Alistair had found her a second dress to keep up the guise, a lavender monstrosity. She hated late-nineteenth century fashion, but she certainly looked the part.

Archie passed her, giving her a brief smile as he headed to the lifts. His part in the mission was ensuring Lillian, Ruby and the rest of their party stayed out of the way. Alistair, Philip and Edmund hurried towards the restaurant, all dressed in fine black coats, cravats and top hats. It was a relief to know they would be close by, should the situation get out of hand.

It wasn't long before Antoine approached. With his long black coat, crisp white shirt, chiselled jaw, glinting eyes and perfectly wavy hair, Anne had to take a moment to catch her breath and remind herself that not only was this handsome man a criminal, but she was happily married too.

Was married. She still hadn't adjusted to the idea that Bill wasn't in her life anymore. She forced down that pain deep inside her and focused instead on the task ahead.

'You are a vision,' Antoine said breathlessly, his smile widening as he reached out to take her gloved hand.

I look like I've been dressed up for the village fair, to be sold off to the local gentry for a bag of grain and two horses, Anne thought. But now wasn't the time to dissuade him.

'You are too kind, Antoine,' she said meekly. 'I hope… you haven't changed your mind?' There was no harm in getting straight to the point.

Antoine offered his arm and she took it, grabbing it firmly as he led her to the restaurant. The more she seemed frail and vulnerable, the better. It would make his defeat all the more satisfying.

'It would be my delight to be your travelling companion,' Antoine said soothingly in her ear as they walked. 'Of course, I can only accompany you as far as Picardy. I hope that will still suffice?'

Anne gave him the biggest of smiles. 'Oh, it will. Paris is so big and I'm just one woman. Helping me find my way out of the city is more than I could ever ask.' She hugged his arm tighter. 'Your company, even just to Picardy, would be delightful.'

'Then I am happy to assist.' Antoine smiled back, keeping his gaze on her eyes uncomfortably long.

She pulled away as they entered the restaurant. The *maître d'* greeted them and led them to their table near the bar. It took a moment for her to spot Alistair and the others, seated at different tables nearby. Not close enough for comfort, but there wasn't much room to make a quick exit. Antoine sat down opposite her, taking her hands in his and it took all her effort not to flinch.

'You are quite beautiful, Anne,' he said, in that infuriatingly silky tone.

You are a creep.

'You are so charming,' she said softly.

'I took the pleasure of ordering us some champagne,' he added, still holding her hands.

She felt trapped, his grip soft but strong. It didn't help that her back was to a wall. Literally as well as metaphorically. Fortunately, Alistair had spotted her and was already making his way to the bar close by.

Glad to have him near, she turned her thoughts to the mission.

'I am so very grateful for everything you are doing for me. Is there anything I can do in return?'

Antoine released her hand, pondering her request.

'Actually, there is.'

That was quick.

'Please, I am in your debt,' she continued in a wistful, meek tone. 'You have been my saviour, my… my hero.'

Antoine held her gaze with those big, impressive dark blue eyes. 'I have a… friend in Lille. I was wondering if you would be so kind to deliver a parcel for me when you arrive at the station? It isn't large and you can leave it with the postmaster. If that isn't too inconvenient for you?'

Anne smiled. Everything was going according to plan. 'Anything for you, my dear sweet Antoine.'

Archie knocked on the door of Lillian's room, waiting impatiently for an answer. With Anne busy with her mission, he was starting to feel a little useless. Babysitting the woman who would be his grandmother, and her friends, made him feel more so, particularly when his great uncle was out there facing off against the Gilded Serpent Society.

The door swung open and Lillian was standing there to greet him, her face somewhat crestfallen.

'Have you seen Ruby?'

Archie felt his mouth go dry. 'No. Is she not here with you?'

'I told her everything. Who this Antoine really was, and I thought she believed me.' Lillian paused, her face pale. 'But then, just a moment ago, she came barging into my room, furious. She… she saw your friend in the hotel lobby and started ranting about how it was all a trick to steal him away and that Antoine really loved her.'

Archie groaned. 'Lillian, tell me what happened next.'

Lillian sighed. 'I think she's gone to find Antoine.'

Despite the rising panic that Ruby could derail the entire mission, a plan came to mind. A converging of two tasks in one. A gamble that might put everything back on track.

'Come with me. I have someone you need to meet. He can help us.'

Lillian nodded and took her hand, closing the door

behind her.

If everything went according to plan, she was going to meet the love of her life…

Anne sipped on the glass of champagne. Just enough to keep up the appearance that she was having a good time, but not enough that she would become intoxicated. She needed her wits about her. Particularly when Antoine was attempting to feed her oysters from the large plate of shellfish laid out between them.

'Come,' he said with a soothing, silky tone, holding up one of the oysters by the shell before her face. 'Indulge yourself a little. This is Paris, after all.'

Anne took one from him and swallowed. She was never much a fan of oysters. But better that she fed herself than have Antoine gently shove a hundred shellfish down her throat. She swallowed and took a quick sip of champagne to clear her throat of the slimy aftertaste.

'Oh, Antoine, they are quite delicious!'

'Almost as delicious as your sweet, delicate eyes.'

His words were nauseating.

'You do flatter me,' she lied. 'Now tell me, what is this package you want me to deliver to Lille?'

'Oh, nothing too important. Some rather dull legal documents. Nothing you should worry yourself about.' He paused to swallow another oyster. 'If this is too much of an inconvenience to you, I would completely understand. I will just have to cut our meal short to post them before we take the train from Paris.'

'Oh, that won't do!' Anne scoffed. 'You have been so very, very helpful to me. I am more than happy to help.'

Antoine grinned, taking his champagne glass and clinking it with hers. 'What a wonderful woman you are, dear Anne.'

'And what a dear, sweet man you are, Antoine.'

Antoine put down his champagne and dabbed the corners of his mouth with a napkin. 'Would you excuse me one moment?' he asked, rising from his seat.

'Of course.' Anne smiled, relieved to have a break from all the sickening falsities.

Antoine gave her a ridiculous bow and hurried away from the table in the direction of the toilets. Anne noticed two men rise from different tables and head in his direction, likely other members of the Gilded Serpent Society. None possessed the curly blond hair of Goff's attacker.

She took a sip of champagne to steel her nerves, wondering if there were other members of the criminal organisation there too. From their two tables, Edmund and Philip were just as interested in the two strangers following Antoine, though they were good enough at their job that she wouldn't have even noticed them if she didn't know what signs to look for.

As soon as Antoine and the two men had vanished, Alistair rose from his seat at the bar and headed in her direction. He slowed his pace as he passed her table.

'Are you okay?' he whispered.

Anne lifted her napkin, wiping her mouth to cover it from any onlookers. 'Yes. He's asked me to deliver a package to Lille. I assume it is the stolen papers.'

'Good work. We'll stay close.' Alistair headed off towards Edmund's table.

A couple of minutes later, Antoine returned.

'Please forgive my absence,' he said, sitting down and grabbing his glass. 'I arranged for the chef to bring us some escargot. They prepare it in this exquisite sauce that you must try before you leave.'

Great. Oysters and snails. Anne was quite fond of fine dining, but this wasn't what she needed to settle her stomach.

'I am sure you have excellent taste,' she said warmly.

Antoine grinned, reaching in to retrieve an envelope from his coat jacket, bound in green ribbon. He handed it to her. 'The package I need passed to my contact in Lille. Are you absolutely certain you are okay to deliver it to the postmaster at the station?'

Anne nodded. 'Of course, Antoine.' She took the envelope.

'My dear English rose, thank you.' Antoine beamed, reaching out to kiss her hand.

Anne smiled back.

I have you now.

The lift doors opened, and Archie and Lillian rushed out into the hotel lobby. Archie grabbed her hand. 'Which way to the restaurant?'

Lillian pointed to the corridor running off to the right of the concierge desk. Archie nodded and together they ran, much to the surprise of the guests and staff around them.

'This man, can he help?'

Archie nodded. 'Alistair is British Military Intelligence too. He'll be able to stop Ruby and save us from Antoine and his thugs.'

'I dearly hope so,' Lillian said, keeping up pace next to him.

As they approached the restaurant, they saw a red-headed woman in a green dress arguing with the *maître d'*. She was irate, demanding entry.

'Ruby!' Lillian cried out.

Ruby turned, glared at them and then pushed past the *maître d'*, running into the busy restaurant. Archie grabbed Lillian's hand again and ran after her, rushing past the surprised *maître d'* too.

'*S'il te plaît, arrête!*'

Archie ignored the man's cries as Lillian reached out and grabbed a surprised Ruby.

'What are you doing?'

'It must have been a mistake!' Ruby snapped back. 'He's not bad. He told me he was going to take me to the Alps. He was going to—'

Archie was surprised by the furious slap Lillian gave her friend.

'This is ridiculous!' she said, quickly lowering her voice as the attention of several diners focused on their little altercation. 'Antoine is a bad man.'

'Your friend is right,' Archie added in earnest. 'Come, we should get out of here.'

Anne noticed the commotion at the far side of the restaurant, but couldn't make out who the staff were trying to escort away. There was a lot of chatter coming from the tables, some guests obviously frustrated at the rude interruption, others gossiping away while trying to feign a lack of interest. Antoine turned, looking to rise from his seat, and that was when Anne caught sight of the man involved in the argument.

She reached out and grabbed Antoine's hand, pulling him back into his seat.

'Tell me more about you. I would love to hear about your many adventures in Paris.'

Antoine smiled and pulled away. 'Let me just check what is happening. I would hate for our lunch to be disturbed.'

'Oh, I am sure it is all fine,' Anne said forcefully, but Antoine wasn't listening. He was already out of his chair and off before she could think of something to entice him back.

The envelope in the green ribbon remained on the table.

Anne wondered suddenly if she could find a way to sneak out with it. If she could put the papers in British Military Intelligence's hands, Alistair could move in to stop Antoine and this whole affair would be over.

He was already heading in her direction, while Edmund was quietly rising from his seat and heading across to Philip. Two tables away, one of the men that had followed Antoine was now watching Edmund. Anne didn't like this.

As Alistair walked past her table, Anne tapped the envelope containing the papers.

'Do you want this?' she whispered.

'Keep it safe,' he muttered back. 'What is Archie doing here with Miss McDougal and Miss Holland?'

Archie had brought his grandmother there? What *was*

he doing? 'I don't know.'

'Let me find out,' Alistair said quietly, striding away from her.

Anne felt her heart racing. She lifted the glass of champagne and took a sip to calm her nerves.

Was this how the meeting between Alistair and Lillian was going to take place? In a restaurant full of spies and criminals?

As she pulled the glass away from her lips, she felt something on her shoulder.

Archie looked behind him as two waiters began escorting Lillian, Ruby and himself out of the restaurant. Ruby's outburst had caught the attention of more than just a few disgruntled guests and staff. Three different men, one of them Intelligence Officer Edmund, was on their feet. The man from Anne's table was also standing, staring in their direction. He began to approach them. Archie didn't like this at all.

He pulled free of the waiter holding his arm and saw Alistair walk slowly past Anne's table. This was it. The moment they had been preparing for.

Without hesitation, Archie grabbed Lillian's hand and pulled her back towards him.

And then something else caught his eye. As Anne took a sip of her drink at her table, a figure dressed all in black, a man in his twenties with curly blond hair, appeared out of thin air directly behind her and tapped her on the shoulder.

There was a brief flash of light and Anne vanished, her glass smashing onto the table.

Antoine turned, coming face to face with Alistair a few feet away.

The man in black vanished again and there was another brief flash of light.

Now someone else appeared, dropping into Anne's chair, a look of surprise on his hairless face.

'George?'

CHAPTER FIFTEEN
From Cave Fighting to Fine Dining

GEORGE LANDED in the chair with a thud. His head span. He tried to catch his breath from the fight. He'd been doing well, until the blond man had turned things around on him, and then… What had happened?

George looked around, gave himself a moment. Everything was warmer, an almost suffocating heat compared to the cave on the mountain. Brighter too. As he blinked, he saw lots of lights and… a smell of fish?

'*Qui êtes vous? Que fais-tu ici?*'

He looked up to see a man in some sort of tuxedo, looking down at him, jabbering angrily in… what was that? French?

George looked away. This wasn't the cave. He was in a restaurant. All around him people were wearing top hats and bonnets, while before him, on a table, there sat a plate of oysters.

There was no sign of Eileen. Wherever he was, however he got here, she wasn't with him.

He lifted his hand and looked at the ring. Had that taken him away from the cave, helped him to escape the blond assassin?

Nothing was making any sense.

There was a shout from a man in a black coat, standing near the table. He had a gun and, for a moment, George thought it was aimed at him. He turned his head. No, the man with the gun was looking at the man behind George, a man who was also pulling a gun from inside his coat.

A shot fired, but it wasn't from the guns held by either of the men. A woman screamed. George turned just as four different men rose from their tables and began shooting at each other.

'Bloody hell! Out of the frying pan, into the flaming inferno!'

Edmund pulled a gun and aimed it at another man rising from a different table. Archie quickly stepped in front of Lillian to protect her.

It took Archie a moment to realise that Edmund had been shot in the split-second Archie had turned his attention to Lillian. He looked around. Philip was close by, rising to his feet, gun in hand, as three other men pulled out weapons of their own.

Guests and staff ran screaming.

Philip took a shot to the face, crashing on to his table, while a limping Edmund threw the round table in front of him, killing one of his attackers before ducking for cover. His table quickly took three rounds.

Across the other side of the restaurant, George crouched down beside the seat that Anne had, barely seconds ago, occupied. Antoine fired three shots in Alistair's direction. Fortunately, Archie's great uncle was quicker, leaping behind another table and using it as a shield too.

Archie had no idea what had happened to Anne, or why George was there, but he knew that he had to trust Alistair. The man was trained for this. That settled in his mind, Archie turned his focus on making sure Lillian stayed alive.

'Come with me… if you want to live.'

He grabbed Lillian's and Ruby's hands and pulled them out of the restaurant.

There was chaos in the lobby too. Cedric was trading gun shots with two men behind the concierge desk. Two others were already dead, one of them Thomas.

There was no way to safely reach the lifts. The only place safe now, was the room Alistair had across the *Place de L'Opéra*.

Once outside it became apparent that the fighting was confined to the hotel, though three men running towards *Le Grand* quickly told Archie it might not stay that way long.

'Follow me!'

The two women joined him, lifting their skirts and running across the *Place de L'Opéra*, navigating through startled passers-by and horse-drawn carriages. Archie dared to look back for any sign of pursuit. More panicked guests were running from the hotel entrance, causing quite the uproar. In the near distance, he heard the ringing bell of a police truck.

Lillian shot him a fierce glare. 'Will you please tell me what is going on!'

Archie sighed. His heart was still racing and he was sure his left knee was about to give out on him. His rugby games with Jimmy aside, he hadn't done this much running in years.

'Something has gone terribly wrong. I'm hoping my associates in British Military Intelligence will be able to put a stop to Antoine and his men. Right now, my priority is keeping you both safe.'

'Oh, it's all my fault!' Ruby cried, rather over-dramatically. There were tears glistening in her eyes. 'I am so sorry, Lilly. I should have believed you.'

'Hush now,' Lillian said softly. 'Now is not the time.' She turned back to Archie; her expression hardened again. 'Matthew, tell me, where are we going?'

'To a safe house.'

So saying, he turned on his heel and strode towards the side of the shop.

'What about my companions?' Lillian demanded behind him.

He turned back, noticing that neither of the two women had followed him.

'I don't know.' The truth was, he had no idea what would happen next. He was completely out of his depth. 'They should be safe, if they stay in their rooms. Right now, my priority is keeping you both out of the fighting. Will you follow me, *please?*'

Lillian considered a moment and then nodded. He gave her a grateful smile and turned away, looking for the side door that led to the safe room. It took him a moment to find it.

It was locked.

Furiously, he shook the handle, but the door was sealed shut. The metal lock looked big and heavy, not something he could so easily break through. Archie groaned.

'What is wrong?' Lillian demanded rather sharply.

Archie looked at them awkwardly. 'I don't have a key. I fear it may be with the men still inside the hotel.'

'Is there somewhere else we can go?'

'This is the best place for us right now. I am hoping the others will come here when the fighting is done.'

Lillian nodded. 'Okay, then we should find somewhere close by.'

'But the criminals!' Ruby gasped, grabbing Lillian's arm.

Lillian gently, but firmly, pulled her friend's arm free. 'Yes, the criminals.' She looked at Archie earnestly. 'Are we a target?'

'Not anymore.'

'Good,' Lillian said with a nod. 'Then we will find somewhere close by to stay and wait for your friends to return. I know a delightful little café a couple of streets away. I assume that is safe enough for now?'

Archie didn't have any better ideas. But he also didn't have any more money on him. He fumbled through his pockets. Aside from his hotel key, the only possession he had on him was James' lighter.

His thoughts turned to his great uncle. If Alistair died in the gun fight… Well, what would that truly change? At least for Archie. Lillian would one day meet Alistair's brother in Cromer, they would fall in love, and Archie's dad would be born. The life Archie had led wouldn't be changed, the only difference is he'd hear stories about a great uncle who died in 1896, instead of 1946.

So, the future of Alistair Gordon Lethbridge-Stewart, his alter ego, would never come to pass, but so what? Despite being on board for the mission, there was still a part of Archie who was resentful of the fact that his life meant less than that of the great hero from the other reality.

He was being selfish, he knew that, but he'd done his bit. Tried his best. Now he had to make sure that, at the very least, Lillian survived, that she went on to become his grandmother.

He had to get Lillian and Ruby out of the city.

Archie looked at the much-treasured lighter. A gift from his sister-in-law, a memento of both her and his dead brother.

They couldn't escape Paris without money.

'I need to find a pawn shop where I can sell this. Then we will wait for my colleagues at this café. And if they don't survive, then I promise you, ladies, that I will get you out of the city and away from the Gilded Serpent Society.'

Lillian looked at him long and hard. Finally, she sighed, nodding her head slowly. 'I remember seeing something like that on the way to the café.'

'Please lead the way.' Archie gave a bleak smile.

George crouched underneath the table while the shooting continued to ring back and forth across the restaurant. He had seen three men die already and the two closest to him were still slugging it out, both hiding behind overturned tables.

The shooting stopped.

George peered nervously over the rim of the table and saw that the man in the tuxedo had emptied his gun, and was quickly trying to reload it.

A flash of green caught George's eye. Next to the plate of oysters was a thick envelope wrapped in a green ribbon. Every instinct told him to grab the envelope. As he did, the man with the gun finished reloading and shouted at George in French. George ducked behind the table once more, narrowly missing a gun shot. The bullet hit a bottle on the table, sending shards of glass and wine everywhere.

Huddled between the chair legs, George stuffed the envelope inside his thick fur coat – which was far too warm for him now. Still it was better than what those men were wearing, and he had to get out of the restaurant without being recognised. Based on the clothing on display, and style of the restaurant, he guessed he was in the past - nineteenth century. Which meant he should try and find Archie.

When no second shot came in his direction, George dared to move. He looked around the restaurant, and saw a small wooden door at the back. Perhaps it led to the kitchen? He might find a way out from there.

Gritting his teeth, he moved to stand. But as soon as he did, a voice shouted out behind him. George froze, panic crippling him. But a second man from behind the other overturned table had already risen and threw a plate across the restaurant. In absolutely spectacular fashion, the plate hit the first man in the shoulder, sending him falling backwards. George grinned and ran for the door.

The man that had saved him was quicker and reached out to grab him by the arm before he could make his escape.

'Do you have the papers?' His voice was unmistakably English.

George nodded – clearly 'the papers' were the contents of the envelope – and the man shoved a gun against his chest.

'Good man, come with me.'

Three men began racing towards George and his new best friend, including the one that had tried to shoot him. George's new best friend kicked open the door and shoved him into the next room. It was, as George had guessed, a kitchen.

He felt something slam into the back of his head. The gun? He lasted a moment before he slumped into the man's arms and all went black…

George blinked against the light when the cloth bag was ripped off his head. He waited a moment for his eyes to adjust to his surroundings for a second time. His arms were tied to the back of a chair and his ankles to the chair legs. He tried not to panic, but it was hard not to. The side of his head pounded from where the gun had struck him. He looked at the faces of the two men staring down at him.

He was in a small room with a large window and a telescope. He thought the man, the one that had saved his life in the restaurant and then abducted him, looked a little like Archie. Though, perhaps not quite like Archie, George decided on closer reflection, as the man leaned towards him, his eyes wide. Menacingly wide.

'Who are you?'

'I'm George,' he said meekly, before forcing a bit of a smile. 'Who are you?'

His abductor did not smile. 'Are you working for the Gilded Serpent Society?'

The what now?

'I don't think so. They sound like a group of A-Level performing arts students, if you ask me. And performing arts is not my thing.'

'Don't mock me, boy.' The man shot him a fierce glare.

'I'm sorry,' George said. 'It's a thing I do. I try to be funny when I'm nervous.' He bit his lip. 'But seriously, they sound like the sort of people that would try and put on an amateur production of *Les Misérables*. We are in France, right?'

'We are. *Les Misérables?*'

'Yeah, the musical. I saw it in London once when I was a boy. Before everything went to… Well, you know.'

'No, I don't think I do. And *Les Misérables* is not a musical.'

'I imagine not the way the Gilded Serpent Society would do it.' George smirked and then thought better of it. His sense of humour often got him in trouble. The man stepped closer, and George tried to lean back into the chair. 'I'm sorry, I'm sorry.'

'You are very strange,' the man mused, stepping back. 'What is wrong with you?'

That was a rude and abstract question to ask. 'What do you mean? I'm just George.'

The man pointed at his face. 'You do not have any hair. No eyebrows. Are you ill, boy?'

'Oh, this?' George replied, trying to wriggle his brows. He never quite knew if that worked without eyebrows. He would have to try it out in the mirror sometime. He couldn't quite believe he hadn't tried before. 'I have alopecia.'

The man took another hasty step back. 'Is it contagious?'

Why did *everyone* ask that?

'No, it's not contagious. It's a condition I have. I'm still human – and you can't catch it. So, relax.'

The man didn't seem entirely convinced. 'If you're not a member of the Gilded Serpent Society, then what are you doing here?'

'Can I ask a stupid question?'

'It depends on how stupid.'

'Where are we? What year is this?'

The man frowned. 'You do not know?'

'I told you it was a stupid question. I think you hit my head pretty hard back there.'

His abductor seemed to take a moment to ponder his question. To be honest, George would have thought it daft if he had heard that question from anyone else. He didn't think announcing he was a time traveller from South Wales in the early twenty-first century, trying to save history and had only yesterday been fighting Yeti in the Transhimalayas in the 1930s, would be met seriously.

'We are in Paris,' the man said slowly. 'It is the twenty-third of May, the year of our Lord Eighteen Hundred and Ninety-Six.'

'1896? I knew it.'

The man raised an eyebrow at him. Now that expression did look familiar.

George grinned. 'That means Anne and Archie are here.'

Surprise shot across the man's face. 'You know Anne? Where is she?'

George frowned. 'I was hoping you could tell me. She

Alistair watched him, his back to the window, arms folded and his eyes narrowed. He didn't look convinced.

'How did you get there? In the restaurant? I've been thinking about what I saw, thinking I'd imagined it, but I saw it. One moment, Anne was at the table, and then the next, in a flash of light she was gone and you were in her seat. Now tell me, George, how can something like that happen?'

George wished he could explain, but even after everything he'd seen in his life, he was only beginning to understand how time travel worked. How could he hope to explain it to a man from 1896? Besides, he didn't know for sure what had happened, but he assumed that if he'd been sent to 1896, then Anne had to have been sent forward to 1935. For some reason, they'd swapped places.

'Maybe if you tell me exactly what you saw…?'

Alistair frowned. 'Okay. Anne was in the restaurant with Antoine, an agent of the Gilded Serpent Society. Her mission was going well. Antoine got up from his seat. There was some commotion at the entrance to the restaurant. And then… And then there was this man. A man dressed in some very strange clothing, all in black, with blond curly hair. It was Goff's poisoner, I'd stake my reputation on it. He turned up, behind Anne.'

The man from 1935. What had the Guardian said? Something about things happening in both time periods concurrently? Which meant the man who was trying to kill Travers was also operating in 1896… *at the same time!*

'The same man jumped me,' George said. 'He brought me here, and… Well, I think he took Anne instead.'

Alistair's eyes were wide with alarm. 'But how? She just vanished. Literally, blinked away, replaced by you.' He stepped towards George. 'Okay, forget that for a moment. Where did he take her? Is he connected to the Gilded Serpent Society?'

'I don't think so. I've never heard of them before.'

Alistair didn't seem convinced. 'How do you know my name?'

'Archie told me,' George said, which wasn't really a lie. 'We need to find him. He knows me. He'll vouch for me.' George rubbed his aching head. He really didn't feel too good.

Alistair nodded. 'My man will find him. You look rather pale. Why don't you get some rest until my man returns?'

Compared to five nights of sleeping in caves and tents, the rickety cot in the corner of the room looked luxurious. George walked wearily across the room and slumped onto it without question. His eyes were closed almost immediately.

George's head was still throbbing when he found himself being shaken awake by Alistair. Light poured through the large windows. He obviously hadn't been asleep long.

Alistair still had his gun in his hand. 'Stay alert. Someone is coming.'

George sat up, his heart racing, keenly aware that he didn't have a weapon to defend himself with. He must have lost his dagger in the cave. Alistair stood in front of him, gun raised in the direction of the door as the handle turned and the door swung open.

It was the man Alistair had sent out during his interrogation. Sighing with relief, Alistair quickly holstered his gun.

'Cedric! Is there any word?'

'Phillip and Thomas are dead.'

'Dear God.'

'The good news is that most of the Society have been rounded up,' Cedric added, a little more eagerly. 'Two Society safe houses have been raided by French Intelligence. We took the third. Are the papers still safe?'

Alistair nodded, pulling out the ribbon-bound envelope from inside his coat.

'Good. Unfortunately, Antoine and three of his associates are still at large. They managed to escape the hotel before we could move in and arrest them.'

Alistair looked worried. 'What about the women? Are

they safe?'

Cedric sighed. 'We have three of Miss Holland's travelling companions in a safe house. I confiscated their train tickets for their safety.' He took out some papers and handed them to Alistair. 'But Miss Holland, Miss McDougal and Archie were not in their rooms. Cecil and Edmund are still looking for them.'

Alistair was about to speak, but was stopped by the sound of footsteps running up the stairs. Without hesitation, Alistair and Cedric had their weapons ready. George could do nothing but wrap himself in the blanket and hope the two men in front of him would save him.

Two more men in black coats entered the room. From the expression on Alistair's and Cedric's faces, however, they were not the enemy.

'Speak of the devils and they shall appear!' Cedric laughed. 'Have you found them?'

One of the men nodded. 'We located them holed up in a café two streets away. It seems Archie managed to get the two women out of the hotel safely.'

George sighed with relief and he wasn't the only one. Alistair smiled, holstering his gun.

'Then our mission is set. We will move the two women to safety and then track down Antoine and the remaining members of the Gilded Serpent Society here in Paris.'

The other three men saluted him. George didn't feel the need to join them. Alistair saluted back and turned to George.

'Come, boy, let us find Archie.'

CHAPTER SIXTEEN
So Close

ANNE FOUND herself falling onto hard ground. It took her a moment to get over her shock, before she took in her new surroundings. She appeared to be in the middle of a cave of some sort. The wind howled outside, and her body temperature plummeted. She was not dressed for this weather…

No sooner had the thought passed through her mind, than her clothes changed. Now she was dressed in the attire one would expect for hiking up a snow-covered mountain. She settled into the warm hood with a smile.

Intuitive, that's what the Guardian said. She removed one of her new gloves and regarded the silver time ring. It must have had some kind of chameleon element. Looking closer she now saw somewhat familiar circular inscriptions all over the surface.

Now it makes sense, she thought. *I should have worked that out sooner. His people do get around.*

She didn't know how, but clearly the time ring must have activated, and based on the temperature and the cave, she surmised she had to be in Tibet. 1935, no doubt. But why? She hadn't completed her 1896 mission.

Taking a deep breath, she looked around the cave, her gaze falling on the pulsating shards of a broken pyramid. Familiar looking thick webbing rippled out from it. It was the same Web that had covered London, which confirmed her supposition. 1935, and the time of the Great Intelligence's first attempt at subjugating the will of humanity.

Which meant…

A broad smile spread across her face.

Her father was out there.

The urge to go to him was strong. Too strong. She had lived with the absence of her father for nine years, and with the death of Bill still rocking her core, the idea of being wrapped up in the arms of her father was almost too much. But… he was dead, in her mind and heart Edward Travers was dead. She couldn't honestly say she was over his death, but she had made it a part of her life. A lingering pain that she could usually ignore, but to think he was out there, so very close.

Only, technically, it wasn't her father yet. She wouldn't be born for a few years. Professor Travers of 1935 was two things, and neither of them was a father. He was a husband and an explorer.

Well, she decided, the time ring wouldn't have brought her forward to 1935 without a reason, assuming it was the Accord controlling it. But, then again, there was that hand on her shoulder mere moments before *Le Grand* vanished… That had to be relevant.

She couldn't sit in the cave thinking. She had to do something.

It wasn't just her father out there, but Eileen and George too. Perhaps they needed her help?

Anne climbed to her feet, and started on her way out of the cave, thinking of Archie. The last she'd seen, he had been in the restaurant with Lillian, barely a few feet away from Alistair. Perhaps that was why she was sent to Tibet. Archie had introduced them, finishing the mission. That made sense.

Once outside, the view took Anne's breath away. Golden sunlight poured over the peaks of the mountains, lighting up the snow before her like liquid gold. But then a freezing wind hit her, and she staggered back. She landed with a thud in a snow drift, immediately grateful for the quick costume change.

'Anne? What on earth are you doing here?'

She looked up at the voice, and gave Eileen a wry smile. 'I got bored in 1896, only so many horse-drawn carriages one wants to see.'

'Where's George?'

Anne frowned. 'He's not with you?'

Eileen's face went pale. 'No, he… he was fighting with that man. The one behind all this, the one trying to stop your father.'

Anne gasped. 'Is my father…?'

Eileen shook her head. 'No, he escaped back to the monastery.'

Anne let out a sigh of relief. 'This man,' she began, a suspicion filling her mind. 'He doesn't happen to have blond hair and dress in black?'

'He does.'

Anne climbed to her feet. 'It's the same man from Paris.'

Eileen was puzzled. 'But how? He was here, in the cave, fighting with George.'

'Who is no longer there… Of course. It had to be him.'

'What did? Sorry, Anne, you're going too fast for me.'

Anne smiled softly. 'Sorry. I thought it was the time ring that brought me here, that the Accord must have decided you needed my help. But, if I'm here and George has gone… Then it's reasonable to assume the blond man is behind our switching.'

'Switching…? You mean you think George is now in Paris?'

'Yes. Now being the operative word.' Anne thought back to Calabi-Yau Space. 'Remember what the Silver Guardian said? That both events are happening at the same time, each weakening the other. This blond man, he must be jumping back and forth through time.'

'Preventing Archie's grandparents from meeting, while at the same time trying to kill your father.'

This was news to Anne. 'That's what he's doing here? Trying to kill my father?'

Eileen frowned, then nodded. 'Of course, you and Archie

left before the Guardian explained that to us.'

'Okay.' Anne took a moment to gather her thoughts. 'Right, well, if my father is in danger, we can't stand here talking.'

'Agreed. Let's head back to your father's camp. I will explain on the way.'

Together the two women walked, and Anne listened with absorbed fascination at the tale Eileen told.

When they eventually arrived at the camp, the tent had blown over and was smothered in snow.

'Poor Mackay,' Anne said. 'Father often spoke of him with fondness.'

Eileen smiled sadly. 'He was a good man.'

'Yes, I believe he was.' Anne looked around. 'Okay, now I'm here, I guess I'll have to pick up where George left off. What do you suggest we do next? I don't suppose it'll be long before that man makes another attempt on my father's life.'

'No, I don't suppose you're wrong, dear. But you must know more about what is happening here on Mount Jampa than I do.'

Anne nodded. 'My father told me stories. The Great Intelligence has taken control of the mountain, possessed one of the monks, I believe...'

'That would explain the man in the robes I saw working with the Yeti this morning.'

'Abbot Songsten. The Yeti are all robots; I assume you know that?'

'George did say. Although... You have encountered them before?'

'I have,' Anne said slowly, wondering where Eileen was going with this.

'Are they alive?'

That was not the question Anne had expected. 'No, they're robots.'

'But they feel pain.'

'They do?'

'Yes. I threw a pick at one. When it struck, the Yeti roared in pain.' Eileen shuddered at the memory. She grasped Anne's hand. 'If they're alive, maybe we can reason with them? If they're being controlled against their will…?'

It was an interesting conjecture, one Anne had never considered before. She'd faced Yeti in London, and since, but never once had she thought of them as living. But if they felt pain… Maybe Eileen was onto something. They wouldn't be the first artificial intelligence Anne had met, and if the Great Intelligence created them to have a certain amount of autonomy, then it was reasonable, and indeed quite probable, that they could evolve beyond their basic programming to the point of gaining sentience. It wouldn't be the first time Anne had witnessed such a thing.

'If we encounter them, or rather when, as it's almost certain,' she told Eileen, 'we'll try. If we can reason with them, we can use them against the blond man.'

Anne expected Eileen to be happy about that, but she clearly was not.

'What's wrong?'

'I just…' Eileen shook her head. 'If we *use* them, we're no better than the Great Intelligence. We have to ask them, let them decide.'

Anne wanted to laugh at the idea of it, but she was a scientist, and she had to accept the possibility.

'You're right. We'll ask them.'

'Good. I'm glad.'

Anne smiled. 'Okay, so… Let's see. Now, we know that the Great Intelligence will be defeated this time by the Doctor, with help from my father and the monks.'

'This time?'

'Another long story, but suffice it to say it will try again in thirty-five years, and that's when the Doctor returns.'

'Right, when you and your father meet Archie's alter ego?'

'Apparently. Not in my timeline, but in timeline zero, yes.'

Eileen looked at her, face filled with hesitation. 'I should warn you, the pyramid in the cave… It did something to your father.'

Anne nodded. Details of his ensuing madness were vague, but she remembered one thing with clarity.

'He will try to return to the cave. He will be most vulnerable then.'

'A perfect time for the blond man to make his move.'

'Yes, but not just yet. If he only recently encountered the pyramid…' Anne thought hard, trying to remember what her father had told her. It had been so long ago. "The Web will spread first, which gives us a little time. We should check in on the monastery.'

'And the Yeti?'

'Well, if we encounter any, it will give us a chance to test out your theory. You know, if they're not attacking us, of course.'

As Anne trudged through the snow beside Eileen, she couldn't help but find herself awestruck at the views around her. Despite the stories of her father, she'd never visited Tibet before, but now she was here… The Transhimalayas, with their sprawling, grand peaks and snow-covered slopes glistening in the sunlight, were every bit as beautiful as her father had said. Seeing it now, as he did, brought her a little closer to him.

Ahead of them though, the slopes were not quite so beautiful. Already the Great Intelligence's webbing had begun to spread from the cave, grey tendrils rippling across rock and snow like a disease. It was almost as far as the path to Det-Sen Monastery, another one of those legendary places from her father's travels.

Two Yeti stood motionless on the main trail.

'Now seems as good a time as any,' Eileen said. 'If the blond man does make a move, it'd be nice to have allies.'

Anne considered. Eileen was right, but the thought of having Yeti on their side bothered her. She remembered how, nine years ago, the Doctor had managed to remote control a Yeti in the London Underground. It had listened to his voice commands, but… Was that the proof of Eileen's theory?

'On the way back,' Anne said. 'Let's not waste time. First I need to make sure my father is safe.'

'I understand that, dear, but you said when he returns to the cave…'

'That was a guess. I might be wrong. Whatever happened to him at the pyramid… It left parts of his memory vague, so the story he told me, it wasn't complete.'

'Then…' Eileen stopped. 'Of course, that might explain it.'

'Explain what?'

'When we first met, last year… Well, seven years from now… He didn't know me. And he hasn't shown any sign of it since. He obviously doesn't remember any of our time together in the last week.'

Anne considered. To lose so much. 'Maybe. He did talk with great fondness of the trip, of the dangers he faced.' She smiled. 'He never really mentioned names, but he did say he met some amazing people on the journey to Det-Sen. Maybe he doesn't remember you exactly, but…'

'I left an impact of sorts.' Eileen nodded, and smiled softly. 'That's better than nothing. I'd hate to think I don't leave a mark on this world.'

Anne squeezed Eileen's shoulder. 'I doubt you'll ever be truly forgotten.'

They enjoyed a small moment of bonding in silence, before turning back to the next part of the plan.

'So, it's agreed, then?' Anne said. 'We'll make sure my father is safe, and then we'll see if we can reason with the Yeti.'

'No, dear, we don't agree. If he's to return to the cave, and the blond man is there, then we need allies.'

'That will take time. If Father is safe in the monastery, then we have a bit of time before he goes to the cave. *Then* we can deal with the Yeti.'

Eileen looked like she was about to argue, but Anne didn't give her the opportunity. Eileen was in her early twenties, a good six years younger than Anne, and she didn't have the experience Anne had. She knew the situation in Tibet better than Eileen, she knew the Yeti better…

Anne turned and continued on her way to the valley housing the monastery. After a while, she heard the crunching of Eileen's boots behind her.

They reached the slope overlooking the valley and were greeted with a warzone. Over the screams and cries below, Anne saw Yeti bursting through the gates, monks desperately trying to fend them off as the enemy rampaged through the monastery. The Great Intelligence was moving against them and her father was down there.

She resisted the urge to rush down and help. History had to run its course. There was no sign of the blond man, which didn't surprise her. Based on what she'd seen in Paris, it didn't strike Anne that the blond man was the kind of person to put himself in direct danger.

Anne and Eileen watched on as the monks bravely fought off the attacking Yeti. Soon the tide of the battle turned. The creatures lumbered away from the monastery, making no sound as they spilled out onto the mountainside.

'What happened?' Eileen asked. 'Were they defeated?'

Anne shook her head. 'No. The Yeti were not the real threat. The heart of the Great Intelligence is still inside Det-Sen. My father and the Doctor will stop it. We need to move.'

Anne stood and Eileen moved with her.

'To the cave?' she asked.

'Yes, Father will head this way shortly, to study the Yeti's next move. And without the Doctor at his side, that's when he will be the most vulnerable.'

'Then let's get a move on.'

Anne grinned at Eileen as the young woman increased her pace. She could see why her father and Eileen had become friends. Now all they had to do was make sure her father lived, not only so that Anne could be born and they could meet Archie's alter ego, but so that one day Edward Travers could meet Eileen Le Croissette.

CHAPTER SEVENTEEN
An Unexpected Meeting

ARCHIE SIPPED on his second cup of coffee, staring out onto the busy Parisian street, and waited for signs of anything out of the ordinary. He wasn't sure whether to expect friends and allies or the enemy. It had been a couple of hours since they had fled the hotel and sold James' lighter. It had hurt more than he thought it would, giving up a relic of his life, of his timeline, now lost to this place.

At least selling the lighter had given him a small sum of cash, by which he might finance a way out of the city. Not enough to make it all the way to England, but maybe to the next town, hopefully far enough from the reach of the Gilded Serpent Society. In the meantime, they waited.

He was worried about Anne too; Goff's attacker had somehow managed to pull her away to God knows where. As for young George, he felt surprisingly protective of the young man. Of course, Archie knew George was quite capable of taking care of himself, but what good were wits when bullets flew around you? Archie dearly hoped that he was still alive. He didn't want to lose him too. Not after Owain.

The two women at his table had been largely silent since they had arrived, traumatised by what they had witnessed and unsure of what was going to happen next. Archie wished he knew what words of comfort he might give, but the truth was he had none for himself. If Alistair had died at *Le Grand,* then his mission was a failure. Of course, as long as he got Lillian to safety, at least his own future was secured.

Ruby had finally stopped crying, some comforting words from Lillian managing to fob off her concerns that this was all her fault. Lillian herself was oddly withdrawn, munching on a small cake with seemingly little appetite. He felt sorry for them both. They had come to Paris, expecting a magical journey across Europe. Finding adventure and passion as they sought to break free of the shackles that society imposed upon them. His grandmother had always spoken so wondrously of her European adventure. He wandered if she still would now. Not with what she had witnessed today.

He set his coffee cup down and grabbed one of the remaining sandwiches, nibbling away absently, with little appreciation for what he was eating. Lillian looked at him, giving him a grateful smile before returning to her coffee. Ruby stared out across the street, seemingly lost in her own thoughts. No, not the Parisian adventure at all.

Archie did a double take as he saw a group of men heading in their direction, marching with grim determination, their long black coats billowing around them as they made their way towards the café. He swallowed his bit of sandwich, chewing quickly as he leaned forward for a closer look.

Alistair led the group, young George at his side. Archie let out a sigh of relief.

He rose from his seat, a big smile on his face. For the first time today, things were looking up.

'These are my friends,' he told Lillian and Ruby. 'Everything is going to be okay now.'

He rushed over to greet the approaching men, and Alistair reached out to shake his hand firmly. George hesitated, looking nervous in his thick fur coat.

'Are you well?' Archie asked.

George nodded, managing a sheepish smile. 'Well, you know. Life isn't boring.'

Archie couldn't help but grin. 'I most certainly agree with that.' He turned to Alistair. 'Anne?'

Alistair shook his head. 'Gone. Taken. George here tells me she was kidnapped by the man that abducted him and brought him here. The man we believe poisoned Goff.'

Archie was confused. The same man?

'He was in Tibet,' George said, 'trying to kill Travers.'

Archie looked at Alistair, who simply nodded. Clearly he'd heard something of the story already, although he probably didn't understand much of it.

'Travers. Anne's father, I assume?' Archie asked.

'Yup. He can't meet… Well, you know who, if he's dead. I think Anne is with Eileen now.'

'Are you saying you and Anne have been… Switched, I suppose?'

'Looks like it.'

'Once again this is over my head,' Alistair said. 'Evidently whatever it is department MI10 does is a little beyond my purview, but I do need to know one thing for sure. Can you vouch for George?'

'Of course. He's a… A trainee, I suppose you could say.'

'I see. Well, okay, a bit rum if you ask me, but nobody has so I'll reserve judgement for now.' Alistair indicated the two women at the table watching them. 'And how are Miss Holland and Miss McDougal?'

This was it, Archie realised. The meeting he had been trying to engineer ever since their trip to the *Palais Garnier*.

He had no choice, circumstances had forced his hand and he'd have to swallow his selfish instincts. The future of Alistair Gordon Lethbridge-Stewart would come to pass. What that meant for Archie's life, he still didn't know.

With a deep internal sigh, Archie laid his hand on Alistair's shoulder and led him to the table, where Lillian was rising gracefully from her seat.

'Alistair Lethbridge-Stewart, allow me to introduce Lillian McDougal.'

Archie stepped back, letting history do its duty. Love at first sight, destiny, call it what you want, this was it in action before his eyes.

'Miss McDougal.' Alistair nodded, and turned his head

towards Ruby. 'Miss Holland.'

Lillian sat down, crossing her arms. There definitely wasn't love in her eyes.

Archie frowned, and looked at George, who raised his hairless eyebrows, equally surprised.

'I presume you are responsible for all of this mess?' Lillian said.

Alistair turned back to her sharply. 'My men have worked tirelessly to ensure your safety, Miss McDougal. Your three travelling companions are protected, and we managed to draw a dangerous criminal organisation away from your friend here.' He crossed his arms in response to hers. 'Without British Military Intelligence, you would have been manipulated into smuggling stolen documentation out of the city. What would have happened to you after you left Paris, I could not say. However, if there is one thing I know about these people, it's that they do not like to leave any loose threads behind.'

Ruby sunk visibly into her seat with a sigh. 'That was why Antoine expressed interest in me? Those documents?'

Alistair nodded, sitting down on the seat next to Ruby's. 'I am afraid so, Miss Holland.' He gently patted Ruby's hand. 'But you have been very brave, and I assure you that I will not allow you to be used by Antoine or any of his men again.'

Ruby wiped a tear from her cheek and nodded. 'Thank you.'

Archie saw Lillian relax a little, her arms falling to her side. 'Are we safe? Will this criminal organisation come for us?'

Alistair paused, taking his hand away from Ruby's. 'We have apprehended most of the group. There are a couple of men still at large, but we are working to track them down. I assure you; we will get you to safety.'

Lillian nodded. 'Okay, Mr Lethbridge-Stewart. I will hold you to that.'

Archie stepped away to join George, who stood with the other three Intelligence officers watching the street.

There was no sign of danger, just the usual bustle of people and horse-drawn carriages navigating their way down the narrow street in front of the café.

George grinned, looking very out of place in his big fur coat.

'Archie! Can you believe what's happening?'

'I'm not sure what to believe.'

'You look rather dapper in your top hat,' George added. 'Very in keeping with the locals.'

Archie removed the hat awkwardly. Give him a simple flat cap any day. 'How are you?'

'Oh, you know.' George shrugged. 'One minute I'm in a cave, avoiding Yeti and trying to save Professor Travers' life. The next minute, I'm in a restaurant in Paris getting shot at, beaten over the head, abducted and interrogated. How about you?'

'I'm… managing. What do you know about Anne?'

George shook his head. 'Not a lot. As I said, that guy must have swapped us. Probably the only way he was going to win the fight.'

Archie raised an eyebrow. 'Fight?'

'Yeah, I totally had him on the ropes.' George beamed. 'Maybe he thinks he stands a better chance against two women?'

'Clearly he hasn't come up against Anne. Well, if she is with Eileen, then there's not much we can do about it.' He nodded over at Alistair and the women. 'We still have a mission to complete. It's taken me three attempts to get them to meet and now they have, I'm not sure what happens next.'

Before he could consider the situation any further, one of the Intelligence officers, the one Archie thought was called Cecil, shouted a warning and pulled out his gun.

A shot rang out over the street, striking the other Intelligence officer in the chest. Just like the restaurant, everything exploded into chaos. Screams from passers-by rang out and diners at the café began to run frantically away. Archie grabbed George and pulled him back to his table, where Alistair was already crouched, gun ready. Lillian and Ruby hid behind their chairs for safety.

Antoine and five other men were charging from across the street, pushing through panicked people, shooting at the Intelligence officers when they had a clear shot. Alistair's men fired back, killing one of the criminals, before backing away to the tables for protection.

Without hesitation, Archie crouched beside Lillian, wrapping his arm around her for reassurance. George did the same with Ruby.

Alistair fired, striking a second man in the arm, but it didn't completely slow them down. Antoine and the other four criminals took up a second defensive position.

'I thought you said there were only three of them left!' Alistair shouted across to his men at the next table.

'I thought so too!'

'Cedric, Edmund. I'm going to lead Archie, George and the two women out through the back of the café. Can you provide cover fire?'

The two men nodded and immediately began shooting furiously at the enemy, the sudden assault forcing them to duck for cover behind their table.

Alistair pulled back, indicating for the others to follow. Archie went to help Lillian, but she was already running, while George was quick to aid Ruby with her escape.

Alistair shoved tables and chairs aside, gun still in his hand, as he cleared a path. At the far side of the café, a large window looked out onto a busy street beyond, where horse-drawn carriages and steam trams were chugging along. There was no door, so Alistair threw a chair against the glass, smashing it.

As he began knocking away loose shards of glass, Alistair turned back. 'Quickly!'

Archie didn't need to be told twice. As the gun fight continued behind them, he joined Lillian, Ruby and George and hurried them through the open window onto the street beyond.

'What do we do now?' Archie asked, once Alistair had

joined them.

Alistair scanned the street frantically. 'Come with me!'

He ran towards the nearest horse-drawn carriage and held up his gun to the driver. 'Police! *Je dois réquisitionner cette voiture!'*

The driver began to protest, but Alistair was already beckoning Archie and the others towards him. The driver continued his frantic debate with Alistair, who turned to address them.

'He won't give up the carriage. But he will take us to the *Gare du Nord.'*

'The *Gare du Nord?'* Lillian asked, following Ruby into the carriage.

'I have your tickets. I am getting you out of the city. You have a train at five o'clock and I intend to make sure you are on it.'

Lillian simply nodded and entered with her friend. George followed. As Archie and Alistair went to enter, they heard footsteps behind them. Antoine and one of his men began charging down the street, guns ready.

Alistair shoved Archie inside and fired a warning shot down the street. A shot rang back, hitting the door of the carriage. Alistair jumped in, slammed the door shut and roared to the driver.

'La Gare du Nord! Aller!'

CHAPTER EIGHTEEN
Goodbye, Paris

GEORGE LURCHED forward out of his seat as the carriage began to rock back and forth violently. He could hear the steady beat of hooves on the street, the sound of the horse picking up speed. With the wheels creaking beneath them, he wondered how long they would stay in one piece. The two women were on one seat, Archie on the other, while Alistair craned his neck out of the small window, gun in hand.

'Balderdash!' Alistair exclaimed, cocking his gun and reaching out of the window. 'They've stolen another carriage and are gaining on us!'

Ruby's eyes were wide with panic, while Lillian seemed more angry than afraid.

'Is the station the safest place for us?' she demanded.

Alistair didn't look back, but leaned his head in a little to respond. 'I am hoping we can lose them. If not, getting out of Paris is still our best option. George, I need you to be a look out on the other side. Tell me if they are gaining on us.'

George was already losing track of how many times he had been shot at since arriving in Paris. He had been safer with the Yeti. He paused, worried that he might get shot in the head.

Archie caught George's eye. 'Seems like yesterday we were in a similar situation. Only then it was the Kruge.'

George almost laughed. 'Simpler times,' he quipped, and cautiously pulled down the window with a thud, and gingerly peered outside.

The busy Parisian street with its row of horse-drawn carriages whizzed past, the air blasting his face. To his right, he could make out the driver tugging furiously at the reigns, the horse almost at a gallop as the carriage weaved between two slower ones. George turned to his left, saw one horse and carriage gaining on them. There were two men on the front seat, one tugging furiously at the reigns, the other with a gun in his hand, the metal barrel gleaming off the sunshine.

He heard a gunshot and ducked, before he realised it was Alistair firing from the other carriage window. Ruby squealed inside as the horse pulling their carriage reacted to the gun fire. George had to hold the edge of the window frame to keep himself from falling. The gun-toting man in the pursuing carriage fired, and the bullet struck the back of their carriage.

Alistair fired again and George ducked before another retaliatory shot struck. The horse was not reacting well to what was happening. The carriage shook violently and this time he fell back into the carriage, landing on Lillian.

'Are you okay?' she asked softly. She wasn't angry that he had almost landed in her lap.

He nodded. 'I better see what's going on,' he said, heaving himself back up to the window and peering out.

Alistair fired again and, this time, the bullet struck the man holding the reigns. The horse pulling the other carriage suddenly began to bolt, pulling free. The enemy carriage tilted severely, crashing onto its side in the middle of the road. The carriages around it struggled not to smash into it and there was a great raucous of cries and neighing as the traffic on the street came to a grinding halt.

George pulled his head back into the carriage. 'Good job!' he cried to Alistair.

'That *should* be the end of it.' Alistair sighed. 'But I do not want to take any chances. We must continue to the *Gare du Nord* and take the train south as planned.'

Lillian was visibly frustrated. 'What about my friends?

We are supposed to be travelling together.'

Alistair smiled. 'I promise you, Miss McDougal. I will arrange for your friends to join us by train later. You will be able to continue your trip to the south of France without any further interruptions.'

Lillian snorted. 'I should hope so.'

George caught sight of Archie. He didn't look happy.

They reached the train station, with no sign of the enemy in pursuit. George couldn't help but feel a little excited as they navigated their way through the busy station to the platforms. There were several impressive steam trains waiting, all jet black and gleaming.

Archie walked beside him. George got a few strange looks. The big fur coat looked somewhat out of place. It was better than a stupid top hat and cravat though.

'How are you holding up, young man?' Archie asked quietly.

George shrugged. What could he say? 'I know life isn't exactly great back home, but I kind of miss it. At least I know what to expect.'

Archie smiled. 'I know what you mean.'

'This is top notch though,' George added, gesturing around them.

'Yes, I suppose it is. Time travel is a remarkable thing. But I would gladly give it up to be home with my wife and children.'

Ahead of them, Alistair brought the group to a halt.

'We have one hour until the train leaves the station,' he announced. 'We should find somewhere discreet to rest before we board.'

They found a long wooden bench behind two large columns that wasn't visible from the main entrance of the station. The moment George sat down, he felt an overwhelming wave of exhaustion. That little nap in Alistair's room above the shop hadn't made up for a night crouched on the side of a mountain, watching Professor Travers and hiding from the Yeti. He was probably suffering from some kind of temporal lag. It had been early morning when he had left Tibet, but now it was already late afternoon in Paris and he had only been there a few hours. Not that it mattered what time it was. If someone showed him to a bed now, he would sleep for days.

Ruby clutched Archie's arm. At least she had stopped sobbing. Lillian and Alistair sat silently, scanning their surroundings. George wondered if they should move on. If the Gilded Serpent Society came to the station, they were surely too exposed, even in this secluded spot.

Lillian turned to Alistair. 'Do you think they will still follow us?'

Alistair sighed. 'I cannot say, Miss McDougal.'

'You can call me Lillian,' she said softly. 'You have saved my life, after all.'

Alistair seemed to hesitate. 'If that is not too forward of me?'

Lillian laughed, holding out her hand. 'No, I should think that it is forward enough.'

Alistair took her gloved hand and gave it a quick, awkward kiss.

George looked at Archie and thought he saw a half smile.

'Are you okay?' George asked quietly.

Archie looked at him and nodded. 'Very mixed feelings. But this is *supposed* to happen. The fate of the universe hangs on it.'

George couldn't ignore the bitterness lacing Archie's words. If George understood things correctly, before Archie's very eyes, the man he had always known as his great uncle was falling in love with the woman destined to be Archie's grandmother, just so that in the future she could have an indiscreet liaison with Alistair's brother to produce Archie's father. And, thus, a timeline would be formed in which Archie would be born as Alistair Gordon Lethbridge-Stewart, and live a life in which he became a war hero and never know Sabina, the woman Archie had married and fathered children with.

George shook his head just thinking about it. At least, if what he and Archie believed was true, then Archie's world would still exist and he would return to it. Forever scarred by the knowledge of the choices his grandmother would have made, had circumstances been a little different.

George thought of his mum in Ogmore-by-Sea. He thought about the life she could have had, if the Clown had not come. And, he concluded, that he wished he had the options Archie had.

Alistair pulled his hand away from Lillian. 'Wait here. I have a contact, someone who is a friend of British Military Intelligence. He will be able to pass a message to my colleagues.' He flashed her a disarming smile. 'I will arrange for your three companions, and all your luggage, to follow on the next available train. In the meantime, I want to ensure you make it safely out of Paris. With Ruby a known target, I cannot take any chances.'

Ruby let out a whimper, and Alistair stood, reaching out to touch her shoulder, giving it a soft squeeze.

'Please, do not worry. My men now outnumber theirs. We might have been taken by surprise at the café, but I will not allow it to happen again.'

'You hope,' Lillian said.

George frowned. One minute she looked as if she might be flirting with the man, the next, she was cold again.

'I assure you, I will do my best to protect you with every breath I have left,' Alistair said, and looked back to Ruby. He cupped her chin in his hand to look into her teary eyes. 'You are both some of the bravest women I have ever met.'

Ruby let her chin be held in his hands as she spoke. 'Thank you, you are too kind.'

Alistair stepped back to Lillian, taking her hand again in his. 'I promise, I will protect you.'

Lillian didn't flinch. She regarded Alistair for what seemed a long while before saying, 'I know you will. Thank you, Alistair.'

*

Archie stared out of the window of the dining cart and watched the familiar sights of Paris pass him by. The sweeping arches and long narrow platforms of *La Gare du Nord* faded into the distance. Grand buildings and spires passed him, distorted images behind soot-stained windows as the carriage began to rock gently back and forth. When he had arrived in Paris with Anne, he had expected to be there maybe a day or two, to put history back on track. Now, days later, he was leaving the city, with no idea what was going to happen next. Yes, Lillian and Alistair had finally met, maybe even sparked a brief romantic interest, but their lives were still in danger. So even if Archie could go, and he supposed he could, after all he had a time ring on his person, he knew he shouldn't.

He let out a long sigh, catching one last look at the Eiffel Tower, majestic in the distance over the rooftops of Paris.

He leaned back away from the window. George sat opposite him, somewhat subdued, as he took in his surroundings. Sitting next to George, Alistair was quiet too. Across the aisle of the dining cart, Ruby and Lillian exchanged a couple of hushed words from their table. Despite the low bustle of conversation from passengers at other tables, there was a sense of morose reflection among the small, weary group.

Archie was tired, so very tired. All he wanted to do was go home, to retreat to his comfortable bed back in Greyhound Lodge. He wondered, for what felt like the hundredth time, whether his family and friends would forgive him for abandoning them the way he had. In truth, he didn't really care. He would gladly look at their faces once more, even if they were filled with anger and not love. He fumbled his hand in his pocket, feeling for James' lighter that was no longer there and felt a gnawing chasm in his chest. Without that tie to home, he had the sinking feeling that the world he'd left may not even exist anymore, not now that Lillian and Alistair had met.

Archie took in his great uncle, full of deeply conflicted feelings.

The train lurched and, for a moment, everyone had a flash of panic on their faces. Only when the carriage returned to its gentle rocking back and forth on the tracks, did the group relax. Ruby, unsurprisingly, was the most flustered and quickly rose from her seat, holding her chest.

'Ruby, what is wrong?' Lillian asked softly.

George and Alistair were looking in her direction too, their eyes alert. No one quite believed that they had left the enemy back on the road to the station.

Ruby took a deep breath. 'Just a little nervousness, that is all. I will be fine.' She managed a weak smile. 'If you would please excuse me, I am going to return to my bunk and get a little rest.'

'Do you want me to join you?' Lillian asked, rising from her seat.

Ruby shook her head. 'No, I should be able to manage.'

She made her way slowly back to the carriage, everyone watching her go. Perhaps the constant rocking and rattling of the train didn't help. Archie had certainly underestimated how unsteady a nineteenth century steam train felt.

'I'm going to go for a walk,' George announced, the moment Ruby had left.

Alistair stood, allowing the boy to leave, and stepped over to Lillian's table, where he sat down in Ruby's place. Archie watched George go and leaned his head back against the seat. A passing waiter brought him a cup of tea, but it was far too sweet for his tastes.

'I must say, I find it quite remarkable,' Alistair said, setting his own cup down.

Archie turned his head slightly, trying to listen without making it appear as if he was listening.

Lillian frowned. 'Remarkable?'

'Travelling across Europe, a group of women, without any chaperone.'

Lillian hesitated to respond, taking a sip of tea instead. As she set it down on the saucer, she regarded Alistair with a hard stare. 'You assume, then, that we need one? That women cannot venture out into the world unaided?'

Rather than back off, Alistair laughed. 'Not at all. I think it is admirable. Many women would feel the need to hide behind a man, let him guide her through life. But not you. I sense that you are quite willing to go out alone. I find that… fascinating.'

Lillian offered a small smile in response. 'It is nearly the twentieth century. Before long, women will do many things that might surprise you. Hopefully, even vote.'

'Oh, I have no doubt about it.' Alistair smiled back. He took a sip of his tea and added, 'Courageous and beautiful. You are quite the remarkable woman, Lillian McDougal.'

That almost seemed to catch her off guard. 'Beauty doesn't come into it, Alistair Lethbridge-Stewart.'

'But it certainly helps.'

Archie saw a glint in his great uncle's eye and an awkward smile on his granny's lips. This was it, the moment they would have captured had they met at the opera.

Archie instantly felt like he was intruding. With an over-obvious cough, he rose from his seat.

'I think I shall join George on that walk. I trust you will keep Lillian safe?'

Alistair nodded. 'You have my word.'

Leaving them to their tea and conversation, Archie quickly navigated his way down the dining cart in the direction George had left.

The young man was not in the small seating area at the end of the carriage, so Archie moved on to the next. The connected walkway between the carriages was a little nerve-wracking to navigate; the mix of thick black smoke from the funnel of the front engine mixed with the blast of cold air as he moved outside, made it hard to step across the two platforms, connected by what he assumed was a thick metal chain. It was something of a relief when he found himself back inside.

The next carriage was full of passenger seats and the majority of them were packed with men, women and children in their finest travelling clothes. Between the large bonnets and top hats, it was obvious to see that George and his fur coat was not among them.

Archie was halfway down the aisle when the far door opened and George burst in, a panicked expression on his face. Ignoring the startled looks from a number of passengers, he hurried towards Archie, panting for breath.

'I think I saw one of them!'

Archie felt his heart skip. He had hoped they'd managed to escape the Gilded Serpent Society at last.

'Come with me. We need to let Alistair know,' Archie muttered, trying not to attract any more attention from the carriage than they had already.

George followed him, racing back along the passenger carriage and jumping across the narrow platforms between carriages. They burst into the main dining area, attracting plenty more startled looks as they ran back to Lillian's and Alistair's table.

'George thinks one of the men from the Society is here on the train,' Archie announced, before he had even come to a halt.

Alistair pulled his gun from inside his coat pocket and jumped out of his seat. Lillian looked alarmed but didn't say anything. She simply stood and took hold of Archie's arm.

At the opposite end of the dining cart, two figures emerged through the doorway. Archie took them in with dread.

One was Ruby, her face white as a sheet. The other was Antoine, his face bloodstained, his eyes wide and a gun fixed firmly against Ruby's temple.

'Give me the papers! Or she dies!'

CHAPTER NINETEEN
Topher Si-William

THE PAIN was real. This was the father she remembered as a child growing up. Young, strong, and oh-so-focused. As she and Eileen carefully followed him from a safe distance, Anne felt tears forming. Nine years since she had to bury him. Sometimes she would look at photographs of him and find she could barely remember what he sounded like, his ticks and body language lost to time.

But now here he was. Her father, Edward Travers, alive again.

He had always been brave; her father was where she got her own courage, but even she didn't think she would be strong enough to dare approach the lair of the Great Intelligence alone. Of course, hindsight was a wonderful thing. Right now, he didn't fully comprehend what he was walking into.

He stopped on a small outcrop of rock that formed a natural observation platform. Picking up the binoculars he had hanging around his neck, he kept his watch on the Yeti which had amassed nearby. Anne's heart swelled with the idea of rushing over to meet him, but he wouldn't know her. She was an adult daughter that he had yet to conceive.

So, she waited next to Eileen, unsure of the next step. She scanned the mountainside for any sign of the man in black. Or, indeed, anything else that might be an immediate threat to her father. She knew the Doctor would come soon, and together they would return to the monastery to defeat the Great Intelligence. But right now, her father was dangerously exposed. If she were the enemy, this would be when she would strike.

Almost on cue, a man blinked into existence on a ridge behind her father. She recognised him immediately. Tall, dressed in black shiny garments, hair blond and curly. But she hadn't expected him to look so young; about Eileen's age.

He held something in his hands. A glint of silver caught the sunlight and she knew instantly what it was. A gun! Anne didn't hesitate.

She moved forward, out from behind their hiding place, before Eileen could even attempt to stop her. Immediately she caught the blond man's attention. He scowled at her, and reached for the metallic device strapped to his wrist. Just like that he vanished.

'What happened?' Eileen whispered.

'Teleportation of some sort,' Anne said.

'Then where did he go? Surely he won't be defeated so easily.'

No, Anne didn't think so either. She looked around and, on the road below, she saw another figure. A man in a large fur coat and a mop of dark hair. Someone she hadn't seen in years, but he looked exactly as she remembered him from the Underground. She was about to point him out to Eileen, when a shadow fell over them.

Anne ducked sideways, knocking Eileen over. A laser beam narrowly missed them. They both stumbled, rolling down the stony slope. The man in black charged towards them, his face filled with fury.

'I thought you would be less bother than that boy, but no, of course not!'

'If you think I am going to let you kill my father, you have another think coming,' Anne snapped back, staggering to her feet.

'Your what?' The man in black laughed, and pointed towards Edward Travers. 'He's your father?' A look swept across his face. Anne could only describe it as rage. 'You're a Travers?' He pointed at Eileen. 'Don't tell me, a

Lethbridge-Stewart?'

'No,' Eileen said. 'Eileen Le Croissette.'

'Never heard of you.' With a sneer, he turned on his heel and began to race up the slope back to the vantage point overlooking the Det-Sen path.

Anne charged after him. A rock hit him firmly in the back, sending him crashing to the ground with a thud. He groaned in pain and Anne turned to Eileen. She was picking up another rock.

'Good shot,' Anne said with a grin.

'I was always good at shot put,' Eileen said, already racing up the hill towards the man in black. 'Are you coming?'

Anne needed no encouragement. She scrambled up the slope by Eileen's side. The man in black was halfway to his feet when they reached him. He shot them a fierce glare and reached for the bracelet he wore. Anne was not going to let him get away again.

She leaped towards him. Eileen did the same…

…and fell, not onto hard rock as she would have expected, but something smooth and shiny. Eileen rolled onto her side, still clutching the rock in her hand.

Anne lay near her, panting for breath, while the man in black sat huddled close by, his mop of blond curls falling over his face. Eileen didn't take her eyes off him, ready to strike should he try to move against them.

'Where are we?'

Anne staggered to her feet. 'I don't think we're in Tibet anymore.'

The room they were in was round, built entirely of metal, with domed windows looking out over a city that was unlike anything Eileen had seen before. Tall, white and silver structures rose impossibly high into the air and between them flew…

Eileen blinked. They looked like cars, but that was impossible.

A beam of purplish white light gleamed over the towers

outside and her mouth fell open. There was not one sun, but two – purple and orange – hovering over the city.

The man in black rose to his feet, sneering as he took them in. His head was bleeding, his eyes wide and menacing. But, Eileen noticed, he had dropped his weapon. Anne saw it, and quickly scooped it up, pointing it at him.

'Where are we?' Eileen asked. She felt impossibly hot under her hat and fur coat, and wished she had a change of clothes. And, just like that, she did. With relief, and a little confusion, she found she was wearing her WAAF uniform again.

'It's the ring,' Anne said, and in a blink of an eye her own outfit changed into something more normal. A nice, smart trouser suit and low heels.

Eileen didn't know what to say. She remembered it had happened in the Accord's realm, and she remembered the Guardian explaining, but hadn't understood how it was possible then, and she didn't now. Still, at least she was cooler, so she didn't complain.

The man in black looked at them, almost seeming to be impressed. 'What kind of technology is that?'

'Don't you worry,' Anne said. 'Where are we?'

'You wouldn't believe me.'

Anne crossed her arms. 'The future?'

'Lucky guess.'

'Quite a good way into the future, I presume,' Anne continued, turning to Eileen. 'Are you okay?'

Eileen nodded. 'I'm ready to throw this rock at his head if he shows any sign of trouble,' she said, locking her gaze on the man in black.

He didn't seem quite so sure of himself now at all.

'Judging by all the contraptions you have on that work bench over there,' Anne said, 'your technology is far more advanced than the twentieth century. So, flying cars, two suns. What planet are we on?'

The man seemed a little put off by Anne's blasé attitude, but he still buffed himself up smugly and said, 'Dagmar Prime.'

'Dagmar Prime.' Anne nodded. 'Never heard of it. Is it nice?'

Eileen fought the urge to smile. Anne was managing to cut through all his bluster, and she didn't want to undermine her. Instead, she quietly removed her uniform cap.

'You think you are so clever,' the blond man said with a snarl. 'You died three thousand years ago. You mean nothing to me.'

'Ah, so the fiftieth century then?' Anne mused. 'Four time periods in about as many days. Well,' she added, glancing at Eileen, 'for me at least.'

'4976,' the man said in as offhanded a manner as he could manage.

'So, just to recap,' Anne said, her voice effortlessly calm. 'You have brought us to Dagmar Prime in the year 4976. Is there anything else you can tell us? Your name perhaps?'

'I will tell you nothing!'

'Except that we're on Dagmar Prime in the year 4976.'

He glared at Anne. More and more, he began to look like a petulant child.

'You can't stop me.'

Anne waved the silver gun slightly. 'I think you'll find I can.'

Clearly not thinking her serious, he moved towards her, so Anne took a step forward, forcing him back.

'Ah, ah, ah! You stay where you are. Remember, I have a gun and Eileen has a big rock. You, young man, have nothing.'

Eileen couldn't help but smile this time.

The man in black hesitated, his eyes wide. He definitely had the look of a teenage boy that had been caught out by his parents for sneaking out to meet with the girl next door. In desperation he reached for his bracelet. No, it was more than that. It was a plastic strip upon which sat a metallic device about three inches in length.

'Stop right there, or I will shoot you in the face!' Anne snapped, her voice like ice. It was enough to cause him to drop his arm. 'Eileen?'

'Yes, Anne?' Eileen asked, eager to join in. She couldn't let Anne have all the fun.

'Would you kindly remove that device off his wrist?'

Eileen nodded.

'Remember,' Anne said, 'she has a big rock.'

Eileen reached over and released the plastic strap. The man looked at her in alarm. Eileen was half tempted to *suggest* hitting him with the rock. Just to see how much he would flinch. When she stepped away, he looked to Anne nervously.

'You wouldn't shoot me.' There wasn't much conviction in his statement.

'Wouldn't I?' Anne said with a glare. 'You tried to kill my father. Not to mention, you've put the universe at risk. Do you know how many timelines are in flux because of what you've done?'

He looked at her with a frown. 'What are you talking about? The universe? I just wanted to—'

Anne took a step forward, the gun still aimed at his face. 'What did you want to do?'

'I…' He lowered his head.

Eileen thought there might be shame in there, buried under all that arrogance. She had known a lot of self-assured people during her time. The war certainly brought out the arrogant side in the majority of men. But he was something else entirely.

Eileen looked around. Everybody knew boys matured slower than girls, so even though he was about Eileen's age, he certainly felt a lot younger. And there had been a glimmer of hesitation in him. She looked at all the toys. And that's what they were, really.

He was just another boy with too many toys. Toys that had, obviously, caused a lot of problems.

Eileen set the rock down on a nearby table, far enough away that he couldn't reach it, and picked up a metal stool from what looked like a work bench. She set it next to the man.

'Sit down, please.'

Anne raised an eyebrow to Eileen, but didn't say anything. Silently, the boy sat.

'Good,' Eileen said, her tone firm but not cold. 'What is your name, please?'

He looked at her nervously, but kept his mouth shut. He obviously wasn't expecting such politeness. He didn't deserve it, but she always tried to lead by example. She folded her arms.

'I will only repeat myself once. What is your name, please?'

'Topher Si-William.'

Odd name, Eileen thought. But then, names did tend to change over time. No doubt there'd be a time when Eileen was out of fashion.

'Good.' She gave him the glimmer of a smile. 'My name, as I've said, is Eileen. This is Anne.'

He looked up at Anne, painfully aware that his gun was still pointed right at him. Eileen brushed down her blazer with her hands, feeling right at home in her old uniform. She could sense Anne's befuddlement as she retrieved two more stools and set them down. Topher watched her, weary. Mindful of the damage he'd caused, and his designs on her father, Anne kept the weapon aimed at him as she sat.

'Now, that's better,' Eileen said. 'Do you realise how much trouble you are in?'

Topher looked at her with a furrowed brow. 'I don't understand.'

Eileen wasn't the expert here. Anne was. She indicated to her companion. 'Would you care to explain the details of this horrid mess to him?'

Anne considered her response and nodded.

'Your mission, as far as I can tell, is to ensure that my father, Professor Edward Travers, dies in Tibet in 1935. You've also worked to ensure that Lillian McDougal and Alistair Lethbridge-Stewart won't meet in Paris in 1896. The result of all this is that my father and Lillian's grandson do not meet in London during the Great Intelligence's attack in 1969.'

'Well, yes… I guess…' Topher said meekly. 'At least, I…'

'Let me finish,' Anne said sharply. 'I can only assume you realise the importance of that event, the impact it has on the future of Earth and, indeed, the very causal nexus of reality itself.'

'Well, no, all I want is——'

'Because my father and the grandson never met,' Anne continued, cutting Topher off, 'history was altered in such a way that it disrupted what the Accord calls the essential timeline. Or, for the sake of simplicity, what I like to call timeline zero.'

Topher was confused. 'The Accord? I don't know what the Accord is.'

'No, I don't imagine you do. They don't appear to many corporeal beings. The Accord are a group of beings that exist in something called Calabi-Yau Space, a realm beyond normal time and space. They protect the universe of causality, among other things. And it was the Accord who assembled Eileen and I, as well as George and Archie, to be agents. We are here to fix your mess.'

'What mess? All I was doing was removing the timelines of two… *families.*' Topher practically spat out that last word.

'Two very important families,' Anne said softly, trying to keep her tone humble, after all she was a member of one of those families.

Topher glared at her. 'Oh yeah, sure, they're always *so* important.'

It was clear to Eileen that something… not so huge was going on, at least in the grand scheme of things. Huge for Topher, perhaps, but not for the rest of them. Although, whatever it was, it had escalated into something much worse.

Eileen leaned forward, looking Topher squarely in the eyes. 'What was your intended purpose? Why are you so angry at Anne's family?'

Topher averted his gaze. His eyes were wide again, filled with a fury that took her breath away. There was so much anger in him.

'Why, Topher?' she asked again.

He looked at Anne with disgust and turned his gaze back to Eileen.

'Because I have lived my life in their shadow. Do you know what it is like to grow up, surrounded by people who worship their legacy? Even here, two and a half galaxies away, you can't escape it. The great Lethbridge-Stewarts and Traverses. Centuries of heroes, soldiers, diplomats, rulers. *Professors.*'

'Well,' Anne said, 'you can't blame them for—'

'Yes I can!' Topher roared the words. 'All my life I worked hard to get where I am today. I was top of my class. I won awards. I achieved the highest commendations.'

'Then you should be proud of—'

'Proud? How can I be proud? No matter what I did, you know who everybody worshipped, who everybody from my class remembered?'

Eileen rather suspected she did.

'Alasdair Travers and Annabel Lethbridge-Stewart,' Topher told them.

Anne rolled her eyes and shook her head. It was enough of a distraction for the rage-fuelled Topher to make his move.

He launched himself at Anne.

CHAPTER TWENTY
Saving the Mission

'**RELEASE RUBY** and I will give you the papers,' Alistair demanded coolly, keeping his gun aimed firmly in the direction of Antoine.

'I don't think so. If you do anything other than pass me those papers, I will put a bullet in her skull.'

Archie held Lillian's hand tightly. She came across as mostly unflappable, but now she looked terrified. He could hardly blame her. He knew he'd been right to stick around. Until Antoine and his men were gone, there was still a risk to Alistair's and Lillian's future.

Alistair, in complete contrast to his future wife, was as cool as a cucumber. There was no sign of fear on his face as he lowered his weapon and reached inside his coat with the other hand, pulling the ribbon-bound envelope free.

'What is so important about these papers?' he asked. 'What secrets have you stolen?'

Antoine smiled a cruel, mocking smile. 'Enough secrets to bring down your government. The chaos those secrets can bring.'

'And yet you risked handing them over to Ruby or Anne?'

'Where is dear Anne?' Antoine asked, pushing the end of the gun barrel harder against Ruby's head, causing her to squeal with pain. 'Oh, it matters not. Anne, Ruby, the rest of your pathetic harem of women,' he added, glaring at Lillian. 'They were a means to an end. Once they had smuggled the papers out of the city, my men and I would have located them and disposed of them.'

Lillian's eyes went wide, but Archie sensed more anger than terror. Poor Ruby, however, was trembling, tears streaming down her cheeks.

Before anyone realised what was happening, a second man reached out and snatched the envelope from Alistair's hands. He spun around and found a gun aimed at his face.

Archie held his breath, wondering if his mission was about to come to a tragic end.

Young George however, not so easily deterred it seemed, propelled himself in the direction of the man, pushing him against a table. Such was his speed, and the fact that nobody clearly considered him a threat, that Antoine's man didn't have a chance to react. The gun went off, the bullet striking the small glass chandelier above Alistair's head. Small beads crashed down all around them.

George was shoved aside, and the man turned and ran down the carriage back the way he had come. Archie pulled Lillian to the floor while Alistair fired back, narrowly missing the man by a couple of inches and hitting a window instead. It cracked and broke instantly, allowing smoke and wind to billow into the carriage. There were panicked screams from passengers as they crouched at their tables, the sound of the chugging steam train thundering through the carriage.

The poor waiter at the far door was shot in the chest as the man made his escape. At the other end of the walkway, Antoine dragged a screaming Ruby away, disappearing back in the direction of the sleeper cabin carriage.

Alistair rose to his feet. 'We cannot let him get away!'

'But Ruby...?' Lillian began desperately.

Archie knew what he had to do. Alistair couldn't do it alone. 'I'll go after the papers with George. You save Ruby.'

Alistair considered a moment and nodded. 'Be careful. I don't have a weapon to give you.'

Archie nodded. He felt sick even thinking about going after an armed criminal, but there was no choice. Besides, George was tough. He looked at the young man.

'Ready?'

George hesitated. 'I guess?'

'Good luck,' Alistair said, moving off after Antoine and Ruby.

'I am coming with you, Alistair,' Lillian added, rising to her feet.

Alistair turned back and nodded. 'Okay, stay behind me.'

Archie and George ran down the dining cart, waving their arms and shouting to keep the path clear. If the passengers didn't understand their words, they at least understood their meaning. Archie's heart was pounding in his chest as they left the small seating area and stepped out onto the two narrow platforms between the carriages. Fighting Yeti in a deserted London, being attacked by strange creatures in the English countryside, struggling against homicidal Clowns, and now chasing armed criminals… What had his life come to?

Again he considered his alter ego, and wondered how much this little caper would be run-of-the-mill for him. If this was Alistair Gordon Lethbridge-Stewart's life, he could keep it.

Without hesitation, George leaped onto the next carriage. Clearly it was a life that George was, however, quite suited for. Taking a deep breath, Archie followed.

They burst into the next packed carriage, but there was no sign of the man and the envelope. They raced through the carriage, clearing the way past the startled passengers.

As George stepped outside onto the next platform, an arm swept out, knocking George to the ground. Archie gasped as the man followed up by kicking George out to the edge, pushing him against the small railing.

One slip, and George would fall onto the tracks beyond.

Archie steadied himself as the train rocked, the track curving around as the train continued to race along. He had no time to worry about panic; he had to act. Now.

He leapt forward, clenching his fist and slamming it against the man's right cheek. The blow was enough to send the gun slipping from the man's grasp. Archie recoiled, grabbing his fist as he felt a sharp pain ricochet down his hand and wrist. That man's face was tougher than it looked.

The criminal stumbled back, trying to regain his step, and spun around, grabbing Archie by the collar and throwing him over his body. Archie slipped, landed with a thud against the platform. He felt smoke and dust sting his eyes as his neck snapped back and his head bobbed up and down above the track. The metal bars whizzed beneath him, bits of stone and dust striking him, forcing him to close his eyes. He tried to move, but another sharp shoot of pain tore through his back.

Something heavy wrapped around his neck. He forced his eyes open. The man bore down upon him, his hands gripping Archie's neck tightly. Archie tried to gasp, but he couldn't get air into his lungs. He began to see specks in his eyes, and pressure built in his head. Furiously, he tried to claw at the man's hands, but his attacker was far stronger.

Alistair raced down the corridor, gun in one hand, Lillian's hand in the other. Ahead of them, the carriage door swung closed as Antoine dragged a screaming Ruby by the hair. A passenger peeped his head out of his sleeper cabin, took one look at Alistair with his gun, and rushed back inside.

Good man. If every passenger could keep out of his way, there was hope yet that they might get through the journey out of Paris with no further civilian casualties. Except Antoine. There was no chance of letting that man live now. Alistair couldn't take the chance that Antoine might escape custody later.

Lillian was a brave woman, willing to throw herself into danger to protect her friend. Alistair was surrounded by brave souls lately. Not just his own men, but Anne, Archie and George. He still didn't really understand their agenda, but he was grateful for their involvement. He was not sure his mission would have succeeded without them. Truth be told, he would probably be floating in the sewers beneath the *Palais Garnier* now if Anne and Archie hadn't come along.

Alistair let go of Lillian's hand and motioned for her to stay. Slowly, carefully, he turned the handle of the door leading to the next carriage, and stepped outside. A rush of smoke and cold wind hit his face. Fortunately, there was no sign of Antoine, so Alistair led Lillian through into the next carriage.

The nearest cabin door flung open, smashed into Alistair's face and sent him stumbling back into Lillian.

A gun shot ricocheted past his brow, so close he could feel the blast on his skin. Luckily for him. Realising it was going to be a fight in close quarters, he flung himself forwards into Antoine, knocking them both into the sleeper cabin.

He was barely aware of Ruby screaming on one of the bunks as they both landed between the beds, hitting the soft rug with a grunt. Antoine immediately raised his gun, smashing the back of the handle against Alistair's face. Dazed but not defeated, Alistair propelled himself up, staggering towards the cabin door. Antoine slowly pulled himself up.

Seeing an opportunity, Alistair reached out and ripped the rug from beneath Antoine's feet. He fell, the gun falling from his hands.

Alistair smiled, raising his own gun towards the man. Antoine had played a good game, but he was no match for a member of British Military Intelligence. It was time to put this member of the Gilded Serpent Society into the ground.

He fired, but nothing happened. The gun barrel jammed. Alistair's heart raced and he scanned the small cabin, considering his options. Ruby was still on the bed, whimpering and in no fit state to help. Antoine was on the ground, looking up at him with a sneer. The man's gun was on the floor, halfway between them. He realised grimly that the odds were no longer in his favour. Whoever got to that weapon first would win. Alistair couldn't allow that. Not with Lillian's and Ruby's lives at stake too.

As Antoine lunged for the weapon, so did Alistair. The edge of the rug slipped at his feet and he found himself propelled forward, landing full force into his opponent. Together they fell back against the cabin window, smashing it.

'Get out!' Alistair screamed at Ruby. He heard her frantic footsteps behind him as he shoved Antoine by the shoulders closer to a broken shard of glass.

He didn't expect Antoine to headbutt him.

Alistair recoiled. The room spun before his eyes. Once again, they both reached for the gun, Antoine barely getting there before him. Alistair grabbed the man's wrist with both hands, forcing the weapon away from his face.

They pushed at each other, slamming against the bunk, the cabin doorway, the window. Somehow, the gun slipped from Antoine's grasp, sailing through the open window.

At least it gave them even footing. Alistair punched Antoine in the face. His opponent retaliated by shoving him back through the open doorway into the narrow corridor. Between them, they kicked and punched, resorting to brute force to knock the other down. Alistair was barely aware of the two women somewhere behind him, but he didn't think either of them could help him now.

Antoine threw himself forward again, knocking Alistair back. His opponent was stronger, broader than he, and his military training would only take him so far. He slammed back against the carriage door. Antoine charged towards him. Alistair turned the handle and together they stumbled out onto the narrow gap. Below them, the track raced by.

So surprised was Antoine by his move, that he wasn't prepared for the punch to the face he received. He stumbled back in shock, slipping over the railing. His hands reached out, grabbing the sleeve of Alistair's bloody shirt.

Alistair gasped as he fell forward. Antoine's grip loosened and he hit the tracks below, slipping beneath the train with a gurgling scream.

Unable to regain his balance, Alistair fell against the

small railing, unable to reach out and grab anything as he plummeted to his own death…

…and was yanked back suddenly by a choking grip on his collar.

He staggered back, gasping for breath, trying not to choke in the thick black smoke, and saw Lillian beside him.

'You saved my life,' he croaked.

Despite the anguish on her sweaty, soot stained face, she managed a wry smile. 'It seemed only fair.'

George choked on the thick black smoke bearing from the funnel of the steam train. After all the crap he'd been through he knew he could easily just lie there and accept his end. He was sorely tempted. But several things kept him going. The need to see this to the end, to be the man Archie wanted him to be, and, most of all, to see if his world still existed. If Reisha still existed. He had his own world to save, and he couldn't do that dead.

Gathering all his strength, he reached out against the thin railing to pull himself up. His stomach hurt where the man had kicked him, and it took a few painful gasps to gain his breath. The train rattled down the tracks. He held on firmly as it rocked back and forth.

He blinked. The man was leaning over the gap, throttling another man.

Archie!

As the train lurched again, something skidded against George's foot. He looked down at the gun on the floor, gleaming silver. He hesitated. He'd never shot someone before, the most he'd used was a bow and arrow. But Archie's life was in the balance.

What choice did he have?

He reached down and grabbed the weapon by the handle, holding on to the railing with his other hand to steady himself again.

His hand trembling, he held the gun up, aiming the barrel towards the man's back. Archie let out one gasp of air and his other hand slipped away as his eyes closed.

He was losing.

'No,' George said, his breath catching on the wind.

His finger pressed the trigger.

A loud bang over the thundering rattle of the train filled the air, screaming in his ears. Archie blinked. The man was no longer on him, instead he was hanging over the side of the platform, his body limp.

Half choking on the smoke in the air, Archie gasped for breath as a shadow loomed over him. Another assailant? How many of Antoine's men were left? Frantically, Archie reached out and grabbed a railing to stop himself from falling back onto the tracks. He closed his eyes and held on for dear life, praying this wasn't the end.

Nothing happened.

'Give me your hand,' said a familiar voice.

Archie opened his eyes and saw George standing over him. With relief, Archie took the offered arm and let George pull him up. He felt a sharp twinge in his back. His head spun and his throat was painfully sore, so he took a few deep, measured breaths. He was lucky to be alive.

'I… I killed him,' George mumbled, his hand trembling as he held the gun. 'I saw him strangling you… and I saw… I saw the gun… and I… I killed him.'

Archie gently took the gun from George's hands and flung it over the side of the railing. He reached out and hugged George, the young man crying as the train rocked back and forth along the track.

Archie knew what it was to take a life. It was one of the things about his National Service that still haunted him, just as this was going to haunt George for a long, long time.

'It's okay, George, you did what you had to do. You saved my life.'

The doors to the carriage opened behind them.

A deep chill spread through Archie at the thought that it might be Antoine, and he had just thrown away the only way of defending him and George.

Fortunately, Alistair stepped through the doorway onto

the platform.

Archie sighed with relief. A painful, wheezing sigh of relief.

Alistair had a fresh cut to the forehead, and blood stained his white shirt. He had obviously been through the wars himself. Behind him, Lillian and Ruby hovered nervously.

Alistair looked towards the body. 'Is he…?'

Archie nodded. Best not explain what had happened when poor George was still in shock. Alistair knelt down beside the body, rummaging inside the man's coat. After a moment of searching, he pulled the ribbon-bound envelope free, half-soaked with blood.

'Hopefully they will still be of some use to Her Majesty's Government.' Alistair gingerly wiped some of the blood onto the man's coat before placing the envelope carefully in his own inside pocket. He turned to Archie, wiping the rest of the blood off his hands. 'Are you both okay?'

'We survived,' Archie said grimly.

The train shook again as it picked up speed. He noticed that the buildings were becoming less packed together and he suspected they were beginning to reach the limits of Paris. He gently pulled George free, giving him a smile of reassurance. George nodded, but didn't speak.

'We should get back inside,' Alistair told them, moving towards the carriage door.

He stopped before Lillian and Ruby and gave them a warm smile. Lillian hugged him gently.

'Is Antoine dead?' Archie asked.

Alistair nodded. 'He took a fall over the side of the train. Would have taken me with him if Lillian hadn't saved me.' He looked at Lillian with a beaming smile. 'She is quite a remarkable woman.'

Lillian reached out and took Alistair's hand.

'It was the least I could do. Without you, we wouldn't have made it out of France alive.'

Everyone was exhausted, and Alistair's suggestion that

they take some rest in the bunks before the next station was met with enthusiasm. Archie entertained the notion of him and George using their time rings to return to Calabi-Yau Space, but decided against it with one look at George. The lad could do with a few hours actual rest.

Alistair buttoned up his coat over his bloodstained shirt and went off to find a conductor and try and smooth things over. Archie had no idea how he would manage that, but that was Alistair's concern, not his.

Archie sat down on his bunk, every muscle in his body on fire, his throat still uncomfortably sore. Even his head hurt, a pounding throb on his temples that he hoped might be cured by a couple of hours rest.

Slowly, achingly, Archie lay down on the bunk, resting his head on the pillow and closed his eyes.

Sometime later, Archie was awoken by a small tap on the door. Alistair entered.

'Have you…?'

Archie pointed to George and placed a finger on his lips, hushing Alistair.

George quickly stirred. 'It's okay. I'm awake.'

Alistair closed the door behind him as George sat up slowly. He lit a small oil lamp, fitted to a small shelf beneath the window. A warm light filled the cabin.

'Have you rested?' Alistair asked.

Archie nodded. Sleep was sleep he guessed, no matter how disturbed it might have been. He did feel a little better for it.

'Did you manage to clear everything up?'

Alistair nodded. 'Yes. Fortunately, two members of French Intelligence were tracking Antoine after the incident near the *Gare de Nord*. They followed him onto the train. They managed to remove the body with minimal disruption to the passengers.'

Archie looked towards George. The young man forced a meek smile. 'I'm okay. Honestly. He deserved it.'

Archie wasn't so convinced by George's words, but

decided not to press the matter further. At least not right now with Alistair there.

'It's almost light and we are not far from the next stop,' Alistair announced. 'I will stay on and accompany Lillian and Ruby to Nice and await her travelling companions there. But you do not have to stay. I'm sure you need to find Anne. I doubt MI10 want to lose some of their best agents. Even trainees,' he added, looking up at George with a smile.

Archie coughed. 'You, ah, never did buy that, did you?'

'No. I've worked in the British Armed Forces for quite some time, and I know British Military Intelligence. There is no department MI10.'

'Not yet,' Archie said softly, but not quietly enough.

Alistair raised an eyebrow. 'You do say the oddest things at times. All three of you.' He let out a sigh and smiled. 'There is much that is familiar about you, and I will confess the three of you are among the strangest people I have ever met. But, whoever you are, I'm glad you're on my side.'

'Yes, well. I suppose the less said the better.'

'Quite.'

An hour later, the train pulled into the next station, a small French village en route to Nice. The sun was rising, golden over the fields that spread out for miles in every direction, but it had yet to ward off the chill of the night. Archie and George accompanied Alistair and the women to the platform as the steam train waited for new passengers to embark.

Alistair and Lillian looked noticeably closer. They weren't at the holding hands stage, but their short time together had obviously forged a bond. Archie noticed the occasional smile exchanged between them as they walked out onto the platform.

Well, at least his alter ego would have the life he wanted, he supposed.

Archie was glad of the fresh air, even with the thick smoke lingering from the funnel of the steam engine.

George huddled in his fur coat and Archie was a little jealous as he rubbed his hands against the early morning chill. As he regarded Lillian, he realised how grateful he was to have seen her in her prime, the courageous, brilliant woman he had always imagined her to be. He didn't really know Alistair that well, but he was impressed by the man.

Archie faced Lillian, his heart heavy at the thought of saying goodbye. Perhaps sensing it too, she reached out to hug him, holding him tight as she whispered a 'thank you' in his ear.

As he pulled away, he gave Ruby a smile and looked to Alistair, who was busy shaking George's hand. With a big breath, Alistair turned to him and gripped his hand, shaking it furiously at the wrist.

'Without you and Anne, we would not be here now,' he said with a warm smile. 'My thanks to you both and to George here. Even in all my years in Intelligence, I have never seen as much courage as I witnessed in you three these last few days.'

Archie almost felt a tear coming. It was very unlike him. 'Likewise. Our lives are in your debt. Thank you for everything.' He looked to Lillian and smiled again. 'To you all.'

'What will you do now?' Alistair asked.

'Find Anne and return home.'

'I wish you all the luck,' Alistair said. 'And when you find her, please pass on my deepest gratitude.'

Archie smiled. 'I will.'

The doors of the train began to close as the last of the passengers boarded. Alistair took Lillian's hand quickly. 'Come, we must go.'

'Goodbye, Matthew. Goodbye, George,' Lillian said softly and turned away with Alistair and Ruby. They quickly boarded the train.

Archie beamed as the others smiled back through the window and waved. With a blast of steam, the train began to pull out of the station, leaving him and George alone, waving them off into the distance.

When the train disappeared around a far hill, Archie turned to George.

'Our mission is over,' he said. 'And, I assume, Anne and Eileen have had as much success.'

'How will we know?'

Archie pulled the silver ring out of his pocket. 'With this.'

George smiled. 'Good. France is nice and all, but I can't wait to get home.'

'If, indeed, we have homes to go to.'

George's smile dropped. 'You don't think we have?'

'I hope we have. And hope is better than nothing at all.'

CHAPTER TWENTY-ONE
Changing Fate

AN ALMIGHTY slap echoed in the lab, and Topher recoiled in shock. Eileen, too, was shocked at Anne's instinctive response.

'You hit me,' Topher said, rubbing his cheek, voice breaking. 'You hit me.'

Eileen watched him closely, the way his face broke like a little boy told off for doing something bad. He turned away, and Eileen lifted her eyebrows at the sound of his sobs.

'You were going to attack her,' she said.

'But...'

'No buts. Looks to me like you've needed taking in hand long before this,' Eileen said, moving towards him. 'No child develops well by mollycoddling.'

Topher pulled away. 'Leave me alone. You're mean.'

Eileen stopped, folded her arms, and looked back at Anne. With a sigh, Anne moved towards Topher.

'Okay,' she said, her voice soothing. 'Let's start again. Maybe a drink? Do you have drinks here?'

Topher stretched out a hand and pointed.

'Eileen,' Anne said.

Eileen said nothing, and simply walked over to the cabinet Topher had indicated. Inside were little capsules of... She lifted one.

'What is a... *Double Shot Flat White with Vanilla* when it's at home?'

'Search me,' Anne said.

'It's coffee,' Topher said, his voice muffled by his arms into which his head was buried.

'I see.' Eileen looked around for some kind of kettle. 'And how does one prepare this coffee?'

With a big huff, Topher walked over to the cabinet and took out three capsules. He looked at Eileen like she was stupid, and then turned to a strange looking contraption. Eileen hadn't seen anything like it before. A plastic-looking box with a gap at the bottom. Topher lifted a lid and popped the capsules in. He flicked a switch, and a small cup materialised out of thin air in the small gap. With a gurgling sound, a light brown liquid poured into the cup. He repeated the sequence, and handed Eileen and Anne a cup each.

Eileen sniffed it. 'This smells very sweet,' she said, smiling broadly. Sweet stuff was in short supply now the war was on, so she eagerly, but tentatively, sipped the coffee. 'Oh, this is delicious.'

Anne clearly did not agree. She set her cup aside.

'Right, let's sit down and discuss this like adults, shall we?' she said to Topher. 'No more threats, no more shouting.'

Topher nodded sullenly, and moved back to his stool. Eileen didn't agree with Anne's new tact. The destruction the boy had created, he deserved a much stronger response. Despite her feelings, it seemed Topher was responding to Anne, so Eileen said nothing, she merely sat and continued sipping her hot but delicious coffee.

'Topher. Tell me about… what did you say their names were?'

Topher looked up at Anne and sniffed. 'Alasdair Travers and Annabel Lethbridge-Stewart.'

'Okay. Not a direct descendent of mine, clearly, since my married name is Bishop. Possibly a descendent of my brother, or my cousins. As for Annabel… Well, plenty of Lethbridge-Stewarts out there I assume.'

'They're all the same,' Topher said. 'Non-achievers. They did nothing with their lives, just coasted along on the legacy of their families.'

'And this is an issue for you… why?'

'Because I worked hard. I was always one of the best students in my school, but did anybody ever recognise that? No. Alasdair and Annabel were the popular ones. But they were nothing special. They did nothing. *Achieved* nothing.'

'What does that matter?' Eileen asked, feeling herself drawn in. 'You said you were the best student. Can't you just take pride in what you've achieved?'

'How can I?' Topher stood, agitated. 'After school, after I invented that…' He pointed at the device attached to the plastic strap on the table next to Anne. 'Do you know what happened? None of my school friends remembered me. We had one of those class reunion things. Most people didn't even remember my name. Oh, but they remembered Annabel and Alasdair, all right.'

'And this…' Eileen sighed, somewhat confused. 'This led you to destroying the universe?'

'I didn't want to destroy the universe!' he spat. 'I just wanted to destroy them. Show them how unimportant their lives are. That being popular shouldn't be about who you are, it should be about what you are, what you can do.'

Anne rolled her eyes behind him. Eileen agreed.

'And I showed them. I showed them all. I was the man to build *that.*'

Anne picked up the device and inspected it.

'What is it?' Eileen asked.

'It hasn't got a name. It's a device that allows me to manipulate the time vortex.'

'You mean a time machine?' Anne asked. 'You created a time machine?'

Topher buffed up with pride. 'I did. I didn't need to be popular, just be brilliant.'

And yet, Eileen considered, it was because of someone else's popularity that this all started.

'Let me see if I understand you,' she said slowly. 'You've built a time machine, and the first thing you do with it is destroy? Travel back to remove people from history just because *they were popular?*'

'No. I…'

'Yes.' Eileen was no longer interested in the sensitive approach. 'This device, this marvel. It could be used for so many wonderful things.'

'And it will, now that the Traverses and the Lethbridge-Stewarts will be gone forever.'

Eileen sighed. She had met many fools, and Topher was one of the biggest.

'Well, speaking as someone born a Travers, I must say I'm disappointed,' Anne said.

Topher lowered his head, chastised.

'Disappointed,' Anne continued, 'that anybody in my family would make another feel so small about themselves.'

Topher lifted his head, a smile forming.

'Now don't get too happy, Topher, you're not off the hook. I can see how they made you feel, but *you* must see how wrong you've been?'

'Why? So, they won't be born. They add nothing, so they won't be missed.'

Anne held back a sigh. 'It's not that simple. You're not just removing them, you're…' She stopped. Just correcting him wouldn't do, she could see that. He was certain he'd done the right thing. She had to show him why it was wrong. 'How did you do it?' she finally asked.

'Well, I'm smart you see.' He rushed across his lab and picked up a small silver device. He pressed a button and the far wall filled with a holographic display.

Anne stood and walked over to it. It was filled with calculations, scientific formula, equations, pictures, notes…

'I studied history. Everybody has heard of the great Lethbridge-Stewarts and Traverses, and all the various families that branched from them. The Bishops, the Greels, the Vyons… It took a while, many journeys into the past, to see how they first met. That was the hard bit. Thousands of years of the two families being bonded. They're practically two branches of the same family now.'

Anne could believe that. It seemed inevitable that if her

family and Archie's remained friends for thousands of years, then eventually there'd be marriages along the way. And, judging by the list of names Topher had reeled out, even some Bishops – descendants of her daughter and any future children she and Bill would—

No. No Bill. No more children for her.

Anne did her best to shake off her sudden despondency.

'Are you okay?' Eileen asked.

She received a cold look from Topher, having interrupted his flow.

'I'm fine,' Anne said. 'Just a momentary reminder. It'll pass. Eventually.' She nodded at Topher. 'Go on.'

'So, I finally traced back the moment where the two families first met. I even tried going back there. All I had to do was somehow waylay one or both of them.'

'You mean, me?'

Topher looked puzzled. 'What? You were there?'

'A version of me, yes. Certainly in the timeline you went back to. That was your mistake, I suppose. It wasn't my father who became the great ally of the Lethbridge-Stewarts, it was me.'

Topher clearly didn't know what to do with that information. 'But… Well, it doesn't matter, does it? I mean, I worked out that I needed to go back further. February 1969 was closed off, something was preventing me from arriving there.'

The fracture point, Anne thought, thinking about what the Accord had told her. Too many time travellers already there, weakening the delicate balance holding it together.

'So, you went back further?'

'Yes, and that was the genius, you see?' Topher was becoming excited. He started pointing at notes, equations, as he told his story. Anne glanced at Eileen behind them. She was barely keeping up.

'I quickly realised that disrupting one event wasn't enough. I tried that, but still the Traverses and Lethbridge-Stewarts encountered each other eventually. So, the trick was to make sure they were no longer around to meet each other. Which meant changing two key moments *at the same time.'*

'1896 and 1935,' Eileen said.

'Exactly! And it was so easy. Well, 1935 was. All I had to do was make sure Travers never met the Doctor. Okay, so yes, it was possible he'd die without the Doctor's assistance, but at least then he wouldn't be around in 1969 to meet Alistair Lethbridge-Stewart. And if he did survive, then he wouldn't be called in to help, as the Doctor wouldn't know him.'

'But you tried to kill him!' Anne snapped.

'Only when you…' He pointed at Eileen. 'And that boy interfered. I wasn't going to kill anybody. I just had to make sure he died.'

'And you think there's a difference?'

Topher wasn't listening, he was too busy explaining. No, Anne thought, not just explaining, but boasting. Oh, he had pride all right, it just wasn't in the right things.

'I determined that he needed to die before he reached Det-Sen. So, I tracked his movements out of Lhasa and then hired a local assassin to finish him off in Tsongkhar, and when that failed, the assassin simply followed Travers up the mountain. Either way he was going to die and not meet the Doctor, and then he couldn't be there in 1969.'

'And the bridge?' Eileen asked coolly.

Topher shrugged. 'I tried subtlety. I wasn't counting on you and that brat to save him. I had to take matters into my own hands.'

'Because you're too small minded to see the damage you've done!' Eileen snapped. She shook her head, and turned away. 'Anne, you deal with him. I can't…'

Anne offered Topher an encouraging smile. She understood how Eileen felt, and wanted nothing more than to slap some sense into him. But she needed to know everything, needed him to express it, before she showed him the true consequences of his actions. And she had an idea just how to do that.

'I'm particularly proud of Paris,' Topher continued

smugly. 'Without them meeting at the theatre, there would be no Lethbridge-Stewart in London in 1969. It required a lot of calculations to determine how to stop those two meeting. I considered breaking up their marriage, but Lillian almost did that herself, so that wouldn't work. I considered going back further and changing their paths as children. But the *Palais Garnier* seemed like the perfect option. When I read Goff's maintenance report, I realised removing him out of the equation, the chandelier wouldn't be repaired and an accident would stop them meeting.'

'Double the damage,' Anne said.

'What?'

'The Goffs are my paternal family. You didn't just stop Alistair and Lillian from meeting, but by removing Frederick Goff's role, you stopped my maternal family having an unseen influence.'

'I didn't even know that. So, 1896 was, sort of, the first time the two families interacted?'

'On a certain level, yes.' She let that sit with him a moment, feeding his false sense of pride. Setting him up for her *coup de grâce*. 'I take it you had a hand in the Gilded Serpent Society's role?'

'Yes. I nudged them towards Ruby. I knew it would end bad. I travelled ahead, saw the fate of the woman Antoine originally targeted. Just not having Alistair and Lillian meet wasn't enough, I had to make sure that Lillian wouldn't meet any Lethbridge-Stewart, anywhere.'

'Cromer. And Archie's actual grandfather.'

'If you mean her meeting Archibald Lethbridge-Stewart in Cromer, then yes. Even that presented a risk of a Lethbridge-Stewart being in London in 1969. I couldn't let that happen.'

'So, you nudged the Society to capture Alistair, and then drag Ruby, and thus Lillian, into their scheme with the envelope, knowing that Antoine and his people would take care of Ruby and her friends later.'

'You do see! It's brilliant, isn't it? I didn't have to get my hands dirty at all.'

'But then Archie and I turned up.'

'Yeah, that was unexpected. I still don't understand how any of you got wind of it. I mean, you shouldn't even have existed.'

'Well, thanks.' Anne needed a sit down, but she had no time for that. 'What you have done is nothing short of brilliant.'

Topher frowned. Anne could feel Eileen's confusion too.

'But it's also wrong. Never mind that it's not up to you to decide who lives and dies, to go back and change history just because you weren't *noticed.* You never stopped to consider the real consequences.'

Topher's expression had changed again. His pride was turning into a frustrated anger. Just when it seemed, to him, that Anne understood and was on his side, she was now dressing him down.

'Give me your hand,' Anne said.

'What?' Topher looked at her with suspicion.

'Just do it. I want you to see something. You've told me what you've done, now I want to show you the results of that.'

Eileen joined her. 'What are you thinking?'

'I assume the Accord is watching, if so, you'll see.'

Reluctantly, Topher took Anne's hand, and the air frizzled around them...

...and the next thing, all three of them were standing in the Quantum Realm at the heart of Calabi-Yau Space.

Anne let go of Topher's hand and watched him for a moment while he took in his surroundings. She caught Eileen's attention, and the other woman nodded, finally understanding.

'What is...?' Topher stopped abruptly at the sight of the Accord.

He staggered back, his eyes resting on the multi-coloured strands of the timelines intersecting beyond the Accord. Things had changed since Anne was last there. The Silver Guardian had gone, for one thing, but it was the state of the timelines that bothered her the most. She was far from an expert when it came to interpreting what she saw, but the difference was stark enough for her to notice. Where before there seemed to be an endless stream of timelines, in colours she couldn't even name, now there only appeared to be several thousand, and of those a few were splintering and disintegrating.

Anne explained about the Accord and the Quantum Realm and what was happening to all the various realities, and Topher seemed too stupefied to do anything other than listen.

'February 1969 wasn't just important because my family and Archie's met properly, it was important for other reasons,' she told him. 'The destiny of Earth, of a thousand other planets, was decided during the London Event. The way I understand it, the Great Intelligence put a target on Earth, declared it open season to many other alien races bent on subjugation and destruction. If it wasn't for my father and me allying ourselves with Archie, then Earth would have remained open to attack. And, I've since learned, our families continued to be united, continued to fight and protect Earth. Setting up generations of defenders, inspiring others. We're the Doctor's legacy, the first line of defence.'

'Yeah, always the Lethbridge-Stewarts and Traverses. And look what happened with your descendants. Lacklustre bores who ride on the coattails of—'

'Two people!' Eileen snapped. 'Just two people in a long, long line of outstanding people. Your condemning untold billions just because you weren't noticed! Don't you understand the damage you've done?'

'I'm just…' Topher cowered beneath Eileen's glare.

'I don't understand you, Topher. You created a wonder, and you've used it for such selfish gain, regardless of the cost.' Eileen took a deep breath, looked to Anne, who nodded for her to carry on. 'I'm no expert on time travel, but I've seen the results of corrupted actions, of true evil. What you've done… It's not evil, but it is naïve and destructive. You could do so much with your machine. You could travel to the future. Save people from disasters they aren't even aware of. You could journey into the past. Experience ancient Rome. Study the dinosaurs. This is a gift, not a weapon.'

'Eileen is right. Why be this man? Why let the selfishness of two people turn you into a monster. A man who would, without any serious consideration, tear apart a multitude of realities. Topher, be better than Alasdair and Annabel.' Anne stepped over to him. 'Yes, my father was a great man. I am proud of my father's legacy, but I don't coast on that. I worked hard my entire life. I earned the respect of those around me. I battled diversity, the jokes at my expense, a woman who wanted to be a scientist, and overcame them. I have saved lives. I am a hero. But I am that because of *my* actions, not because of my family name.'

'Yeah, but Alasdair and Annabel—'

'Don't worry about them,' Anne said. 'Consider what you've achieved. You've battled diversity. You worked hard when everyone ignored you. This thing you have created, this vortex manipulation device, it should never be used against those you hate. Otherwise you will be remembered, not as a great man, but a monster. And there are too many of those out there already.'

'I…' Topher lowered his head, his eyes tearing up. 'I didn't mean…'

'Yes,' the Accord said in its multi-layered voice. 'I see your future. It is uncertain, but it doesn't need to be.'

'What is it?' Anne asked.

'Time travel. There was a race who monitored such a thing, but they have gone, destroyed in a war.'

'And Topher can change that?'

'No,' the Accord said. 'But he can help monitor time travel. Create an… agency to safeguard the timelines.'

Anne grinned. 'Yes, brilliant. Turn your weapon into a force for good.' She took hold of Topher and lifted his head with her hand. 'What do you think? You can help millions. Create your own legacy.'

'On my own? I wouldn't know where to start.'

He was clearly excited about the idea, though.

'I can help,' Anne said, the idea appealing to her too. 'I have some experience in setting up such a huge outfit, and back home I was considered brilliant too. Probably not up to your standard, but…'

Eileen gently took Anne's arm. 'A word, please.'

'Have a think,' Anne told Topher, and moved aside with Eileen. 'What is it?'

'You can't be serious, Anne. After what he has done? He tried to kill your father!'

'I know, but…' Anne watched Topher, looking around him in awe, his face a frown of concentration. 'You said it yourself, he's not evil, just naïve. Jealousy burned him, but it doesn't have to.'

Eileen thought a moment. She placed a hand on Anne's arm. 'You're right. We did stop him, so why not try and turn this into something good.'

'Exactly. And besides, after Bill… I need something to focus my mind on. I have this,' Anne said, wiggling the time ring on her finger. 'I can always return home to my daughter when I'm ready. No time need pass for her.'

'Can you do that?'

'I think so.'

Eileen didn't look wholly convinced, but Anne was set now. She patted Eileen's hand, and then walked back over to Topher.

'So, what do you say? Shall we make a difference?'

Topher grinned, and Anne couldn't help but think he looked like a kid who'd just won the biggest bar of chocolate in the world. He had much maturing to do, but Anne always found that responsibility did that to a person.

CHAPTER TWENTY-TWO
Saving the Universe

'WHERE IS Anne and Eileen?'

Archie and George were back in the nexus of Calabi-Yau Space, both once again dressed in their normal clothes.

'Eileen has been returned to her correct time and place,' the Accord said. 'Her memory of the mission erased.'

'What?' Archie couldn't believe it. 'Why?'

'She is destined to meet Alistair Gordon Lethbridge-Stewart in April 1970, and when she does, she must not know him.'

That made sense. For Eileen at least.

'And Anne?' Archie asked, looking around.

'She accompanied Topher Si-William to the fiftieth century to help him develop his time travel agency.'

'Are we missing something?' George asked.

'I rather think we are. Perhaps an explanation or two wouldn't go—'

Archie stopped abruptly as Anne blinked into being before him. She was wearing clothing the likes of which Archie had never seen before, in materials he couldn't quite place. She looked older, too, by at least ten years.

'Archie!' Delighted to see him, Anne wrapped her arms around his neck. 'It's been too long. And George…' She clasped George's hand. 'You look just as I remember you.'

'Maybe that's because we've only just returned from Paris,' George said.

'Only just…?' Anne looked puzzled for a moment, then laughed. 'Time travel! You'd think after the last ten years that nothing would surprise me.'

'Anne, the Accord said…' Archie looked to George for some help.

'Some kind of time agency? And some guy called Topher… something or other?'

'Of course. Okay, let me explain from the top…'

Archie and George listened as Anne explained about Tibet, about Topher and why he'd set about altering the timelines. Archie couldn't believe it was over something so petty as jealousy, but then he reflected how it was often the little things that set people off. She explained about returning to the fiftieth century with Topher, and how she'd spent the last ten years helping him create a new time agency to monitor time travel, to turn all the bad he'd done into something truly good.

'He's grown a lot in ten years,' Anne finished. 'Seeing the downside of time travel, the unexpected consequences… Well, needless to say, we set in place some stringent rules for our agents.'

'I see,' Archie said. 'And now we've all succeeded…?'

'Time to return home.'

They turned to the Accord. Behind him the timelines were no longer in flux, the multitude of threads streaming and intersecting gracefully.

'The temporal shockwave has been erased,' the Accord continued, 'the fracture points are sealed. Timeline zero is once more stabilised.'

'And the other worlds?' George asked. 'Is my world better?'

The Accord looked out into the rainbow of infinity. 'Your world is as you left it. Some timelines have been erased, others fixed. Timeline zero itself has been altered in subtle ways due to your mission in Paris.'

'You mean, Alistair and Lillian didn't meet each other as history originally recorded, don't you?' Anne said. 'And this changed things?'

'Subtle things. Moments, events. But Time has fixed what it can, made it so that once again timeline zero is the essential timeline of the quantum universe. It is more or less as history once recorded.'

Archie wasn't sure he liked the more or less part of that, but there was little he could do about it. The mission had succeeded, that was the main thing. What had been changed, what minor events were now different, were not things he would have to worry about. Timeline zero wasn't his world.

'So,' he began, 'what's next?'

'You will be returned to your own worlds.'

Archie nodded. 'Good. Well…' He clasped his hands together and turned to his companions. 'Wait,' he said, looking back. 'You erased Eileen's memories for a good reason, but… Well you can't just erase *our* memories. These events have changed us, what happened to us on our worlds before we were sent on the mission… Owain's sacrifice must be remembered. Honoured. I can't go back to the man I was.'

'Me too,' George said. 'If I'm going home, and if anything is going to matter, then I need to remember it.'

'Do all three feel this?' the Accord asked.

Archie and George nodded. They glanced at Anne.

'I…' Anne swallowed. 'I suppose, yes.'

Archie smiled, and took Anne's hands in his. He knew what she was going back to. 'It'll be almost ten years, Anne, but look me up when you get back. I'll be waiting.'

'Yes. I will.' Anne told him the exact date, and then looked over at the Accord. 'If I'm going back to a world without Bill, then I have to at least…' She stopped, frowned. 'You said that timeline zero was changed, that Time fixed things. Can it fix things in my world? Surely Bill is still needed by… the world.'

Archie knew she really meant 'by me'. Tears filled her eyes. Archie stepped forward and placed a comforting hand on her shoulder.

The Accord said nothing. Instead, Anne simply vanished and Archie found his hand resting on thin air.

He looked at George.

'Well, then, I guess—' Archie began, but was cut off by George who stepped up to the Accord.

'If we're asking for favours, I have a kind of big one to ask myself.'

The Accord and Archie both listened, and Archie smiled. George had changed, and yet in many ways he was still the same young man Archie had met on that bridge. He still liked to hold all the cards, be the one with the answers, one step ahead of everybody else.

Some might say what George was asking for was cheating, but Archie couldn't blame the lad. He had helped save the entire universe, after all.

'It will be done,' the Accord said.

With a huge grin, George turned to Archie and offered his hand. 'Thank you,' he said.

'For what? All I did was—'

George blinked away, leaving Archie holding air. He gathered himself together, cleared his throat, and looked at the Accord.

'My turn then. You know, I do hope I never have to meet you again.'

He sat in *The Blind Beggar*. It wasn't the kind of place that George usually found himself in. There hadn't been a trading pub in London, or anywhere else in the country, since the start of the Great Occupation. While abandoned pubs had been a part of the resistance network since day one, George generally preferred somewhere with a more eclectic jukebox. But *The Blind Beggar* had been standing, in one incarnation or another, since 1896, and things that had been alive for a very long time like that had a curious habit of staying that way, no matter what circumstances they might find themselves in.

His hoodie pulled up to cover his bald pate, his eyes covered with dark glasses, a makeshift fake beard covering his lower face, George sat and nursed a half of sickly looking lemonade and an out-of-date packet of cheese and onion crisps as he waited for her.

The only person in the place was Ron, the publican who George suspected might have been here at least as long as the pub, only bothering to update his look sometime around the mid-'70s. If Ron was aware that there was a revolution going on outside his front door, he didn't let on.

George checked his watch. If he'd got it right, and he nearly always did, she'd be coming through that door any minute now.

On the wall, an old television silently played the news on an endless loop. The flotilla had moved and was heading up the Thames, the rest of the world seizing the opportunity as if it had been holding its breath all this time, finally coming to the rescue of dear old Blighty. The Clown, the Kruge, the Volpertinger… it was all coming to an end at long last. George watched as the picture faded out, replaced by shaky mobile phone footage of him and Archie on London Bridge.

George couldn't remember exactly what he'd said before he threw himself off that bridge and into the wild adventure that had awaited him, but it had obviously had an impact. As predicted, the revolution was indeed being televised.

The picture changed again, footage of an interview with a group of children from the school where George and Archie had tried to liberate Lucy Wilson. She was there, front and centre, and while George couldn't hear what she was saying, he recognised the look in her eyes. Archie got it from time to time as well, a look that could stare down an alien battleship. She might have run the first time, but George guessed that blood would out with that one, sooner rather than later. Another Lethbridge-Stewart to pick up the mantle.

Battleships are one thing, George thought, *but there is a lot of country to liberate, and this is just the beginning.*

Luckily for George, he had a head start.

The door of the pub swung open and, right on time, Reisha Travers arrived.

She had fresh military fatigues on, and a crossbow slung over her shoulder. George smiled when he realised that she'd kept the kid's skull-and-crossbones eyepatch she'd picked up when they were in Henley-on-Thames, a bittersweet reminder of their adventure with Archie and how Reisha had lost her eye.

George kept his head down. Hiding from people was different to hiding from aliens, but he'd become good at not being seen. He watched as Reisha interrogated Ron, slapping her newly minted UNDER credentials on the bar. Hushed words went back and forth, and George wondered, for just a moment, how this was going to play out. Then he realised that, reflected in the glass behind the bar, Reisha was smiling.

'You can take that stupid beard off,' she said, turning to face him. 'Please, for the love of all that's good in the world, tell me it *is* a fake.'

'I can't even grow eyebrows,' George said sardonically, peeling the fake beard off.

'And for your next trick?' asked Reisha, sitting on a stool opposite him.

'What do you mean?'

'I mean, three weeks ago you jumped off a bridge and disappeared. A little magic trick that started a revolution, brought the rest of the world back to our door, brought what was left of the resistance out of the shadows, and even re-ignited UNDER. We're taking it all back, George.'

'You're… welcome?' said George slyly.

'I've checked our London rendezvous points every day since you disappeared. Where have you been, what happened and why the hell were you wearing a fake beard?'

George winced. 'Promise me you won't be mad.'

Reisha reached across the table and put her hand on George's. 'I've got you back, Hobo,' she said softly. 'How could I be mad?'

'Because I'm about to tell you that I've actually been back for six weeks.'

'This crossbow is loaded, you know.'

'It wasn't planned,' George said hastily. 'Reisha, when I went to rescue Archie at the school, we both thought we'd never see each other again. And when I jumped off that bridge, I thought… I hoped… that whatever was going to happen, it was going to do what Archie had said from the beginning. It was going to put this world back to the way it was supposed to be.'

'So, what went wrong?'

'Nothing. When it was over, when it was time to come home, I didn't even question it. This world, for all its horrors, is where I belong. It's home. You're… home.'

'Do I need to remind you about the crossbow?' said Reisha, blinking back a tear in her good eye.

'The point is, the world did get fixed, or at least it's getting there. We'll fix it, I know we will. So, I asked the Accord for a little favour. A little sidestep, just so I could see how things panned out and make some preparations.'

'Preparations?'

George reached into his pocket and pulled out a battered street map of London. He spread it out on the table between the two of them and Reisha tried to follow the mass of annotations and notes that had been written all over it.

'This is what you've been doing?' she asked. 'Making a spotters guide?'

'The world is so much bigger than we thought. The Clown, the Kruge, even the Volpertinger. They're just the tip of the iceberg. There's so much more.'

'Such as?'

'Well,' said George with a grin. 'Let me start by telling you what I've found in the Underground…'

Everything changed. Archie was no longer in Calabi-Yau Space. He looked around, his eyes taking a moment to adjust to the light provided by the moon. Immediately he recognised the place. He was standing outside Greyhound Lodge.

Archie Lethbridge-Stewart was home.

He glanced down at the silver band on his finger. The time ring. Putting it out of his mind, for now, he considered his surroundings.

It was night-time, but when? No light on in either the Lodge or *The Rose & Crown* next to it. And judging by the position of the moon in the sky, it couldn't be any later than 2am.

Can it be?

Archie barely dared to consider the possibility. But now he was, he noticed his car was missing.

A spring of hope welled up, and he dashed inside. He glanced up the stairs. All was quiet. He snuck into the dining room and there, on the table, exactly where he'd left them, was the small pile of letters he had written.

Was it possible? Had he really been returned to the same night he'd left Bledoe?

He picked up the letters. Closed his eyes.

This was his chance. He didn't have to live with the guilt of leaving his family in the lurch. He could just go to bed, wake up in the morning like usual, and nobody would be any the wiser.

Except… His car was missing. Which had to mean that out there a slightly younger version of him was two hours away from Bledoe, heading towards London with Bill and Owain.

Owain.

In a couple of days, the lad would be dead. Bill would be returned to his own world and Archie… Well, he'd be off to meet George Kostinen.

How could he just return to his ordinary life now, knowing that Owain was dead? What would he tell the Vines? He could pretend ignorance; say he knew nothing about where 'Daniel' and Owain had gone. Say they must have stolen his car…

No, that would do both of them an injustice.

Archie left the dining room and the house. He would shred the letters, make sure nobody ever found them. He'd hide the time ring, keep it safe for a rainy day. And he would come up with an excuse for the absence of both Owain and Bill, make up a story that would put minds at rest. And then…?

He couldn't just return to his old life, could he? After what he'd been through, he was no longer that ordinary man who had first met Bill Bishop. No, he decided, changes needed to be made. And they would start with him contacting Spencer Pemberton in a couple of days...

Anne stood outside the lift. She wanted to visit Bill, spend some time with him. Talk to him, but the thought of looking on his face. If it wasn't for the lack of colour, she would believe him asleep, but...

She stopped, her hand resting over the call button. Ten years had passed. She had lived this before. She was back in the French hospital, she'd just been to visit Copeland, and was arguing against going to see Bill's body in the morgue.

A sharp intake of breath.

She looked at her hands, studied herself in the reflection of the lift doors. Ten years showed on her face. How would she explain that when she returned to her mother and daughter? She retained all her memories of the last ten years, travelling through time, Paris, Tibet, nurturing Topher Si-William. And now, after everything, she was back...

Back without her husband.

She had in the last decade managed to come to terms with his absence. But it had been easy then; she'd been so far away from everybody that would remind her of him. Now she was back, though, back in France, and would soon be home. Soon be around her family, and the loss would come crashing down on her again. The old wound opened once—

'Anne?'

She froze. Her heart seemed to stop a moment. That voice. Last heard so long ago, almost forgotten now...

She smiled, tears stinging her eyes. She whispered a silent thank you to the Accord, to the universe itself for giving her this small, but so important, reward.

She turned, and standing there was her husband.

'Oh, Bill,' she cried, and launched herself into a very long embrace.

Archie glanced up from his marking as the phone rang. His eyes shifted over to the calendar on the wall. The date was underlined in red.

The date.

Could this be it?

He stood and crossed the lounge to the hallway where the phone continued to ring. It had been nine years since he'd returned, nine years since Owain went missing. Life had returned to normal, more or less. He continued on as a teacher, although he also worked with Pemberton from time to time, advising UNIT, that sort of thing. He may not have been Alistair Gordon Lethbridge-Stewart, but he could still do his part. In secret, of course, after all he couldn't have Anne learning about him before they even met.

As for Bledoe. Nothing changed, really. He still had his family. Katherine had met a man and married him, moved on to Liskeard. Jimmy got a rugby scholarship and was out there living his dream. And Archie and Sabina…? Well, life was good for them. Life was normal.

Sadly though, a cloud persisted over the Vines. They had held out some hope that Owain would return, but, of course, he never did. Archie wanted to tell them why, tell them their son died to save the world. But he couldn't. And so, they carried on, until finally the hope died and they decided to move away. They'd be gone next week.

Archie picked up the phone.

'Hello, Greyhound Lodge?'

The voice on the other end was just the one he had expected. 'Archie?'

'Anne,' he said, smiling. 'It's been a long time.'

'Not for me. Hours at the most.'

A pause, and Archie wondered what to say. She had just returned to the world, where she had to once more face the fact that her husband was dead.

'He's alive,' Anne said. 'Archie, Time fixed things for me. Bill's alive.'

Archie was glad. Just like him, she'd been given a reward for fixing the universe. At the thought of that, Archie smiled. Smiled because it had been nine years, and not once in that entire time had he been able to talk about his experiences. Sometimes he even wondered if he'd imagined it – but the absence of Owain was a constant reminder that he hadn't.

He lifted the phone off the reception desk and walked it over to a more comfortable chair.

'Anne. I have much to tell you,' he began…

'**Sir? Brigadier?** Shall we inform Dr Arnold?'

Brigadier William Bishop blinked, and glanced at Bonnie. 'Yes. Sure. We need UNIT's biggest brain on this.'

Really speaking, Dr Arnold should have been there anyway, as UNIT's head science officer, but he knew she was busy with Colonel Obasi Lethbridge-Stewart arguing UNIT's case in light of budget cuts brought on by the latest round of the Brexit fiasco. If Dr Arnold had been there, then Anne wouldn't be… His wife was retired. Neither of them should have been involved with this.

His eyes roamed the room. Rested on the machine. In a small aperture sat a plain ring. They jokingly called it a time ring, because of the small crystal imbedded in it. A crystal that enabled the wearer to travel in time. There were two of them; one in Ogmore-by-Sea in the safekeeping of Lucy Wilson, and the other… Right there in front of him.

He moved forward, ignored by the scientists who were all preoccupied. He reached for the ring, closed a fist tightly around it.

'I'll save you, Anne. I'll save you all…'

…

Bill blinked. Looked down at the ring. Cast his eyes around the lab, around the bustling team of scientists.

He was back. The ring had returned him from that alternative 1969.

He wondered if Archie, Eileen and the other Anne had succeeded. If they had managed to fix the…

'Bill?'

He swallowed. His mouth suddenly dry. He turned.

She was there. His wife. Not the younger Anne of an alternative 1978, but the woman he'd spent most of his life with.

They had done it.

Bill put the ring down and walked across to Anne, took her in his arms. 'Anne, it is so good to see you.'

Anne was confused. 'What do you mean? I haven't been anywhere.'

And at that, Bill just laughed.

All the instruments showed the temporal disruption had ceased, everybody erased had been returned. Colonel Lethbridge-Stewart and Dr Arnold wanted to be debriefed, so UNIT could, in turn, brief the government, but Bill had insisted he and Anne had a few things to do before that happened. He wouldn't explain, not at first, but after a brief visit to Bentley Priory where a statue of Eileen Younghusband (nee Le Croissette) stood, he explained everything on the train journey to south Wales.

And now they were in Ogmore-by-Sea. They stood on the slope by the beach and watched as two young teenagers played around on the sand and pebbles.

'So,' Anne said, 'everything is back in its place.'

For a short while longer they watched Lucy Wilson and George 'Hobo' Kostinen. Then they turned and walked away.

'The future is in safe hands,' Anne said. 'Obasi will sort things out, and then UNIT can do what it was made to do. As ever, the Lethbridge-Stewarts continue to protect Earth. The next generation.' She grinned. 'And, I daresay, one day they'll encounter other members of my family again. My brother and cousins have children after all, and some of them are old enough to do their bit now. And, just think, one day our son may want to take up the mantle too.'

'Or his children. That is if they don't just coast along on the family name.'

'Oh, Bill. That's a horrible thing to say. Nobody in my family would do such a thing.'

Bill grinned. 'Let's hope not.' He wrapped his arm around his wife. 'Lucy and Hobo won't remain in Ogmore-by-Sea forever. A big wide world out there. No doubt at least one Travers is out there waiting.'

'Yes. A world of Lethbridge-Stewarts and Traverses. Protecting Earth. Just like those kids in Ealing, and the ones in Coal Hill…'

Bill smiled. 'Sir Alistair would be happy. His grandchildren leading the way.' He glanced back at Lucy and Hobo.

'They're our future now,' Anne said with feeling. 'Our job is well and truly done.'

Lucy's and Hobo's adventures continue in
The Lucy Wilson Mysteries
Available now from Candy Jar Books